PATRICIA WENTWORTH
WEEKEND WITH DEATH

PATRICIA WENTWORTH was born Dora Amy Elles in India in 1877 (not 1878 as has sometimes been stated). She was first educated privately in India, and later at Blackheath School for Girls. Her first husband was George Dillon, with whom she had her only child, a daughter. She also had two stepsons from her first marriage, one of whom died in the Somme during World War I.

Her first novel was published in 1910, but it wasn't until the 1920's that she embarked on her long career as a writer of mysteries. Her most famous creation was Miss Maud Silver, who appeared in 32 novels, though there were a further 33 full-length mysteries not featuring Miss Silver—the entire run of these is now reissued by Dean Street Press.

Patricia Wentworth died in 1961. She is recognized today as one of the pre-eminent exponents of the classic British golden age mystery novel.

By Patricia Wentworth

The Benbow Smith Mysteries
Fool Errant
Danger Calling
Walk with Care
Down Under

The Frank Garrett Mysteries
Dead or Alive
Rolling Stone

The Ernest Lamb Mysteries
The Blind Side
Who Pays the Piper?
Pursuit of a Parcel

Standalones
The Astonishing Adventure of Jane Smith
The Red Lacquer Case
The Annam Jewel
The Black Cabinet
The Dower House Mystery
The Amazing Chance
Hue and Cry
Anne Belinda
Will-o'-the-Wisp
Beggar's Choice
The Coldstone
Kingdom Lost
Nothing Venture
Red Shadow
Outrageous Fortune
Touch and Go
Fear by Night
Red Stefan
Blindfold
Hole and Corner
Mr. Zero
Run!
Weekend with Death
Silence in Court

PATRICIA WENTWORTH

WEEKEND WITH DEATH

With an introduction by
Curtis Evans

DEAN STREET PRESS

Published by Dean Street Press 2016

Copyright © 1941 Patricia Wentworth

Introduction copyright © 2016 Curtis Evans

Cover by DSP

First published as *Unlawful Occasions* in 1941 by
Hodder & Stoughton

ISBN 978 1 911413 29 5

www.deanstreetpress.co.uk

Introduction

BRITISH AUTHOR Patricia Wentworth published her first novel, a gripping tale of desperate love during the French Revolution entitled *A Marriage under the Terror*, a little over a century ago, in 1910. The book won first prize in the Melrose Novel Competition and was a popular success in both the United States and the United Kingdom. Over the next five years Wentworth published five additional novels, the majority of them historical fiction, the best-known of which today is *The Devil's Wind* (1912), another sweeping period romance, this one set during the Sepoy Mutiny (1857-58) in India, a region with which the author, as we shall see, had extensive familiarity. Like *A Marriage under the Terror*, *The Devil's Wind* received much praise from reviewers for its sheer storytelling élan. One notice, for example, pronounced the novel "an achievement of some magnitude" on account of "the extraordinary vividness...the reality of the atmosphere...the scenes that shift and move with the swiftness of a moving picture...." (*The Bookman*, August 1912) With her knack for spinning a yarn, it perhaps should come as no surprise that Patricia Wentworth during the early years of the Golden Age of mystery fiction (roughly from 1920 into the 1940s) launched upon her own mystery-writing career, a course charted most successfully for nearly four decades by the prolific author, right up to the year of her death in 1961.

Considering that Patricia Wentworth belongs to the select company of Golden Age mystery writers with books which have remained in print in every decade for nearly a century now (the centenary of Agatha Christie's first mystery, *The Mysterious Affair at Styles*, is in 2020; the centenary of Wentworth's first mystery, *The Astonishing Adventure of Jane Smith*, follows merely three years later, in 2023), relatively little is known about the author herself. It appears, for example, that even the widely given year of Wentworth's birth, 1878, is incorrect. Yet it is sufficiently clear that Wentworth lived a varied and intriguing life that provided her ample inspiration for a writing career devoted to imaginative fiction.

It is usually stated that Patricia Wentworth was born Dora Amy Elles on 10 November 1878 in Mussoorie, India, during the heyday of the British Raj; however, her Indian birth and baptismal record states that she in fact was born on 15 October 1877 and was baptized on 26 November of that same year in Gwalior. Whatever doubts surround her actual birth year, however, unquestionably the future author came from a prominent Anglo-Indian military family. Her father, Edmond Roche Elles, a son of Malcolm Jamieson Elles, a Porto, Portugal wine merchant originally from Ardrossan, Scotland, entered the British Royal Artillery in 1867, a decade before Wentworth's birth, and first saw service in India during the Lushai Expedition of 1871-72. The next year Elles in India wed Clara Gertrude Rothney, daughter of Brigadier-General Octavius Edward Rothney, commander of the Gwalior District, and Maria (Dempster) Rothney, daughter of a surgeon in the Bengal Medical Service. Four children were born of the union of Edmond and Clara Elles, Wentworth being the only daughter.

Before his retirement from the army in 1908, Edmond Elles rose to the rank of lieutenant-general and was awarded the KCB (Knight Commander of the Order of Bath), as was the case with his elder brother, Wentworth's uncle, Lieutenant-General Sir William Kidston Elles, of the Bengal Command. Edmond Elles also served as Military Member to the Council of the Governor-General of India from 1901 to 1905. Two of Wentworth's brothers, Malcolm Rothney Elles and Edmond Claude Elles, served in the Indian Army as well, though both of them died young (Malcolm in 1906 drowned in the Ganges Canal while attempting to rescue his orderly, who had fallen into the water), while her youngest brother, Hugh Jamieson Elles, achieved great distinction in the British Army. During the First World War he catapulted, at the relatively youthful age of 37, to the rank of brigadier-general and the command of the British Tank Corps, at the Battle of Cambrai personally leading the advance of more than 350 tanks against the German line. Years later Hugh Elles also played a major role in British civil defense during the Second World War. In the event of a German invasion of Great Britain, something which seemed all too possible in 1940, he was tasked with leading the defense of southwestern England. Like Sir Edmond and Sir William,

Hugh Elles attained the rank of lieutenant-general and was awarded the KCB.

Although she was born in India, Patricia Wentworth spent much of her childhood in England. In 1881 she with her mother and two younger brothers was at Tunbridge Wells, Kent, on what appears to have been a rather extended visit in her ancestral country; while a decade later the same family group resided at Blackheath, London at Lennox House, domicile of Wentworth's widowed maternal grandmother, Maria Rothney. (Her eldest brother, Malcolm, was in Bristol attending Clifton College.) During her years at Lennox House, Wentworth attended Blackheath High School for Girls, then only recently founded as "one of the first schools in the country to give girls a proper education" (*The London Encyclopaedia*, 3rd ed., p. 74). Lennox House was an ample Victorian villa with a great glassed-in conservatory running all along the back and a substantial garden--most happily, one presumes, for Wentworth, who resided there not only with her grandmother, mother and two brothers, but also five aunts (Maria Rothney's unmarried daughters, aged 26 to 42), one adult first cousin once removed and nine first cousins, adolescents like Wentworth herself, from no less than three different families (one Barrow, three Masons and five Dempsters); their parents, like Wentworth's father, presumably were living many miles away in various far-flung British dominions. Three servants--a cook, parlourmaid and housemaid--were tasked with serving this full score of individuals.

Sometime after graduating from Blackheath High School in the mid-1890s, Wentworth returned to India, where in a local British newspaper she is said to have published her first fiction. In 1901 the 23-year-old Wentworth married widower George Fredrick Horace Dillon, a 41-year-old lieutenant-colonel in the Indian Army with three sons from his prior marriage. Two years later Wentworth gave birth to her only child, a daughter named Clare Roche Dillon. (In some sources it is erroneously stated that Clare was the offspring of Wentworth's second marriage.) However in 1906, after just five years of marriage, George Dillon died suddenly on a sea voyage, leaving Wentworth with sole responsibility for her three teenaged stepsons and baby daughter. A very short span of years, 1904 to 1907, saw the deaths of Wentworth's husband, mother, grandmother and brothers Malcolm and Edmond, removing much of her support network. In 1908, however, her father, who was now sixty years old, retired from the army and returned to England, settling at Guildford, Surrey with an older unmarried sister named Dora (for whom his daughter presumably had been named). Wentworth joined this household as well, along with her daughter and her youngest stepson. Here in Surrey Wentworth, presumably with the goal of making herself financially independent for the first time in her life (she was now in her early thirties), wrote the novel that changed the course of her life, *A Marriage under the Terror*, for the first time we know of utilizing her famous *nom de plume*.

The burst of creative energy that resulted in Wentworth's publication of six novels in six years suddenly halted after the appearance of *Queen Anne Is Dead* in 1915. It seems not unlikely that the Great War impinged in various ways on her writing. One tragic episode was the death on the western front of one of her stepsons, George Charles Tracey Dillon. Mining in Colorado when war was declared, young Dillon worked his passage from Galveston, Texas to Bristol, England as a shipboard muleteer (mule-tender) and joined the Gloucestershire Regiment. In 1916 he died at the Somme at the age of 29 (about the age of Wentworth's two brothers when they had passed away in India).

A couple of years after the conflict's cessation in 1918, a happy event occurred in Wentworth's life when at Frimley, Surrey she wed George Oliver Turnbull, up to this time a lifelong bachelor who like the author's first husband was a lieutenant-colonel in the Indian Army. Like his bride now forty-two years old, George Turnbull as a younger man had distinguished himself for his athletic prowess, playing forward for eight years for the Scottish rugby team and while a student at the Royal Military Academy winning the medal awarded the best athlete of his term. It seems not unlikely that Turnbull played a role in his wife's turn toward writing mystery fiction, for he is said to have strongly supported Wentworth's career, even assisting her in preparing manuscripts for publication. In 1936 the couple in Camberley, Surrey built Heatherglade House, a large two-story structure on substantial grounds, where they resided until Wentworth's death a quarter of a century later. (George Turnbull survived his wife by nearly a decade, passing away in 1970 at the age of 92.) This highly successful middle-aged companionate marriage contrasts sharply with the more youthful yet rocky union of Agatha and Archie Christie, which was three years away from sundering when Wentworth published *The Astonishing Adventure of Jane Smith* (1923), the first of her sixty-five mystery novels.

Although Patricia Wentworth became best-known for her cozy tales of the criminal investigations of consulting detective Miss Maud Silver, one of the mystery genre's most prominent spinster sleuths, in truth the Miss Silver tales account for just under half of Wentworth's 65 mystery novels. Miss Silver did not make her debut until 1928 and she did not come to predominate in Wentworth's fictional criminous output until the 1940s. Between 1923 and 1945 Wentworth published 33 mystery novels without Miss Silver, a handsome and substantial legacy in and of itself to vintage crime fiction fans. Many of these books are standalone tales of mystery, but nine of them have series characters. Debuting in the novel *Fool Errant* in 1929, a year after Miss Silver first appeared in print, was the enigmatic, nautically-named *eminence grise* Benbow Collingwood Horatio Smith, owner of a most expressively opinionated parrot named Ananias (and quite a colorful character in his own right). Benbow Smith went on to appear in three additional Wentworth mysteries: *Danger Calling* (1931), *Walk with Care* (1933) and *Down Under* (1937). Working in tandem with Smith in the investigation of sinister affairs threatening the security of Great Britain in *Danger Calling* and *Walk with Care* is Frank Garrett, Head of Intelligence for the Foreign Office, who also appears solo in *Dead or Alive* (1936) and *Rolling Stone* (1940) and collaborates with additional series characters, Scotland Yard's Inspector Ernest Lamb and Sergeant Frank Abbott, in *Pursuit of a Parcel* (1942). Inspector Lamb and Sergeant Abbott headlined a further pair of mysteries, *The Blind Side* (1939) and *Who Pays the Piper?* (1940), before they became absorbed, beginning with *Miss Silver Deals with Death* (1943), into the burgeoning Miss Silver canon. Lamb would make his farewell appearance in 1955 in *The Listening Eye,* while Abbott would take his final bow in mystery fiction with Wentworth's last published novel, *The Girl in the Cellar* (1961), which went into print the year of the author's death at the age of 83.

The remaining two dozen Wentworth mysteries, from the fantastical *The Astonishing Adventure of Jane Smith* in 1923 to the intense legal drama *Silence in Court* in 1945, are, like the author's series novels, highly imaginative and entertaining tales of mystery and adventure, told by a writer gifted with a consummate flair for storytelling. As one confirmed Patricia Wentworth mystery fiction addict, American Golden Age mystery writer Todd Downing, admiringly declared in the 1930s, "There's something about Miss Wentworth's yarns that is contagious." This attractive new series of Patricia Wentworth reissues by Dean Street Press provides modern fans of vintage mystery a splendid opportunity to catch the Wentworth fever.

Curtis Evans

Chapter One

IT WAS VERY COLD in the waiting-room. Sarah Marlowe pulled her fur coat up round her ears. There was no more that she could do. Skirts being what they were, her admirably shaped legs in their thin silk stockings had just to bear the arctic temperature without making a fuss. The stockings were of a deep tan colour, the shoes on the slender feet dark brown and noticeably well cut. The fur coat was brown too, and so was the small round pill-box hat tilted to exactly the right angle at the side of Miss Marlowe's head. When she moved to pull up the collar of her coat the other occupant of the waiting-room could see that the hair under the pill-box was of a dark bright brown. After breaking into two neatly rolled curls it swept smoothly down to a coil on the nape of the neck. Lashes a shade darker than the hair set off a pair of eyes which were generally considered to be Miss Marlowe's best feature. Sarah herself had even got a little tired of hearing about them. They had been used so often by candid relations to disparage a charmingly irregular nose and a widely humorous mouth. "If it were not for Sarah's eyes she would be positively plain"—Great-aunt Louisa when she was twelve. "The child certainly has fine eyes. Pity her nose turns up"—old Cousin Tom Courtney at the top of a powerful voice on the occasion of his daughter Winifred's marriage. Sarah had been a bridesmaid, and all the way up the aisle, instead of looking at the bride, she was trying to see her own nose sideways on and wondering just how badly it did turn up.

Miss Emily Case, on the opposite bench, permitted herself to shiver. She thought the girl in brown looked very warm and comfortable. Her own coat of black serge with its small collar of grey opossum was not really thick enough for the weather, and of course, coming from Italy, one was bound to feel the cold. It was some years since she had wintered in England, and she was afraid that she was going to find it extremely trying. She leaned forward and addressed her fellow traveller.

"I really do feel that there should be a fire in a waiting-room in weather like this."

Sarah Marlowe smiled.

"Well, there is a war on."

Miss Case looked abashed.

"Oh, yes—one should not grumble—you are quite right. It would not matter at all if the trains were not running so late. And then of course the fog—such a peculiarly penetrating sort of cold. But I seem to remember that the waiting-rooms on this line were always very insufficiently warmed."

Sarah nodded.

"Waiting-rooms always are," she said. "Funny how they all have the same smell—a kind of deadly cold stuffiness, and every time anyone opens the door you get an icy draught all mixed up with smoke and engine oil. Post offices are pretty bad, but they don't have as many draughts as waiting-rooms, and you get gum instead of oil."

Miss Case was not listening. She did not wish to listen, she wished to talk. She glanced in the direction of the waiting-room door and shivered.

"I have had a very uncomfortable journey, and now—it is so cold— after being abroad—"

Sarah began to wish that she had not responded. This was obviously a person with a grievance, and people with grievances can be such terrible bores. She looked at Miss Case, and did not feel any great desire to continue the conversation. A neat, shabby little woman with a pale, plump face and pale blue eyes—one of those people you always seem to meet when you are travelling. Impossible to imagine them with a life of their own, impossible to imagine that anything of the slightest interest has ever happened or can ever be going to happen to them. A passing wonder as to what this rather shabby elderly woman had been doing abroad and why she was now returning to England just touched the surface of her mind. It deepened a little when Miss Case said,

"I've been in Italy for five years. It isn't much of a welcome coming home like this, with the war on and getting held up by a fog at an inconvenient station with nobody knows how long to wait for a train."

Henry Templar had once told Sarah that she had a heart like a hot mutton pie, grateful and comforting. Sarah, revolted, at once flung the nearest book at his head. "And what's more," Henry had declaimed from half way up the stairs, "it'll land you in a mess one of these days—you just see if it doesn't!" It was this fatally warm heart which now caused her to say in a sympathetic voice,

"It sounds horrid—but perhaps we shan't have very long to wait. Are you going to London?"

Miss Case shook her head. A rather limp-looking black felt hat slipped down over one ear. A hand in a shabby glove came up and pulled it straight again.

"Oh, no. I have come from London, or I should say, through London—after landing at Folkestone, you know. I am going to stay with a married sister at Ledstock—it is quite a small village. And then I shall have to try and find another post. I was five years with Lady Richards. She made her home in Italy—the climate, you know—so delightful. But she died in November, and so of course I shall have to think about another post."

Sarah suddenly felt so sorry that she did not know what to do. How devastating to spend five years nursing a possibly grim old woman and then have to start all over again—and again—and again—and again! She said,

"Oh, I do hope you will find someone very nice. Would you like to tell me your name in case I hear of anyone?"

"Miss Case—Miss Emily Case. I'm sure it's very kind of you—"

Kind.... Sarah felt as if the word had stabbed her. Stray cats, stray dogs, stray people—you were sorry for them, but you weren't kind to them, because you were afraid of being let in for more than you could manage. So you couldn't be kind—you had to look the other way and pretend that they weren't there. Sometimes it was all too much for you and you did bring in the wretched wisp of a kitten which rubbed, purring, against your ankle, or the dreadfully thin mongrel puppy which wagged its stub of a tail and looked at you with brightening eyes. But people—what could you do with people, when you were twenty-three and hadn't a penny in the world except what you earned and that didn't go quite far enough to make its two ends meet? She did not know what to say. A faint apologetic smile touched her lips.

But Miss Case was not looking at her. The same nervous glance as before had gone towards the waiting room door. Sarah turned to see what she was looking at. The upper half of the door was of glass. Beyond it was the platform, a darkness just touched with ghostly blue from the shaded light which was all that was allowed by the black-out regulations. But of this darkness there was to be seen no more than a narrow streak where the blind which screened the glass had slipped aside.

Miss Case turned back.

"Did you see anyone? I thought there was a man." There was alarm in her voice.

Sarah said as gravely as she could, "Well, it might be a porter or a passenger—"

Miss Case produced a large handkerchief and blew her nose. Her hand was not quite steady.

"He's been walking up and down," she said in a dismal whisper.

"Why shouldn't he?"

She rolled the handkerchief up into a ball and clasped it in her black gloved hands.

"He makes me feel so nervous," she said. "I didn't think of it before, but suppose he's been following me—it would be quite easy, wouldn't it?"

Sarah allowed herself to sigh. Henry was perfectly right. That was what was so aggravating about him—he nearly always was. She had let herself in. The poor thing was certainly unhinged. Here she was, let in for a heart-to-heart talk that might last for hours if the trains went on not arriving. Her worst fears were realized when Miss Case leaned forward and said in an earnest voice,

"If you would let me tell you about it, I think it would be a help. You see, I haven't had anyone to talk to since it happened, and I keep wondering if I did the right thing—only I'm sure I don't know what else I could have done. You see, there was no time to think. And then I really was feeling faint—the—the blood, you know—and the poor young man looking just like death—"

Sarah felt as if a drop of cold water was running down her spine. It was the most uncomfortable feeling. She said "Oh!" and Miss Case sniffed.

"That is just what I said. He was holding his handkerchief pressed against his side and the blood quite soaking through it, and he said, gasping all the time poor fellow, 'They've got me. I've got something they mustn't get.' And then he said, 'You're English', and he pushed it into my hand and said, 'Don't let them get it.' And he said 'Go!' so I went back to my own compartment, and I was just wondering whether I ought to press the bell or not, when I saw the guard coming along—" She stopped and gazed at Sarah. "I do hope you think I did right—"

Mad as a hatter—

Sarah said in a soothing voice,

"I'm sure you did."

The pale blue eyes looked into hers without blinking.

"He seemed so anxious I should go. And of course I have no idea who he was. I only happened to be passing his compartment. I had been tidying up—and I thought he seemed ill—you quite understand that, don't you?"

"Oh, quite," said Sarah, who did not understand anything at all.

"And of course," pursued Miss Case, still gazing—"*of course* I should not have left him if he had not been so very urgent about it, though it would have been most inconvenient and awkward if I had been detained as—as a witness, or even suspected of having injured the poor young man myself. I could not really be expected to take the risk of anything like that, do you think? Actually we were just running into the station, so it was not like leaving him without any help. It was quite certain that someone would find him, and I really could not risk becoming involved in anything so unpleasant as a stabbing case. Fortunately I had been alone in my compartment, and no one saw me either when I left it or when I returned. People were looking out of the windows and getting their luggage down—because we were coming into the station."

Sarah thought, "She doesn't say what station. I'm not going to ask her. She's mad, or she's making it up."

"It was most fortunate," said Miss Emily Case.

"What was?" said Sarah. She hadn't meant to ask any questions, but it was beyond her to let a remark like this go by.

Miss Case maintained her pale, unwinking stare.

"I was not delayed at all," she said. "It was most fortunate. I got a porter almost at once, and there was no delay at all."

Sarah's resolution gave way a second time.

"What happened to the young man?" she enquired.

"I really have no idea," said Miss Case. "I hope the wound was not a fatal one, but he looked like death. I was so anxious not to be involved that I avoided passing his compartment. It was possible to alight at the other end of the carriage and I did so. At the time, I am afraid, I only thought of getting away without becoming involved in any unpleasantness. It was not until afterwards that I began to be uneasy about the packet."

A little doubt crept into Sarah's horrified mind. It was quite small and vague, and it said in a small, vague voice, "Perhaps she isn't mad—perhaps it really happened."

She shooed it out and shut the door in its face. Things like that *didn't* happen.

Miss Case went on talking in her tired, flat voice.

"He didn't tell me what to do with it. That makes it so very, very awkward—you do see that, don't you?"

Sarah said, "It would," in the earnest tone of the puzzled but polite.

"Because of course I don't want to get mixed up with the police. If my name once got into the papers, I should find it so very difficult to get another post. If it were not for that, I should take it to the police. My sister tells me that they have a new superintendent at Ledlington—a most charming man. But that would never do. One cannot be too careful when one has one's living to earn."

How more than true. And Sarah Marlowe had her living to earn. Even if she didn't earn it in as dull and exiguous a fashion as poor Miss Case (companion—could anything be gloomier?) she still had it to earn. Bread and butter, board and lodging, a warm fur coat and the rest, a little money to play with, and the rent of Tinkler's cottage. More especially the rent of Tinkler's cottage. At a pinch the other things could go short, but Tinkler had got to be housed. Old ladies with fifty years of hard work behind them can't be turned out on to the highway because you have played the fool and lost your job. Therefore Sarah studied to approve herself the perfect secretary to Mr. Wilson

Cattermole, and therefore it behoved her not to get entangled with stray lunatics babbling of murdered men and mysterious packages. "A tale told by an idiot, full of sound and fury, signifying nothing." Odd how bits of Shakespeare came into your mind. Henry called him the universal William. Anyhow, and to come back to bedrock fact, Tinkler was her job, and not Miss Emily Case.

Sarah had reached this point, and Miss Case was murmuring things like "I'm sure I hope I did what was right—but it is so difficult to know—" when the door was flung open and the fog came billowing in. A large young porter loomed between the jambs.

"Your train, miss." He was addressing himself to Sarah. "She'll be in in two minutes. Number four platform. Here on the left."

He caught up her suitcase and retreated, leaving the door open. The ineffectual voice of Miss Case pursued him.

"Porter—oh, porter! What about my train—the Ledlington train?"

Sarah had got up. She was settling the brown pillbox in front of what she decided must be the most unflattering mirror in the world. The porter's voice came back along the stream of icy air from the station.

"Ledlington train—number five—on the right. She's signalled. About five minutes. I'll be back."

The rumble of the London train came up out of the foggy distance.

Sarah Marlowe turned from the glass with relief, picked up the brown handbag which she had left on the waiting-room table, and stopped for a moment to bid her fellow traveller farewell.

"Goodbye. I'm so glad your train is coming in too. And—and I shouldn't worry—I'm sure it will be quite all right."

Miss Case sat primly upright on the shiny wooden bench. Her hat was a little on one side again—a companion's hat, limp and discouraged, in black felt. Her black gloved hands were clasped together over her shabby black bag, but she had a kind of perked-up look. You couldn't exactly say that there was colour in her cheeks, but they did not look quite so pale. She met Sarah's smile with an unwavering light stare and said quite brightly,

"Oh, yes, it will be quite all right now. Good evening."

The London train came clanking in on the left.

Chapter Two

IN THE MIDDLE OF WHAT felt like a crowded compartment Sarah Marlowe pursued her way to town. She had her back to the engine. Outside the cloudy window the fog flowed away on either side in an unending stream. The windows themselves were fastened, and covered by dark blinds. It was only with the eyes of her mind that she could see the river of fog go streaming by. With her ordinary, everyday bodily eyes she could at first see practically nothing, but as they became accustomed to deep dusk inside the carriage, she was able to identify the man over whose outstretched boot she had tripped and the girl who had said "Damn!" when she hacked her on the shin. The boot was so large that she wondered how she had ever got past it. The shin belonged to something in uniform—an A.T. or W.A.A.F. Beyond them other shapes, one of considerable bulk. These were between her and the door by which she had entered. On the other side a young man nudged and a girl giggled. In the opposite corner a fat voice soothed a yapping Peke.

Sarah sighed. There was of course no hope of getting a compartment to oneself on this train, but it wasn't always as crowded as this. She leaned back, wedged between the giggling girl and the man whose outsize in boots was matched by the width of his shoulders.

She thought about Tinkler—*darling* Tink—"I shan't see her again for a fortnight. Heavenly to have a little flat and find her waiting for me when I got home instead of retiring to my ghastly attic or sitting out the evening with the Cattermoles. But it's no use—she'd never transplant, and the money wouldn't run to it either. It's the board and lodging and everything found that saves our financial lives."

She thought about the Cattermoles. Wilson Cattermole. Joanna Cattermole. Mr. Wilson Cattermole. Miss Joanna Cattermole. Brother and sister—elderly, cranky, stuffy, but undeniably kind. One wouldn't perhaps cling to a Cattermole if one didn't have to, but there were worse ways of earning a living—Emily Case's way, for instance. It was better to be the secretary of the president of the New Psychical Society than to wait on an old lady's whims.

There were moments when the Society amused Sarah quite a lot. There was the time when they had investigated the case of a flat which was haunted by a canary—some very bright moments there—and the time the car broke down and they had to spend the night in the local inn and Joanna swore to an interview with a genuine eighteenth-century smuggler—"Such a very, very, very handsome man, my dear." Poor old Joanna!

It was a little later that Sarah felt convinced she had a smut on her nose. She declared afterwards that she had distinctly felt it settle. The large man on her right had gone to sleep practically on her shoulder. She had to slide sideways and lean well forward before she could open her bag. A smut on the nose is frightfully undermining to one's self-respect. She slipped off her glove, managed to get the bag open, and groped in it for compact and handkerchief.

The handkerchief should have been right on the top, but it wasn't. Instead her fingers touched something quite unfamiliar—something smooth, cold, and glithery. She touched it, and instantly recoiled. It was rather like touching a snake. As the thought rushed through her mind, Sarah pringled all over. She shut the bag in a hurry and sat there. It couldn't be a snake. It felt like one. "How do you know what a snake feels like? You've never touched one, thank *goodness*! You don't need to touch a snake to tell what it feels like—smooth, and cold, and glithery. How could there possibly be a snake inside my bag? Well, there's something there that doesn't belong." And all in a blinding flash she thought of Miss Emily Case.

Miss Case saying, "He pushed it into my hand."

Miss Case saying, "I don't know what to do about it."

Miss Case all perked up and saying, "It will be all right now."

All right now, because whatever the smooth, cold, glithery thing was, Miss Case had put it in Sarah's bag. She had got rid of it by planting it in Sarah's bag when Sarah was putting her hat straight in front of that revolting glass. "That was the only single moment I ever turned my back on her. And she must have been as quick as lightning. Who would have thought she had it in her? It only shows you can't go by what people look like."

And now what?

Sarah kept firm hold of the clasp of her bag. Smut or no smut, she wasn't going to open it again until she was alone and could see what she was doing. She sat on the edge of the seat because the large man was now slumbering over most of her share of the back of it and thought bitterly of Miss Emily Case.

It was at this moment that Miss Case, alone in a third-class carriage about seven miles from Ledlington, heard the sound of the wheels on the track become suddenly louder. They were louder because the left-hand door was opening. Even in the semi-darkness she could see that it was swinging in. And not of itself. Someone was climbing into the compartment. She saw a black shape rise, and she opened her mouth to scream.

Nobody heard her.

Chapter Three

THE CATTERMOLES LIVED in Chelsea. A tall, narrow house, so near the embankment that Sarah could just see the river from her attic if she craned dangerously far out from the left-hand window.

The fog, capricious as fogs can be, was actually less thick in London than it had been in the country.

Sarah let herself in with her latchkey, felt her way across the hall— Mr. Cattermole had personally removed the electric light bulb on the day that war was declared—and ascended to the next floor, where a very faint blue light was permitted.

The drawing-room door opened as she went by. Joanna Cattermole in black velvet, her pale hair frizzing wildly out all round her small head, stood there beckoning. A thin, dry hand caught at her wrist.

"Marvellous results whilst you've been away—really marvellous! My smuggler, you know—quite a long message. He has been *longing* to come through."

Sarah spoke soothingly.

"I'll be down in a minute. It's not frightfully early, so I'd better change, hadn't I?"

She escaped, ran up two more flights in a hurry, and arrived at her attic. She had called it ghastly, but that was merely the irritation of feeling how nice it might have been if the Cattermoles hadn't spoiled it. She liked being at the top of the house with a bathroom next door, and she liked the feeling that she could see the river if she didn't mind risking her neck. The trouble was that the Cattermoles had put all the furniture they didn't want into this large attic room, and there was so much of it that there was not a great deal of room for Sarah Marlowe.

She came in now, switched on the light, and crossed over to the dressing-table, a massive Victorian structure with a two-tiered mahogany mirror planted squarely upon it. There were three chests of drawers, two of them full of hoarded rubbish—Cattermole rubbish— two wardrobes, one mahogany and the other yellow maple, a swing-mirror, and a big brass bedstead. There were black velveteen curtains at the two windows, a black velveteen bedspread exactly like a pall, and three armchairs upholstered in faded crimson damask. The walls were covered with one of those papers on which an elaborate pattern contends with the smoke and grime of years. A lovely bonfire of all the furniture and a pot of whitewash were visions with which Sarah sometimes cheered herself.

At this moment however she wasn't thinking about the ghastliness of the attic. She wasn't even noticing it. She flung off her hat and coat, ran back to the door, and locked it. Then she sat down on the edge of the bed and opened her handbag. Her heart beat a little faster. Of course she had had to open her bag to get out her purse and her latchkey, but they were on one side; whatever it was that Miss Case had wished on her was on the other. Between the two lay a centre compartment for handkerchief and compact. She opened the bag as wide as it would go and saw what it was that she had touched in the train, a small package about four inches by three, very neatly sewn up in dark green oiled silk.

Oiled silk.... Of course—that was what her fingers had touched in the dark, slipping from the clasp to its cold glitheriness. No wonder she had thought about snakes. Nothing except a snake could feel so like one as oiled silk. She picked the little parcel up. It weighed lightly. If there had been thoughts in her mind about jewels, they were gone before she had time to consider them. Paper was more like it. She felt the thing gingerly. Yes, paper—or should one say papers. Sheets torn out of a notebook, sewn up in oiled silk, and passed from a dying man to Emily Case, and from Emily Case to Sarah Marlowe.

Fantastic, ridiculous, incredible story. And the vagueness of it! "If I'd known she was going to plant it on me, there are simply heaps of things I could have asked about. The young man who was stabbed on the train.—Well, Emily was coming from Italy, but she didn't say where it happened, or what station they ran into. And she didn't say if the young man was English. She only said that was what he had said to her—'You're English'."

Life with the Cattermoles had developed in Sarah a strong resistance to what she termed boloney. You either had to become a credulous fanatic or develop a healthy scepticism. With all the healthy scepticism at her command Sarah Marlowe now stigmatized Miss Case's story as boloney.

But the package in dark green oiled silk was a present and concrete fact. What was she going to do about it?

After a few moments' thought she dropped it back into her bag and pushed the bag under a pile of pyjamas in the middle drawer of her own chest of drawers. She then proceeded to interpret her remark to Joanna rather liberally by spending half an hour in a deep hot bath.

Dinner was at eight o'clock. Wilson Cattermole partook of stewed fruit, nuts, and a cereal which resembled chopped hay. At their first meeting he had reminded Sarah irresistibly of an ant. So earnest, so busy about what did not really seem to matter very much. His arms and legs too, brittle and tenuous. And then the thin neck, the bulging forehead, the prominent eyes. Oh, certainly an ant. But such a hairy ant. Wilson was fairly smothered in hair, fine and frizzy like Joanna's, but brown instead of flaxen. A dreadfully hairy ant, but harmless.

He sat at one end of the table and consumed stewed prunes, whilst at the other end his sister Joanna manipulated a little pair of scales. So much of Vitamin A, so much of Vitamin B, so much of Vitamin C, so much of Vitamin D, the quantities in each case so microscopic that Sarah was never able to understand just what terrible consequences might be expected if the scales were to be weighed down a little too far in either direction.

Sitting half way between the two, Sarah reaped the reward of having made friends with Mrs. Perkins. Mrs. Perkins was the cook, a majestic yet human autocrat. She regarded Wilson and Joanna with something between pity and contempt, and she made it her business to see that Sarah was served with what she termed Christian food. Tonight it was soup—beautifully hot, a mushroom omelet—perfect, and a lemon-curd tart.

When the tart made its appearance Wilson Cattermole breathed the word "Pastry!" in a horrified undertone, and averted his eyes. The meal, ceremonious in its service, went on.

"Tomorrow," he said, "I propose to go over the notes of the Gossington case. The Society for Psychical Research may say what they like, but I am convinced that the disturbances point to a poltergeist. As you will remember, Miss Marlowe, my disagreement with them over a very similar case was the reason for my resigning from the Society. 'Credulous' was the expression Eustace Frayle permitted himself to use. 'An accusation of that sort, my dear Eustace', I said, 'is one that I will not take from anyone, no matter how old a friend he may be. And if, as I have reason to suspect, my ears did not deceive me and the word which they distinctly heard you add was "Fool", let me tell you,' I said, 'that to be abusive in controversy merely exposes the weakness of one's case, and that I would rather be called a credulous fool than prove myself a purblind and ignorant sceptic.' Rather well put, I think, Miss Marlowe."

Sarah had only to smile and nod. Wilson, once started on the reasons which had led him to resign not only from the Society for Psychical Research but from every other society of the kind, needed no more than sympathetic attention to maintain a steady flow of narrative. He appeared to have formed such associations only to break away from them again, and had now arrived at the proud position of being president and secretary of a society of his own. At present the membership was small, but as he said in his most earnest voice, "It is quality that counts, Miss Marlowe—quality, not quantity. There is, I believe, a Syrian proverb to that effect." He laid a finger against his forehead and cogitated.—"Ah—let me see—yes, I can give you a rough translation.—'A crumb of bread is better to the hungry than ten thousand grains of sand.' You do not know Syriac, I suppose? A pity. It is an interesting language."

Miss Joanna looked across her scales at them.

"Wilson is marvellous at languages, but I was never any good at them. I think it so providential that spirits who want to communicate always seem to know English even if they've been Chinese or Red Indians before they passed over. Such a good arrangement, because I've never really been able to get on very far even with Esperanto. I find it too confusing, some of the words being real ones and some with bits cut off. It reminds me of a boy cousin when I was quite a little girl. I had three dolls that I was very fond of. He cut their legs, and arms and noses off. I remember I cried dreadfully, and we had a funeral service at the bottom of the garden with shoe-boxes, and I made a wreath of cowslips. But I shall never forget how dreadful they looked, and somehow Esperanto always seems to bring it back."

Dinner wore to an end.

Afterwards, in the drawing-room, there was a sheaf of scribbled sheets to be gone through, the record of Joanna's interview with her smuggler.

"Nat Garland—short for Nathaniel—you see how clearly that comes out. Automatic writing is sometimes so very disappointing, but this evening I had hardly sat down, when the pencil began to move. And that is what it wrote: 'Nat Garland'—just like that. So I said, 'Who are you?' and the pencil wrote 'snug', so of course I knew it was my smuggler. They often seem to make a mistake like that when they are coming through, and you just have to be clever and guess—and I guessed at once."

Joanna gazed at her across the tumbled papers. The sack-like garment which she wore fell away from the thin arms and emaciated neck. Her little face seemed to be all bones, the skin strained over them, chalk-white with powder except where high up on either cheek a ghastly patch of carmine stood alone. The eyes behind their pale lashes burned with an odd fire like a flame trembling in the sunlight. Her hair, fine as thistledown, seemed to hover like a nimbus. "If I wasn't so sorry for her, she'd make my flesh creep," Sarah thought. Aloud she said,

"Don't you think it would be a good thing to put it all away for tonight?"

"Oh, *no*! I must tell you about it! Because I asked for his name, and the pencil began to move at once, and this is what it wrote: 'Nat Garland'—oh, yes, I told you about that, didn't I? And then he said he had been longing to come through, and he began to tell me about his smuggling days. My dear—most exciting and romantic. Look—it's on this piece!"

Sarah looked at a muddle of disconnected words straggling across the page: dark—kegs—beach—hide—church....

Joanna pointed with a long scarlet finger-nail.

"You have to translate it a little, you know. They landed the kegs on the beach in the dark and rolled them up to the church and hid them in the crypt—that word is really meant for crypt, I am sure."

"Yes, Miss Cattermole—they told us all that at the inn when we stayed there. Don't you remember?"

The light flame in Joanna's eyes flickered a little higher.

"Yes—yes—yes. But to get it all first-hand—to hear his own account of it—that is what is so wonderful! And to know that he wants to tell it to me!" The fire went out of her suddenly. Her eyes were dull and shallow. She put up a claw-like hand and yawned, once, twice, three times. Her nails were as red as the pips on a playing-card.

Sarah thought, "The five of diamonds—they're like that—and nearly as pointed—"

The hand dropped. Joanna said in a fretful voice,

"It's gone. And I'm tired—don't you think a fog makes one feel tired? I'll just listen to the news, and then I think I'll go to bed. Wilson is always so late."

Chapter Four

UPSTAIRS IN HER ATTIC, in the dark between sleeping and waking, Sarah slipped from thought to thought easily, dreamily. It was like sliding down a long, smooth slope—no hurry, no check, just a steady, easy glide.

"If she was always as balmy as this, I don't think I could stick it ... Wilson always works late—but he doesn't expect me to—he really expects very little.... Not a bad ant—hairy, but considerate.... Four guineas a week for a couple of hours' work a day and putting up with Joanna.... Are letters about haunted houses work?... Sometimes it's only about half an hour, but putting up with Joanna goes on all the time.... I suppose I really am a companion like Emily Case.... Horrible thought.... Four guineas a week.... I'd like to be an A.T. or a Wren.... They don't get four guineas a week.... Must have Tinkler's rent.... Companion—four guineas—Emily Case...."

Sarah reached the bottom of the long incline. Dark waters of sleep closed over her.

She began to dream. She was having a tea-party with Tinkler and Emily Case. Tinkler had on her grey Sunday dress with the blue and white cross-over shawl which Sarah had knitted for her. Her hair was in tight little silver curls all over her head, and her eyes were as bright and as blue as forget-me-nots. It is only old ladies who have eyes that colour—old ladies like Tinkler, who have never had an unkind thought about anyone in all their lives.

Sarah purred in her dream. Lovely to be with Tinkler—lovely.... And then it wasn't so good, because Emily Case said in her flat voice, "The blood dripped down from between his fingers," and that wasn't at all the thing to say, when you were having tea with Tinkler. And Tinkler said in her darling voice, "Pray let me give you a little more sugar in your tea." Then something happened. Sarah didn't know what it was, but she felt it coming up, black like thunder, and all at once John Wickham, who was Mr. Cattermole's chauffeur, had her by the wrist and they were running for their lives. Anguish of failing strength, failing breath—

She woke up choked, her face in the pillow.

When she had beaten the feathers out flat she slept and dreamed again, but nothing that she could remember—incoherences of flight and turning wheels—Wickham calling her—and Joanna turning over an endless pile of scribbled papers....

At the breakfast table Wilson Cattermole remarked that she looked pale, a circumstance for which she was presently to be thankful, because it would have been horrid to come down all milkmaid and then turn the colour of a bad cream cheese. No, the fact of her pallor had been well and truly established before she picked up the paper and read the first disturbing headline:

WOMAN MURDERED IN LEDLINGTON TRAIN

Joanna asked twice for the salt whilst she gazed at it.

"I'm so sorry, Miss Cattermole—"

Sarah passed her the mustard. Her eyes were fixed upon the sharp, black print:

The deceased has been identified as Miss Emily Case—

Something in Sarah said, "Oh, no!"

Joanna's voice echoed it. "Oh, no—" But this was a plaintive voice, not the violent one which rang through Sarah's mind. "I don't ever take mustard. If I might just trouble you for the salt—"

Sarah passed her the salt. It went down the table and out of sight. Her eyes came back to the paper:

When the 5.30 down train arrived at Ledlington nearly an hour late yesterday evening, Mr. A. J. Snagg made a terrible discovery....

She skipped the next few lines, because she was not interested in Mr. Snagg, and didn't want to know how many years he had been a porter at Ledlington, or his reactions to the discovery of what he himself described as a murdered woman. There was, however, no getting away from them. Mr. Albert Snagg and his emotions were inextricably entangled with the narrative. You could have knocked him down with a feather when he opened the carriage door—he said so himself. Never had such a thing happened in any train he'd ever had anything to do with, and he hoped he'd never have anything happen like it again.

There was the pore thing all of a heap with her head smashed in. Looked regular like one of these motor accidents. And dead as a door-nail, as the saying is. You wouldn't think anyone would do a thing like that—only a lunatic. But seemingly it was robbery he was after, for there was her bag turned out and her pockets turned out, and everything in the two cases she'd got with her thrown out all over the carriage.

The print of the paper ran and dazzled before Sarah's eyes. She had the horrifying thought that she might be going to faint, and she remembered about putting your head down and letting the blood run into it. She let the paper slide on to the floor and stooped down to pick it up. Her head cleared. She heard Wilson Cattermole say,

"I see Cyrus Hoxton is dead. A very contentious fellow. Did I ever tell you, Miss Marlowe, how I was able to set him right on the date of the Ankerton affair—a particularly interesting series of phenomena with which he should have been conversant? I put him right—he was at least a dozen years out—and I do not think he ever forgave me."

Sarah responded mechanically. His voice flowed on. He was telling her without the omission of a single word just what he had said to Cyrus Hoxton, and what Cyrus Hoxton had said to him, and what they had written to each other, and how they had both resigned their membership of some society which she had never heard about.

And under all this, like a dark current moving against the tide, her thoughts surged in fear, in horror, in a kind of obstinate scepticism. It wasn't Emily Case.... The papers said it was.... But why should anyone murder Emily Case? Because—Sarah cut across that sharply. She didn't believe it. She didn't believe a word of Emily Case's story. She didn't believe she had been murdered for the sake of a package done up in dark green oiled silk. The package was upstairs inside Sarah's bag, in Sarah's middle drawer under a pile of pyjamas. Emily Case hadn't got it. Why should anyone murder Emily Case for something she hadn't got?

The telephone bell rang. She got up and went into the study to answer it. Wilson Cattermole called after her.

"One moment, Miss Marlowe—if it is a man called Smith, I will speak to him myself. A really interesting case of haunting in Essex. I wrote to him whilst you were away, and I am rather expecting him to ring me up."

She went on across the hall to the back room where she wrote letters and listened to monologues and earned her four guineas a week. Sometimes when the monologues were very long she didn't feel she was earning it any too easily.

The telephone bell rang again as she came in. She put the receiver to her ear and wondered what Mr. Smith's voice was going to be like. And then it wasn't Mr. Smith at all. It was Henry Templar saying,

"Hullo! That you, Sarah?"

She said, "It will be in a minute," and went over to shut the door.

When she came back Henry sounded indignant.

"Why did you go away? Don't you know that people who drop telephones in the middle of conversations are the off-scourings of the human race?"

"All right—I'm an off-scouring. Next time I shall leave the door open and the Cattermoles can listen in. Anyhow it wasn't the middle of a conversation, because we hadn't begun. I suppose you didn't just ring me up in order to tell me that you mustn't be interrupted?"

"It would have been quite a good idea. Actually, I rang up to ask you to lunch."

"I thought you went on doing Economic Warfare all day long."

"Not as unremitting as that—an hour for lunch isn't frowned upon. The economic army also marches on its stomach. Well then— the Green Tree at one?"

"I don't know about one—"

"I shall hope," said Henry, and rang off.

All through the morning Sarah was wondering about Henry. She had known him since she was fifteen, but she wasn't sure whether she was going to tell him about Emily Case. They were very good friends, and every now and then the friendship strayed in the direction of something a little warmer, a little more romantic. Since Henry had acquired his new job with its really substantial rise in salary there had been moments when she suspected him of serious intentions. That was Tinkler's expression, "But, my dearest child, has he any serious intentions?" Until a month ago she had always been able to laugh and say, "Not an intention, darling—and nor have I." There was something frightfully stuffy about linking your romantic feelings to a rise of salary.

Sarah said, "Yes, Mr. Cattermole," and went on taking down a long, dull, pompous letter to a man in Australia about the ghost of a donkey.

She hadn't made up her mind when she set out at a quarter to one. The brown bag was under her arm, but the oiled-silk packet still reposed beneath the pyjamas. Because if she took it out to lunch with Henry, he was perfectly capable of marching her round to Scotland Yard, and she wasn't at all sure about getting mixed up with the police. The thing she was quite sure about was that she mustn't get mixed up with the murder of Emily Case. If it came to inquests, and snapshots, and paragraphs in the paper, and a murder trial, she was going to lose her job with Wilson Cattermole.

The right sort of publicity—yes. "Mr. Cattermole, president of the New Psychical Society"—"Mr. Wilson Cattermole, speaking to our correspondent, maintained yesterday ..."—"'Ghosts I have known', by J. Wilson Cattermole." This sort of publicity by all means, and as much and as often as you please—an academic publicity, a literary publicity, a scientific publicity. But not the sordid publicity of crime, and coroner's courts, and a limelighted, headlined murder trial, with his secretary telling a fantastic tale in the witness-box. No—long before that could happen Sarah Marlowe would have ceased to be his secretary. Sarah Marlowe would be out of a job, because nobody wanted to get mixed up in a murder trial. *And what about Tinkler's rent?*

By the time she reached the Green Tree her mind was quite made up on one point—whatever Henry said or Henry did, she wasn't going to risk her job. For the rest—well, wait and see.

The minute she saw Henry it came over her that they were going to quarrel. He had that sort of look about him. *"Totalitarian"*, said Sarah to herself. Her eyes brightened, but she smiled her wide, delicious smile.

"Hullo, Henry!"

Henry gloomed and said, "You're late."

"Darling, I told you I would be."

"It leaves us so little time."

Sarah sat down and began to take off her gloves. Henry gloomed more deeply.

"I don't make pretty speeches."

Too, too true. Sarah had sometimes sighed over this. But you can't have everything. Henry making pretty speeches wouldn't have been Henry, and on the whole she liked him as he was. A tall young man with a good pair of shoulders and a certain air of forcefulness about him. Quite ordinary features, quite ordinary hair of a nondescript shade of brown, but rather good dark grey eyes and noticeably well shaped hands.

He gave his order to the waiter and gazed moodily at Sarah.

"I don't know what you call a week-end. You've been away four days."

A becoming colour mounted to Miss Marlowe's cheek. So that was what it was. Gratifying of course, but if Henry Templar thought he could come it over her like that he would have to learn to think again. She said sweetly,

"I had Mr. Cattermole's leave. I didn't know I had to have yours too."

"Look here, Sarah—"

They were certainly going to quarrel.

"Look here, Sarah—"

"Darling, there isn't anything to look at—I only wish there were. I'm most frightfully hungry. What did you order? Soup? I could do with really boiling soup."

The soup arrived, and the quarrel was for the moment averted. You cannot quarrel and eat very hot mulligatawny soup at the same time. There was a short armistice, during which Sarah prattled about Joanna and her smuggler. This, however, was not at all a safe subject. As soon as he had finished his soup Henry said in an exasperated voice,

"She's quite mad—they're both mad. I don't like your being there at all, and I wish to goodness you'd leave."

"Oh, there are worse jobs. They're awfully kind, and anyhow—"

The waiter took away their plates. When he had gone Henry said with subdued violence,

"You've no business to be with people like that!"

"Nonsense!"

He looked past her, frowning.

"I suppose it's not my business."

"I was just wondering when that would strike you."

He pushed that away with an odd impatience.

"You haven't got anyone else."

Sarah looked at him with exasperated affection.

"Darling, a whole family of parents, brothers, uncles, aunts, and cousins all put together wouldn't fuss worse than you do. Besides, I've got Tinkler." Her voice changed. "Henry, I do wish you wouldn't quarrel, and I do wish you'd be reasonable. There's Tink. You—you know what she's done for me, or perhaps you don't. I don't think I've ever told you in so many words, but I didn't know all of it myself till the other day. Anyhow when the smash came and my father and mother died—well, I was twelve. There weren't any near relations left, only an odd cousin or two, and they made the foulest suggestions—institutions and things like that. And then Tink bobbed up. She'd been my mother's governess. They'd always kept up, and she used to come and stay, and of course I loved her awfully, but there wasn't any reason in the world why she should have bothered about me or taken a hand, but she did. She was just going to retire—she'd got her savings all ready to put into an annuity. She had been governessing for forty-five years, and she'd managed to save quite a piece. And then I came along without one single claim on her, and instead of buying her annuity she used her savings to bring me up and put me out in the world. Do you think I mind who I work for or what I do as long as I can keep her going? She has hardly got anything left, because she spent it all on me. Don't you see I've got to have a job that will keep her going?"

When Sarah looked at him like that Henry experienced emotions of a conflicting nature. He wanted to be alone on a desert island with Sarah. He would have eliminated the rest of the human race without a qualm. Let them go and have their stupid wars and blow each other off the face of the earth—he didn't give a damn for any of them. He wanted to drag Sarah by the hair, and beat her over the head, and kiss away the tears that were shining in her eyes. He had a moment of pure savage exultation.

And then the waiter thrust between them with hot plates and something in a casserole. It might have been indiarubber for all that he knew, but Sarah commended it highly. She was a little ashamed of having got all worked up about Tinkler. As a sedative to the emotions there is nothing like really good food. The thing in the casserole was superlatively good. There was chicken in it, or perhaps pheasant—it was too sublimated to be easily identifiable—and there were certainly mushrooms, and very small, very succulent sausages. In the midst of her warm appreciation the bit of her mind which had not been quite made up set as firm and hard as cement. Not for anything on earth would she tell Henry about Emily Case and the oiled-silk packet.

She wouldn't tell him, but on the other hand it would be amusing to fish for probable reactions. She cut a minute sausage in half, pinned it to a mushroom, and ate it thoughtfully. Her expression was womanly and charming in the extreme. Henry Templar thought so, and his mood softened. If he had been alone with Sarah on a desert island at this moment he would have relinquished the more violent points of his original programme.

Sarah looked sweetly at him and said,

"Suppose you were in a lift and someone put something in your pocket and got out, and the lift went on, and then you heard a shot and you found someone had committed suicide—"

"What are you talking about?"

"A hypothetical case. You know—one of those what-should-A-do sort of things. Well, in this particular case, what *should* A do? The person who put the thing in the pocket is dead—"

Henry bent a severe frown upon her.

"Sarah, what on earth are you talking about?"

She was brightly flushed and animated.

"You haven't been listening. I'll say it all over again. Just concentrate. It's quite easy really."

She said it all over again.

"But what's it all about?"

"What should A do?" said Sarah.

Henry's mind appeared to grapple with the problem.

"It would depend what was in the packet."

"Oh, they wouldn't know that."

Henry stared.

"Who are *they*?"

"The person whose pocket the packet was put into."

He held his head.

"Then it isn't *they*."

Sarah waved this aside.

"It's what everyone says."

"You'd better stick to A," said Henry. "What's inside the packet?"

Sarah said, "A doesn't know," in a complacent voice.

"Then A had better find out."

Sarah began to draw a pattern on the table-cloth with the point of her fork.

"They mightn't want to."

"*A*," said Henry—"*A!*"

"Well, then, A mightn't want to."

"Why not?"

"Well, they mightn't want to know."

"I do wish you would stick to A!"

"It's so difficult," said Sarah.

"You're not trying."

She looked up with a sparkle between her lashes.

"Why should I? It's only a hypothetical case anyhow, and if I like to make it part of the case that A doesn't want to know what is in the packet, well, I can, can't I?"

The sparkle did something to Henry. In the four days that Sarah had been away he had been struggling with feelings which he didn't want, didn't like, and thoroughly resented. He was a great deal too busy to fall in love. He had known Sarah for eight years, during the whole of which time he had successfully avoided being in love with her, yet during a four days' absence something had blown their relationship to blazes—nothing that either of them had said or done, just a bomb from a clear sky. For a month or two he had been thinking quite calmly and dispassionately that if and when he married, Sarah would suit him very well. His heart contracted with rage when he remembered how thoughtlessly, how fatuously he had dallied with the idea. Suit him! She had smashed him up!

It was in this pleasant frame of mind that he had played the host. She might, and probably did, think him an ill-tempered boor, but like a more famous person he was astonished at his own moderation.

When she looked up at him, however, something happened. Their eyes met. He experienced a sudden release. The tormenting struggle within him ceased. There flowed in quiet, and an assuaging calm. He was able for the first time really to give his mind to what they had been saying. His expression, from being ferocious, became intelligent. He said in a voice that alarmed Sarah very much,

"Look here, what is all this about? Hypothetical case my foot! What have you been up to? Has anyone been putting things in your pocket?"

Sarah answered the easiest of these demands.

"Of course they haven't! Why should they?"

"I don't know. The point is, *did* anyone put anything in your pocket?"

"Oh, no."

A bag is not a pocket.

"It really was a hypothetical case?"

"Of course it was!" Sarah said this without a blush. The lift, the pocket, and the suicide were most purely hypothetical. She sustained a searching glance with perfect calm.

"Then I call it damned silly," said Henry. Everything in him relaxed. He felt superior. He felt happy. He was assuaged. "Why are we wasting time on hypothetical cases?"

"I don't know," said Sarah. "They're interesting. One has to talk about something, and you were looking like a jungle gorilla getting ready to bash my head in with a stone." She now desired to lead him as far from the dangerous subject as possible.

"I felt like it." His tone was complacent.

Sarah gurgled.

"I should hate to be a headline in the papers—Victim of Economic Warfare."

The danger-point was past. They recovered their old footing. Lunch went smoothly on. But when the hour was up and they were saying goodbye under the green tree from which the restaurant took its name Henry bent on her a disconcerting look and said rather hurriedly,

"If any of that case wasn't hypothetical, A ought to go to the police, you know."

Chapter Five

SARAH WALKED HOME briskly. She was pleased with herself, and not too pleased with Henry. After a most inauspicious beginning lunch had gone off well. They hadn't quarrelled. She hadn't told Henry anything to matter, and the food had been very, very good. She appreciated the absence of hay, prunes, vitamins, and the scales with which Joanna weighed out her scanty food. Agreeable to see people enjoying a hearty meal.

And then all at once something happened. No, it didn't quite happen, but it very nearly did. There was a little crowd round a bus stop. Someone jostled Sarah rather roughly—a big man in a heavy coat. But it wasn't he who tried to snatch her bag, because he had pushed past her and the snatch came from behind—she was quite sure about that. The bag was under her arm so as to leave her hands empty. It jerked against her side and very nearly jerked free. There was a second tug just as she got her hand to it. By the time she managed to turn round there was no possibility of identifying the snatcher. It might have been the weedy youth with the loud scarf, or the draggled elderly woman with the antique feather boa, or the girl with the magenta lipstick, or any one of half a dozen others.

Sarah kept hold of the bag and told herself that anyone might tempt a bag-snatcher in a London crowd. Nonsense to suppose that the attempt had anything to do with Emily Case and the oiled-silk packet.

All the same it set her wondering what she was going to do with the thing. It couldn't just go on lurking under her pyjamas. The answer to that was, "Why not?" She stuck her chin in the air and laughed.

After tea she wrote letters for Wilson Cattermole. Two of them were awfully dull letters, haggling about dates and data. Was a certain person in a certain place at a certain time, or was it somebody else? Could the appearance of Mr. Edward Ranelagh at a public house in the Mile End Road at 7.54 on the evening of February 25th in the year 1901 be considered a genuine phantasm of the living? Or, unlikely as this might seem, was Mr. Ranelagh corporeally present on that occasion? One Joseph Cassidy maintained that he was, whilst the Reverend Peter Brown contended with asperity that he was not. Sarah didn't care a snap of her fingers about Edward Ranelagh or Peter Brown. She considered the whole thing dull and tedious to the last possible degree. There was a long letter to Mr. Cassidy, and an interminable one to the Reverend Peter, with whom there had also been some correspondence about rather a promising haunted house. Mr. Brown was most anxious to induce Mr. Cattermole to make a personal investigation. Mr. Cattermole was toying with the idea.

"These long, dark nights—most favourable of course—I really do feel very tempted. Joanna, I think, would be interested. Well, well, I must see if I can manage it. And meanwhile just leave it open, Miss Marlowe—it must depend on circumstances."

Sarah left it open in the most tactful manner. When she had read the letters over to Wilson and he had signed them, he said in an embarrassed voice,

"Er—Miss Marlowe—you will be free to do anything you like tomorrow morning. I am—er—going away. I shall not be returning till lunch-time tomorrow. The fact is, my—er—brother is dining here. He will spend the night. My sister is attached to him, but—well, it is best to be candid—he and I are better apart." He ran his hands through his hair, a gesture which appeared to relieve his feelings, and began to walk up and down in the room. "Family ties only serve to accentuate real incompatibilities. We are twins, and physically we are considered not unlike, but no two characters could be more divergent, more antagonistic. Morgan is everything that I am not. He is a man of violent temper, a sceptic, a flesh-eater. He has an extreme partiality for alcohol. My scientific pursuits excite his contempt. I make this explanation because otherwise you would naturally think it very strange that I should absent myself from a family reunion. I can only assure you that I have found it to be the wisest course. Joanna can then enjoy her brother's society without being under the constant apprehension of some serious disagreement between us. Since you have been with us Morgan has been abroad, and now that he has returned, Joanna and I consider that the circumstances should be explained to you."

Sarah really did feel sorry for him—so embarrassed, and trying so hard to appear at his ease. She said in a warmer voice than she had ever used to him before,

"Thank you, Mr. Cattermole. It's very nice of you to explain, and of course I quite understand."

If this was, at the time, only a sympathetic form of speech, she had no sooner set eyes on Mr. Morgan Cattermole than it became a reality. She heard him arrive. The door-bell proclaimed him with peal after noisy peal, and as soon as he had been admitted the house was full of him. Doors banged. There was a clatter on the stairs. She heard him call in a yodelling voice, "Jo-a-an-na! Jo-a-an-na!"

The voice was not unlike his brother's, but imagination boggled at the thought of Wilson Cattermole making such an unholy row. The drawing-room door burst open and banged again.

When, a tactful twenty minutes later, she descended and made her entrance, he was standing on the hearthrug with his back to the fire, holding his sides and laughing uproariously, whilst Joanna gazed fondly up at him from the fender-stool. Sarah looked at him with interest which immediately passed into distaste. Whereas Wilson Cattermole invariably paid his company, and his prunes and hay the compliment of a dinner-jacket, and Joanna wore her sack-like garments of black or purple velvet, their brother Morgan stood there in baggy tweeds, loud of pattern and looking as if they had been worn night and day during the whole time of his absence. He went on laughing in a boorish manner whilst Sarah crossed the room, and only stopped when Joanna put a hand on his arm.

"Oh, Morgan—this is Miss Marlowe."

He did not offer to shake hands, but gave her first an appraising look, and then a kind of offhand nod.

The gong sounded and they went down to the dining-room, Joanna hanging on her brother's arm. She was in purple tonight, with a draggled bunch of violets at her breast, fastened with a brooch containing several fine diamonds in a dirty setting.

If Morgan Cattermole was addicted to the flesh-pots, Mrs. Perkins gave him no cause for complaint. He did complain however, and loudly, when he discovered that a small bottle of grocer's claret was the only drink the house afforded.

"I'd as soon drink ink and water," he announced. Then, banging the table, "Oh, take it away, take it away, can't you! I'll bring my own tipple next time, and you can tell Wilson I said so—the damned skinflint teetotaller!"

And then all in a moment he was telling a gross, vulgar story and laughing at it as he rolled about in his chair. Extraordinary that he should be Wilson's twin brother.

Sarah sat there aloof and slim in a full-skirted dress of dark red silk. The tight bodice, square neck, and long sleeves gave her the formal air of another century. She felt at least as far as that from Morgan Cattermole and his vulgarities. From her distance she regarded him. How strange for twins to be so alike, and so different—the same features, the same slender hands, and every mental characteristic at opposite poles. Morgan was a little the broader of the two—or was it only the baggy clothes? His skin was deeply tanned where Wilson's had the scholar's pallor. And Wilson had the scholar's stoop, the scholar's peering sight. Obvious at a glance that Morgan would never waste the midnight oil over a book. His hair was darker than his brother's, or perhaps it merely seemed so because he had sleeked it down with some horrible pomade, the smell of which filled the room.

Sarah had got as far as this, when his voice broke in, jovial and familiar.

"Well, Miss Sarah—think I'm like my brother? We're twins, you know. Would you know us apart?"

She turned her eyes on him in a steady look.

"You are alike—but of course I should know you apart."

He laughed.

"And I'll bet you wouldn't if I took the trouble to dress up a bit. I see myself doing it!" He gave a kind of guffaw. "Fancy me minding my step and picking my way like a hen on a muddy road!" He slapped his thigh noisily. "Yoicks! That's it! That's Wilson to the life—isn't it, Jo? A damned faddy old hen, scratching for maggots on a rubbish heap!"

Joanna put in a feeble protest.

"Morgan—*dear!*"

"Well, isn't he? Now, Miss Sarah, let's have your frank opinion."

"I'm afraid I haven't got one."

"Oh, come—you must have."

"None that you would care about, Mr. Cattermole."

Miss Joanna said, "My dear!" and Morgan laughed boisterously.

"Snubbed!" he said. "Well and truly snubbed! Done like a duchess too! But you can't take me down that way. Indiarubber—that's what I am. You ask Jo—she'll tell you. The harder I'm hit, the higher I bounce. Well, well, we won't spoil our food by quarrelling over Wilson. I'll say this for him, he's got a damned good cook."

Whatever he might say, Sarah considered that her snub had not been without its effect. He appeared to have reached and passed the peak of his insufferable behaviour. Ill-bred and noisy as he continued to show himself, the offence was now more in voice and manner than in any actual word. Joanna, weighing out her vitamins, watched him with what actually appeared to be admiration. Her eyes had brightened and her cheeks were flushed with excitement. As they went upstairs again, she slipped a hand inside Sarah's arm and whispered,

"Dear Morgan—he always has such high spirits. It quite does one good."

Chapter Six

WHEN COFFEE HAD been served and Thompson the elderly parlourmaid had closed the door behind her, Morgan began a long, boastful yarn about an encounter with brigands in the Balkans. He had, Sarah noticed, one trait at least in common with his twin, the faculty for entangling the simplest narrative in a mass of irrelevant and uninteresting detail. Wilson's spooks and Morgan's bandits were alike in this, that no one could possibly get up any interest in their doings. Even Joanna's attention appeared to wander. Her eyes strayed to the small baize-covered table on which, as always, paper and pencil, and a planchette board lay in readiness. When Morgan burst out laughing she turned a pleading look upon him.

"If only you were not such an unbeliever. You know, I've always felt that you would be wonderfully successful, and just now it would be especially interesting, because I have been having some really wonderful communications—no, don't laugh—if you would only just try for yourself. His name is Nat Garland—short for Nathaniel. A smuggler, Morgan, and he passed over just before the battle of Waterloo. That does bring it so home to one, doesn't it?" She clasped her hands about his arm and stood looking up into his face, her eyes fever-bright.

Sarah thought that he was rather startled. He said,

"Hullo! What's all this about smugglers? You'll be getting yourself run in if you don't take care."

"Oh, no!" Joanna's voice went high and sharp. "Oh, Morgan—if you *would*! They told us about him down at Ryland Bay—a most charming little inn. And that night I had an *experience*—but I won't tell you about it in case you might scoff, and I don't think I could bear it—I really don't. And then when we came back here he began to come through—automatic writing, you know—most, most enthralling, but just a little bit disconnected, so I thought perhaps some other method. And if you and I and Sarah were to sit together and try with planchette, I do believe we should get results. Oh, Morgan—if you *would*!"

He stood looking down at her with a comical, half-laughing face.

"Well, well, well—what a to-do! Why, Jo, you needn't look at me like that. Bring out your hocus-pocus and we'll have a stab at it. But I warn you I'm no good. Wilson—now I expect Wilson's a dab at all this jiggery-pokery."

Joanna was all smiles.

"Oh, no, he despises it, and the pencil won't write at all when he is in the room. But you—oh, I have always felt that you would be marvellous! Sarah dear, you will join us, won't you?"

When they were seated round the table, Morgan looked doubtfully at the little heart-shaped board.

"What do we do with it?"

"Put our hands on it. No, no, only the finger-tips. And you mustn't push or guide it at all—just sit quite still and wait to see what happens."

He frowned.

"What does happen—what does it do?"

"Sometimes nothing at all. But you see, it runs on wheels and there is a pencil underneath. It writes if there's a message coming through."

Sarah sat back in her chair.

"Do you know, I think I'll just watch. It's really only meant for two people."

She had all at once a great distaste for the whole thing. Their hands would be so close together. She could imagine Morgan taking advantage of that. "A cockroach," she thought—" that's what he is—cockroach to Wilson's ant. Revolting!"

Rather to her surprise, neither of the Cattermoles made any demur. They leaned towards each other across the green-topped table, Joanna brittle and eager, Morgan uneasy. His boisterous joviality seemed to have fallen away. He took a hand from the board to fumble for a handkerchief and wipe a shiny forehead.

"It gives me the jitters," he said. "Sure it doesn't bite, Jo?"

"Morgan—*dear!*" She pulled his hand back to the board. "Now keep perfectly still, and remember not to press, or push, or anything like that. Just keep still and relax, and wait to see if a message comes through."

Silence fell upon the room. Sarah, her chair pushed back, watched it and them—an L-shaped London room with two tall windows looking to the street and one to a narrow strip of ground behind. All three were curtained with a velvet so dark that only the line of the folds disclosed a shade of sombre green. The carpet stretched drearily from wall to wall with an endless pattern of blue and green and brown, all the colours dimmed and lost in a general effect of gloom. As in every other room in the house, there was too much furniture. Chairs, couches, small occasional tables, jostled one another for floor space. Pictures and engravings crowded together upon the walls. A profusion of small ornaments littered every table. An entire tea-set was displayed upon the mantelpiece. A dismal room, made more dismal by the new chair-covers of which Miss Joanna was so proud. Sarah shuddered as she looked at them. Joanna must have searched London to find anything so ugly, and as she said, the stuff would never wear out—a mustard and brown damask, practically indestructible.

Her focus narrowed to the faces of the two at the table—Morgan's still half scared, Joanna's vacant. She looked down at the hands stretched out to the heart-shaped board. Startlingly alike, those two pairs of hands—and so like Wilson's too. Unexpected for Morgan to share those thin, nervous hands which belonged of right to Wilson and Joanna. His should have been coarser—stronger—blunt-fingered and insensitive.

Just as she thought that, the board began to move. She leaned forward, watching intently. It was hardly a movement. There was a quivering. She thought, "One of them is pushing it—" and then, "No—it's pushing them." And even as the words came into her mind, the thing really was moving, with the up and down, to and fro motion of a clumsily handled pencil. The hands went with it—they did not appear to guide it. The pencil attachment ran off the edge of the paper and stopped. Morgan Cattermole dropped his hands from the board as if they found it hot.

"Look here, I don't like this. But you were pushing it, Jo—you were, weren't you?"

She looked up, flustered and scandalized.

"Oh, no—of course not! Morgan, *dear*—that would be cheating!"

"You didn't push it? Honest injun?"

"Oh, no."

"Well, that's a queer start. If it was anyone else, I'd say you were having me on."

The tears came into Joanna's eyes. She flushed painfully.

"Morgan—*dear!*"

He laughed and patted her hand.

"Don't be silly, old dear. You're O.K.—I know that. I only said if it was anyone else."

For the first time Sarah came somewhere near liking him, or at any rate to understanding why Joanna liked him. They really did seem fond of one another.

He laughed now and picked up the sheet of paper with its trail of scrawled writing.

"Here—let's see what we've got. String of rubbish it looks like to me—*a, b—ab ... b, a—ba...* like a kid's spelling-book.... Hullo, here's a word—'*bark*'. Does your smuggler keep a dog, Jo? '*Bark—beach—tar—boots—sand—*' And that's where we ran off the paper. It doesn't turn a corner very pretty. Here, let's have another go and take the long way of the paper."

Joanna beamed.

"I knew you would be interested once you made a start! You see, he's just trying to get through—that's what makes it rather disjointed. But if we persevere he may come right through, and that would be so marvellous. And *bark* wouldn't be anything to do with a dog, dear. It's just one of those old-fashioned words for a boat—the mariner's barque, you know."

The board was set again. This time the movement started at once. With no preliminary tremor, it seemed to run away, reaching the paper's edge almost as quickly as if the pencil had been driven by a practised hand.

Sarah watched, not the hands, but the faces. Joanna's blank—eyes fixed, lips parted. Morgan's interested now, but with a strange look of uneasiness. She thought, "He's like a schoolboy doing something he knows he oughtn't to—and rather enjoying it."

The board stopped. He picked up the paper and read from it:

"'*Night—dark—fog—case—night—fog—*'"

Joanna woke up.

"Oh, that's quite new! He's trying to tell us about landing the cases of rum—only he's always called them kegs before. And the fog is new. Do, pray, let us go on!"

Sarah became aware that her feet were cold—icy cold. How wretchedly silly—*dark—fog—case....* For a moment she was back in the cold, narrow waiting-room listening to Miss Emily Case whilst the fog thickened the blank window-panes and a man's footsteps went to and fro outside in the dark. *Fog—dark—case—*and even as the words were in her thought, Morgan Cattermole had picked up the paper again and was reading them aloud:

"'*Fog—dark—case—*' Hullo! Oh, he's repeating himself.... No—here's something new: '*Where is it—*' And he's written it twice, only it's slipped off the edge a bit at the end. Come on—he's getting going now. What is it, Bogey? Speak up—we're all attention!"

The finger-tips came down on the planchette again. Joanna's trembled slightly, but the movement gave no impetus to the board. It was not until the tremor died that motion began. There was a jerk, a smooth rhythm, another jerk, and so on while the paper lasted.

Sarah found herself watching with strained attention. And yet it was all nonsense—it *must* be all nonsense. She didn't believe a word of it. Joanna's mind was running on her smuggler. She wouldn't consciously cheat, but somehow these words which called up pictures of a dark beach—a landing in the fog—somehow these were transmitted to the paper. She didn't know how it was done. She only knew that it must be something like that. Anything else was ludicrous—out of all bounds of possibility.

Morgan pulled his hands away. There was still that effect of a recoil. He read again:

"'*Fog—dark—*' A bit of a harper, isn't he?... '*Emily—where is it—*'"

Sarah's heart knocked so hard against her side that it frightened her. *Emily—*it wasn't possible. She leaned back and felt the hair damp against her temples. There was an icy chill somewhere. Was it in the room, or in the empty places of thought? She didn't know. She heard Morgan say, "Getting a bit mixed, aren't you, Bogey? Who's Emily? And what's the betting the last thing ought to read, 'Where is she—'? 'Emily—where is it—' don't make sense to me. "Let's have another go and see what we get this time."

Joanna put up a hand to her light, floating hair.

"I don't know—" she said in an uncertain voice. "I'm tired. He's not coming through very well."

"Jealous because he's got a lady friend! That's it—isn't it, Miss Sarah?" His eyes ran over her with a sly smile in them. Then he turned back to the board. "Come on, old dear—open your mouth and shut your eyes and see what Bogey'll send you."

Joanna's fingers shook a little as she placed them on the board. Then, as before, her face took on its blank look. Morgan leaned forward, laughing.

"Come on—get a move on! Jibbing, are you? Wait till you hear me crack my whip! Off with you! Yoicks! Tally ho!"

The board did not move. Sarah felt her pulses steadying. Actually, a little surprise crept upon her. The board had moved so immediately and so freely that she found she was expecting it to move again, to go on moving. Now it did not move at all. It was as dead as a telephone with a cut wire. It was as dead as Emily Case. The sweat came to her temples again. What a horrible thought to have! She heard Morgan Cattermole exclaim impatiently,

"Well, I'm not going to sit here all night waiting for your darned smuggler, old girl. Let's have out the cards and rook Miss Sarah at cut-throat."

Chapter Seven

MORGAN CATTERMOLE was gathering up the cards for his second deal, when the telephone bell rang. Though there was only one fixture—in Wilson's study—though a bell rang on every floor.

Sarah pushed back her chair.

"Hi! What's wrong with the servants answering it?" said Morgan. "Or let the darned thing ring—ten to one it'll be some of Wilson's claptrap, and no loss to him or anyone else—eh, Jo? What's the odds it's some nobody from nowhere ringing up to tell our eminent brother that there's a spook walking in his back garden, and will he please come along and interview it?"

Sarah had reached the door. She looked over her shoulder and said,

"I am afraid that is why I must go. You see, it happens to be my job."

She ran downstairs to the study and picked up the receiver. A voice she did not know said,

"Is that Miss Marlowe?"

As soon as she had said "Yes", she heard it say, "She's on the line, Mr. Cattermole," and at once there was Wilson, speaking.

"Miss Marlowe, I am so sorry to trouble you, but I have had a good deal on my mind, and I am not quite sure whether I asked you to post the letters I dictated this afternoon. If they are posted, never mind. But if by any chance I forgot, perhaps you would send Thompson to the post with them. I am afraid I can't wait just now, but if you will just see to it, that will be quite all right. I am sorry to have troubled you. Good-night."

There was a click as the receiver was hung up at the other end. Sarah put back hers and looked about her. The letters…. No—they were in the post. He had given them to her and she had pushed them through the slit in their own corner letter-box with a feeling of good riddance. Joseph Cassidy, Esq., and the Rev. Peter Brown—a pair of bores who would be certain to reply at length and in the most tedious manner. It would be pleasant to think that their letters had gone astray. But no such luck—the perfect secretary had posted them with her own methodical hands.

She thought, "He was worried enough to ring up, but he didn't wait for an answer. Fancy worrying over Joseph and Peter!" And on that the telephone bell rang again and brought her back from the door. She banged it behind her and groped without waiting to put on the light. It would probably be Wilson again, to ask whether she had remembered to shut the inkpot, or put his address-book away.

She got hold of the receiver, and it wasn't Wilson, it was Henry Templar.

"Sarah—is that you?"

Sarah said "'M—" and added in a resigned voice, "It always is. But all the same you'd do better to make sure before you come out with your Sarahs like that."

Henry sounded impatient. Not that that was anything new.

"Look here, I want to talk to you. But before I start I want to know whether there are any extensions your end."

"Why?"

"I don't want anyone listening in—that's why. Are there any?"

"No—only for the bell."

"That's all right. Did you listen to the nine o'clock news?"

"No. We were interviewing Miss Cattermole's smuggler with planchette—all eighteenth-century. Why—was there anything special?"

"Not in the news. Sarah, what train did you come up by last night?"

"Last night? Well, it was supposed to be the 5.17, but it was about three quarters of an hour late because of the fog."

"5.17 from Craylea?" Henry sounded relieved.

"No—from the junction. All the trains were behind, and I thought I was going to be late for dinner—a *frightful* crime."

"When you say 'the junction', you mean Cray Bridge?"

"Yes, of course. What is all this about?"

Henry said in what she stigmatized as a stuffy voice,

"What did you do while you were waiting for your train?"

A little warning bell rang in Sarah's mind. She spoke lightly and at once.

"Darling, what does one do? I got frightfully bored, and my feet froze solid."

It wasn't any good. Henry was thorough both by nature and by training. He just went on.

"Were you on the platform, or in the waiting-room?"

Well, she wasn't prepared to lie—not to Henry. She said in an exasperated voice,

"My good Henry, I'm not quite cracked. Why should I wait on the platform in a fog with the temperature heading for zero?"

"You were in the waiting-room?"

"I was in one of them."

She oughtn't to have said that. It would sound as if she knew what he was driving at. But it didn't matter, because he just drove on.

"What platform did your train go from?"

"How should I know?"

"You *must* know—and I mean to."

Well, they could quarrel about that. But even a quarrel wasn't going to stop Henry if he was really set. She said,

"A bit totalitarian, aren't you? As a matter of fact I believe it was number four—it generally is."

"Then your waiting-room was between number four and number five—is that right?"

"Henry, what's all this about?"

"Sarah, listen! Was there anyone in the waiting-room with you?"

"Yes."

"Can you describe her?"

"I didn't say it was a her."

"But it was, wasn't it?"

"Yes."

This conversation was going all wrong. She was letting him drag it out of her bit by bit. She ought to have kept the talk in her own hands. She ought.... What was the good of saying what she ought to have done? She hadn't done it.

"There was a woman there when I went in—the sort of person you do find in waiting-rooms. I can't imagine why you want to know."

"Can't you? Didn't you read your paper this morning?"

"Of course."

"Didn't you see that a woman had been murdered in the train between Cray Bridge and Ledlington? That train left number five platform at five minutes past six. The woman was a Miss Case, and she had been waiting for her train at Cray Bridge for the best part of an hour. The porter says there was another lady there with her most of the time—a young lady in a brown fur coat. He knows her quite well by sight, but he doesn't know her name. The initials on her suitcases are S.M. He put her into the London train at six o'clock."

Sarah said in a dry, shaky voice which didn't sound at all like her own,

"Well, thank heaven for that, or I suppose they'd be saying I murdered her."

Henry went on implacably.

"It was you."

"You knew that all the time! How did you know?"

"There was a police message in the nine o'clock news—that's why I asked you if you had been listening to it. You'll have to ring up the police at once—Ledlington 3412."

"Henry, I can't!"

"My dear girl, you've got to. Don't be silly!"

"It isn't—you don't understand—if I get mixed up in a police case I shall lose my job. And I *can't*—because of Tinkler."

Henry attempted to be soothing. It was not his happiest manner.

"My dear, there's really nothing to be afraid of."

"I am *not* afraid!"

"There is no reason why you should be. You have only to ring up the police and answer a few simple questions. I don't suppose they will call you at the inquest. It is really only that you must have been one of the last people to see the poor woman. There is no question of your getting mixed up in a police case."

Sarah's temper boiled over suddenly and fiercely.

"That's all you know about it!" she said, and banged the receiver back.

Chapter Eight

SHE HAD TO DO things to her face before she went back to the drawing-room. Even so, her colour was higher than it had any reason to be, and her eyes were much too bright. Joanna had an air of fretful impatience, but Morgan evinced an odious admiration.

"Well, well, Miss Sarah, that was a good long call. Convenient things telephones, aren't they?"

Sarah let a cold glance slide over him. She spoke to Joanna.

"It was Mr. Cattermole. He wanted to know if I had posted some letters."

Morgan was slipping cards across the table. He laughed and said, "Took quite a time over it too, didn't he?"

Sarah's anger had iced over. She said in her most indifferent voice, "I had a call from a friend of mine. You must have heard the bell."

Morgan picked up the cards.

"Oh, well, it's my deal," he said.

When the evening was over Sarah, going up her attic stair, considered quite dispassionately that she had never endured a more disagreeable three hours or disliked anyone so much as she disliked Morgan Cattermole. Next time he came—if there was a next time—she would take a leaf out of Wilson's book and go away. He could hardly blame her for following his own example.

She came into her room and shut the door on the rest of the house with a feeling of relief. It was over. She became aware that she was very tired. She sat down on the edge of the bed and thought how nice it would be not to have to undress. She didn't feel in the least like undressing. How much better if you could just curl up like a dog and sleep when and where you pleased. It was much too much trouble to undress.

But as soon as she sat down all the things she didn't want to think about came crowding in. She didn't want them, but she couldn't bar them out. Planchette—Morgan's and Joanna's hands balancing—white fingers—brown fingers. Which of them had pushed the board? It seemed to be pushing them. But that was nonsense. Nothing and nobody was going to make her believe that it was the spirit hand of Mr. Nathaniel Garland, hanged for smuggling and the murder of a Preventive Officer in 1815, which had guided the scrawling pencil. Anger and disbelief welled up in her as she thought about it. Morgan was of course the obvious one to suspect. But Joanna had had these messages before. She had them when she was sitting quite alone. That cut Morgan out. Or did it? She wasn't sure. She thought it would take a lot of practice to make the thing write what you wanted it to. She swung back to the idea that the writing was in some way produced or at any rate influenced by Joanna—not consciously, but in some way that transmitted the thoughts which obsessed her.

This was, of course, a very reassuring explanation. It accused no one and it accounted for everything. Emily Case's name had got into the message because Joanna had seen it in the paper, and it had got mixed up in her mind like getting a fly mixed up with the currants when you were making a cake. What a perfectly revolting thought!

She got up from the bed and took off her red silk dress. The last thing on earth she wanted to do was to begin thinking about Emily Case. She hung the dress on a painted hanger with a lavender bag dangling from it—a Christmas present from Jessica Grey. The lavender was nice, but the dress slipped on the painted wood. Enraging to find your dress on the floor when you had hung it up.

Emily Case.

What was she going to do about Emily Case?

She went and stood against the foot-rail of the bed and looked at the drawer which held her pyjamas. One pair on the bed, waiting for her to put on. Three pairs in the second long drawer of the shabby bow-fronted chest with the broken inlay. And under the bottom pair the packet which Emily Case had put into her bag.

She went over to the door and put up her hand to turn the key.

There wasn't any key.

All in a moment Sarah stopped feeling tired. She opened the door and looked on the other side of the keyhole. She went down on her knees and searched the floor.

There wasn't any key.

Anger came up, and behind the anger fear. Because there had always been a key, and the key had been there last night. She remembered coming in—and locking the door—and getting Emily Case's packet out of her bag—and putting it back inside the bag at the bottom of the pile of pyjamas in that middle drawer. And this morning she had taken the bag, but she had left the packet under the pyjamas. And she had locked the door again then, so the key was not only there last night, it was there this morning. At 12.30, to be precise. The point was, where was it now?

There was no answer to that. Unless the fact that it wasn't in the door could be called an answer.

A bright flush of anger came up into Sarah's face. She pushed one of the solid Victorian chairs up against the door and wedged the handle. Then she opened her middle drawer and felt under the pile of pyjamas for Emily Case's packet. As her hand was slipping in, she thought, "Suppose it isn't there." She had been out of the house for two hours in the middle of the day, and anyone could have taken it then. It was such a horrid thought that she stopped, her hand just touching the top of the pile.

Anyone could have taken it, but that meant someone in the house—Wilson, Joanna, Thompson, Mrs. Perkins, or Mrs. O'Halloran who came in to oblige from nine to one.

Sarah said, "Rubbish!" and something inside her said, "Who took that key?" She pushed her hand down to the bottom of the drawer and found the packet.

She put on her dressing-gown and sat down on the bed. Well, there it was, the horrid little object, about three by four in the way of inches, neatly sewn up on two sides with white linen thread. A man had been stabbed for it, Emily Case had been murdered for it, and Sarah Marlowe wished it very heartily at Timbuctoo. This being the kind of wish which relieves the feelings but produces no other result, Miss Marlowe set herself to think along more practical lines. She could ring up Henry Templar—she could ring up the police.... No, she couldn't. There was her job, and there was Tink.

If she could be sure that Henry wouldn't, as it were, hand her over to the police, Henry would do.

At this moment, with the clock close upon midnight, and the key of her room gone missing, Sarah wasn't feeling quite so haughty about Henry as she had done round about half-past nine. But there was nothing more certain than the fact that to ring up Henry would be practically synonymous with ringing up the police. It would be a complete climb-down, and before she knew where she was she would be telling a police inspector all about Emily Case.

There were, of course, other possibilities. She could send the packet anonymously to the Ledlington police, or to New Scotland Yard. She was rather taken with this idea. The only bother was, suppose the police were to track her down, it might seem rather a suspicious sort of thing for her to have done, because if they did track her—and at any moment one of the Cray Bridge porters might remember having seen her name on a label—well, the only possible line for her to take was, "I really haven't the slightest idea what this is all about." She wouldn't tell any lies, but she wouldn't tell any more of the truth than she could help. If she had to tell them about the packet, well there she was, as innocent as the driven snow—"I found it in my bag, and I didn't know what to do with it". Pure, beautiful truth without a speck on it. But if she had already posted the miserable thing anonymously to Scotland Yard, the truth wouldn't look so spotless—there is something furtive about an anonymous communication. It seemed to her that there was a case for compromise. She could mark time and see what happened. If the police came, there she was, all innocent, and they could have the packet. And if they didn't come, she could post it at Tooting, or Surbiton, or somewhere like that.

Sarah sat with her blue dressing-gown tucked round her and approved this plan. It was not perfect, but it would do. Anyhow she couldn't think of a better one.

Then all at once a dangerously bright idea came jigging into her mind. After all, people aren't stabbed or murdered just for nothing. The young man who had passed the packet on to Emily Case probably knew what was inside it. No, not probably—certainly. Emily Case may or may not have known more than she had told Sarah, but Sarah Marlowe meant to know what was in that packet before she did anything with it. If a thing is going to put you in the way of being murdered, you do have a right to know what it is all about.

As she picked at the stitches with her nail-scissors she reflected that she had a reel of strong thread in her work-box, and that she could sew the packet up again so that no one would know it had ever been opened. No need to unpick more than just the narrow end.

She peeled back the oiled silk and saw what she had expected to see, a wad of tightly rolled-up paper. Just for a moment she hesitated, and then she was unrolling it and spreading it out on her knee.

Flattened out, the wad was a manila envelope. There was nothing written on it, but it seemed to be full, and the end was firmly stuck down. She went into the bathroom, let the hot tap run, and steamed the shut end until it opened easily. Then back to her room again, with the chair against the door.

The envelope was full of papers. She pulled them out and sat down to look at them. There were sheets and sheets and sheets of thin paper covered with writing—very thin paper, covered with a small, neat writing. Names and addresses—just ordinary names and addresses. She turned the pages over, surprised and puzzled. Quite ordinary names. Quite ordinary addresses—London, Birmingham, Portsmouth, Manchester, Liverpool, Leeds, Bristol, Plymouth, Woolwich.... Dozens and dozens of names, dozens and dozens of addresses all over England.... And a man had been stabbed and a woman murdered to prevent these names and addresses from reaching an unknown destination.

A shiver went over Sarah. There was someone who valued the possession of these lists so highly that he had done murder to get them. There was someone who was expecting to receive them. There was a young man who had been stabbed and who might or might not be dead. And there was Emily Case.

There was also Sarah Marlowe.

As she turned the pages over, a photograph slipped out and lay against a fold of her blue gown. It was a snapshot, and it had been taken with a good modern camera. It showed a man coming out of a house with his hat tipped back and an attaché case in his hand. Every line of the picture was hard and clear. There was a bald forehead with the hat pushed back off it, a large smooth face with all the contours rather flat—an expressionless face, heavy and hairless. Unpleasant without any especial reason. Perhaps it was the lack of hair. There were no eyebrows or eyelashes to be seen, no sign of hair on lip or chin. This, and the unsparing clarity of the photograph, gave an effect of nakedness. Sarah had a flash-back to a family of young pink pigs. She could think of nothing else as bare as this man's face.

She turned the snapshot over and saw that there was writing on the back. Not the hand of the addresses—a bolder one. The writing was in pencil.

"Paul Blechmann, alias Paul Black."

That was on a line by itself. Below, in a scrawl which ran diagonally across the paper,

"Pretty sure he's the boss."

Somewhere down in the house a clock struck twelve. The strokes had a faint, lingering sound. Between the first stroke and the last Sarah had made up her mind what she was going to do. Before the last stroke had died away she was tense, keyed up, busy, all her indecision gone.

Queer to spend thirty hours not knowing which way to turn and what to do, and then all of a sudden to be quite, quite sure. It was like a load off her mind. She felt light, and free, and eager again. All her movements were quick and controlled. She came and went in the room. She threaded a needle with the steadiest of hands. A good thing she had the right sort of thread—you must have strong linen thread for the buttons on your canvas shoes. It matched the original thread exactly, and she had a fitful moment of wondering whether the original thread had been bought for some girl's shoes, and who that girl might be.

She finished sewing up the packet and cut the thread. There was an inch or two left. She struck a match and burned it, and smeared out the ash upon the carpet by the bed. With the needle back in her workbox and the scissors on the dressing-table, no one could ever know that she had opened the packet and sewn it up again.

She had pushed it back under the pile of pyjamas, when something made her look round. If it was a sound it was a very soft one. She could not have said that she had heard anything, but in the act of pushing home the drawer she turned her head towards the door and saw the handle move. At once her mind was cold and clear. She shut the drawer, stepped back from it, and said,

"Who is there?"

There were only four people besides herself in the house. Mrs. Perkins and Thompson slept in the basement.

If it was Morgan—well, in that moment of cold anger she felt quite capable of annihilating Morgan.

Chapter Nine

IT WASN'T MORGAN. It was Joanna.

Her plaintive "Are you awake?" brought Sarah to the door with the least possible delay. The Victorian chair pushed aside, she threw it open and revealed Miss Cattermole in a reassuringly solid camel-coloured dressing-gown, with her hair screwed up tight to her head in

aluminium curlers. Her eyes looked large, and vague, and frightened.
She clutched at Sarah and said,

"Oh, my dear—forgive me—I do hope you were not asleep. Oh, no,
I see you have your shoes and stockings on. But, my dear, I had such a
terrible dream. That is the worst of being so psychic—it makes one too
receptive. And when I woke up I had such a palpitation, and I thought
perhaps if you would come down to my room and stay there a little, I
shouldn't feel so nervous—only I am really very sorry to disturb you."

As she spoke she came a little way into the room, peering to right
and left with an odd, startled glance. It slid over the chair which had
guarded the door and slid away.

Sarah said quickly, "Of course I'll come. Why, how cold you are!
Would you like some tea, or a hot water bottle?"

Joanna was trembling. She looked very small and shrunken
without her wild halo of hair.

"No—no—oh, no, I don't want anything. If you would just come
down with me and stay a little—"

Sarah went down with her and got her into bed. There was a
gas fire in the room, burning brightly and throwing out a good heat.
Joanna, in the large double bed which had belonged to her parents,
looked smaller than ever. She sat up against three immense pillows
in frilled linen pillow-cases and told Sarah all about her dream. Now
that it was over and she had company, she was able to derive a good
deal of gloomy pleasure from it.

"I don't quite know where I was, but it was an empty house and
I couldn't get out. There were a great many doors and windows, but
they were all locked and I couldn't get out. I have always been very
much afraid of being shut in anywhere. I could never understand how
people could go down into the catacombs and places like that—I am
sure I should faint—and in my dream this place was much worse,
because there was the *sense of an evil presence*—" Joanna's voice
dropped to a rustling whisper.

"But it was only a dream. Would you like a little more light?"

Sarah could have done with more herself. A heavily shaded lamp
by the bedside did very little to relieve a pervading gloom. The room
was dark—L-shaped like the drawing-room. Round the corner it ran

away into a black cave. The gas fire struck a cheerful modern note. Sarah found herself with an affection for it.

Miss Joanna said in a creeping voice, "And what made it so much worse was that I was quite sure something dreadful was going to happen. It was coming nearer every moment, and the dreadful thing was that it was always just behind me—just out of sight."

"Don't you think we had better talk about something else?"

"No—I think it does me good. I learned a piece of poetry about something of the same sort when I was a child. I don't think it was a very suitable piece for a child really, and I know it kept me awake for hours at a time after I got it by heart. I don't remember it all now, but it was something about a man who was walking across a moor and was afraid to turn his head—'As one who fears a frightful ghost doth close behind him tread.' I used to know it all off by heart, but that is the only bit I can remember now. And I am not sure whether it is Coleridge's *Ancient Mariner* or *The Dream of Eugene Aram*. I think it was one of them, but I can't be sure, because we had a governess who was very fond of poetry and always made us learn a great deal of it."

It was a relief to have got Joanna away from her dream, but Sarah began to wonder if she was feverish. There was a flickering colour in the hollow cheeks, a fixed brightness in the sunken eyes, and the voice was like the voice on a gramophone record—it went on, and on, and on.

She said, "Would you like me to read to you a little?"

Rather to her surprise, Joanna said, "Yes."

"What would you like?"

The bright eyes dwelt on her, but not at all as if they saw Sarah Marlowe.

"Oh, anything—it doesn't matter at all."

There were books in a trough by the head of the bed. Sarah stood up and picked one out. Then she knelt down under the light, found a page at random, and began to read:

> "Art thou not void of guile—
> A lovely soul formed to be blessed and bless—
> A well of sealed and sacred happiness,

Whose waters like blithe light and music are,
Vanquishing dissonance and gloom—a star
Which moves not in the moving heavens, alone—
A smile amid dark frowns—a gentle tone
Amid rude voices—a beloved light—
A solitude, a refuge, a delight—
A lute which those whom love has taught to play
Make music on to soothe the roughest day,
And lull fond Grief asleep—a buried treasure—
A cradle of young thoughts of wingless pleasure—
A violet-shaded grave of woe?—I measure
The world of fancies seeking one like thee,
And find—alas! mine own infirmity."

Sarah paused slightly and went on, her voice soft and grave:

"She met me, Stranger, upon life's rough way,
And lured me towards sweet death—"

There was a small choking sound. Sarah leaned out of her circle of light and saw that the tears were running down Joanna's face. Such a poor wizened little creature, with her face all puckered up like a baby's.

Sarah's soft heart smote her.

"Is anything the matter? I'm so sorry—I'm afraid it's rather melancholy, but I just began where the book opened, and I liked the singing sound it made. Did it upset you?"

Joanna's thin fingers fastened upon Sarah's wrist. They were very cold. She said in a weak, stifled voice,

"No—no—it is very beautiful. I have always been fond of poetry. I once had some verses printed in the parish magazine. That was Shelley, wasn't it? A friend gave me the book—a long time ago—"

"Would you like me to go on?"

Joanna shook her head.

"No—it brings things back. He used to read—very beautifully. Just put the book away and stay a little longer, and then I think I shall be able to go to sleep."

As Sarah turned with the book in her hand, something fluttered out from between the pages and lay on the table under the light—the small unmounted photograph of rather an arty young man with longish hair and a small pointed beard. The features were without character, the photograph a faded snapshot. Sarah put it back and replaced the book.

After a few minutes Joanna began to talk about other things—a book she had read, a book she wanted to read, a letter she meant to write, and would Sarah please remind her about it. All very gentle and trivial. There were no more tears. Presently she yawned once or twice, and at last sent Sarah to bed.

"You are sure you are all right now? Shall I leave the fire on or not? You won't be too hot like that?"

"No—I am always cold. But I shall sleep now."

"I can stay a little longer if you like."

"No, no—it won't be necessary—I shall sleep. Good-night."

Sarah said, "Good-night."

It was cold on the landing, and black dark. She felt for the newel-post and the bottom step of the stair. Half way up she had the horrid thought of how very unpleasant it would be to bump into Morgan coming down. It was not only an unpleasant thought, it was a crazy one, because it was ten thousand a year to a halfpenny that Morgan was asleep in the back room over the study, and self-evident that he could have no possible business on the attic floor. All the same, she kept a hand well out in front of her till she came to the top of the stair and the sight of her own lighted room.

A yard from the door she stopped. So that was why the stair had been so dark. The door was not shut. But she thought she had left it wider open than this. She tried to remember exactly how she had left it. She couldn't be sure—Joanna was clutching her. She couldn't remember stopping to close the door, and yet here it was with only a chink of light showing against the jamb. She opened it now, and left it wide whilst she looked inside the wardrobe and under the bed. Then she barricaded it again with the stout Victorian chair. It was as heavy as lead, with a solid curly frame and faded damask upholstery. It would at any rate give fair warning if anyone tried the door. But she didn't think anyone would—not now—*not again*. She was as sure as she could be sure of anything that someone had been, and gone.

She was laughing a little as she opened her middle drawer. And then she stopped laughing. Her hand went down into the drawer and came back again. Sarah stared at it in amazement. Because she had expected her hand to come back empty, and it wasn't empty—it was holding the oiled-silk packet.

She went on staring at it for quite a long time. And then all at once a bright colour came into her cheeks and her eyes began to sparkle. She held the packet close under the light and examined it. Not her thread—and not her stitches. Pretty good, but not good enough. The thread was ordinary cotton, not linen thread, and the stitches were not so neatly taken. Someone had opened the packet and sewn it up again. If they had removed what was inside it, they had put something in its place. She could feel the sharp edge of an envelope. There was nothing in the feeling to show that it was not the original envelope. That was clever. And it was very clever not to take the packet—it gave the thief quite a lot of margin. If it hadn't been for the difference between cotton and linen thread, a difference which probably didn't exist to the male mind, Sarah would never have known that the packet had been tampered with, and by the time anyone did find out, the tampering might have taken place anywhere and been effected by anyone. By the stabbed young man, by Emily Case, or by Sarah Marlowe.

Sarah sat down on the bed with the packet in her lap and laughed till the tears ran down her face.

Chapter Ten

SARAH SLEPT THE SLEEP of the just. When she woke the burr of the telephone bell was in her ears. With an outspoken comment on people who ring up before eight o'clock in the morning, she emerged upon an icy landing, pulling on the blue dressing-gown as she went. It would be somewhere between half past seven and a quarter to eight, because that was when she always did wake. The thinning gloom at her open window bore out this conjecture.

The light was on upon the next floor, and when she was half way down the stairs Thompson came into sight, very clean and starched, in lilac print and a large white apron. She was coming out of Miss Cattermole's room, and she had a small round papier-maché tray in her hand with Sarah's own cup of tea upon it. Secretaries don't get early morning tea-sets, but the cup was a breakfast-cup and it was always scalding hot.

At the foot of the stair Thompson looked up.

"If it's the telephone, miss, it was for Mr. Morgan and he's gone down to it."

Sarah went back to bed with relief, taking the tray with her.

As she drank her tea she made all her plans for the day. The very first thing as soon as she was dressed she would go down to the study and ring Henry up. She had laughed last night, because if you have a sense of humour you can't help laughing when something really funny happens, even if it is all very dangerous as well. She had laughed, but she knew very well that fundamentally this wasn't a laughing matter. It was a dangerous, murderous business, and she couldn't stand in it alone. Names and addresses which were worth doing murder for must mean something very serious in the way of crime, and she thought she could make a guess at what that something might be. If that guess was right, then her job, from being all-important, became just one of those things which have to go when the pinch comes. Henry would have to be imported into the affair. If the worst came to the worst, Henry would have to lend her the money to pay Tinkler's rent. She wouldn't have any scruple about it at all. After all, what was he for?

She dressed like lightning and ran blithely down to the telephone. The light was still on in the passage, but the study gloomed in a faint, reluctant daylight. It wasn't ever what you would call a bright room, but this morning, with a heavy leaden sky hanging low over the backs of the houses opposite, there was hardly light enough to see what you were doing.

The telephone was not in its accustomed place. It had been dragged across the writing-table and left rather precariously upon the left-hand edge. Morgan of course. It just went through her mind to wonder if he was left-handed. She lifted the receiver and listened for the dialling tone. Nothing happened. She put the receiver back, shook the telephone for luck, and tried again. Not a sound. She dialled Henry's number and depressed the rest. Nothing happened.

It was at this point that it first occurred to her that nothing was going to happen. When she had done everything all over again, and done it several times, suspicion crystallized into most unwelcome certainty. The telephone was dead.

Sarah put the thing back on its stand. It had been all bright and lively about three quarters of an hour ago. Less. It was about three quarters of an hour since the bell had waked her, and Morgan must have had quite a long conversation, because the bell outside her bedroom door had tinkled in sympathy with his ring-off after she had got out of bed and begun to dress. She lifted the receiver and tried all over again. It wasn't any good. The line was as dead as Canterbury lamb. Exit Henry.

She stood by the writing-table and made the necessary readjustments in her plans. There was nothing to get fussed about. It was all too easy. She would have breakfast, and then she would walk out of the house in hat and coat and take a bus to the Ministry of Economic Warfare. Of course Henry would be extra official if she had to see him in his office, but that was one of the things that just couldn't be helped. In any case she hadn't any very great hopes of being able to mould him.

Sarah had a naturally hopeful disposition. It had buoyed her up on quite a number of tiresome and difficult occasions. It buoyed her up now as she entered the dining-room and found Joanna gazing limply at yesterday's *Times*, which she held in one hand whilst the teapot, imperfectly controlled by the other, wavered between a breakfast-cup and the table-cloth. There wasn't much tea in the cup, but there was a good deal on the cloth. It was not of course real tea, but a horrible synthetic product of a Health Laboratory.

Joanna greeted her with relief.

"Good-morning, my dear. Oh, yes, do take it! I am not at all fond of pouring out tea. There are so many things to remember, and Wilson is so very particular. You see, for this health tea the water must not be boiling and the milk must on no account be put in first, and it must stand for just so long—and of course no sugar."

"But you are not expecting Mr. Cattermole for breakfast?"

Joanna was mixing a tea-spoonful of something that looked exactly like bone-meal with an equal quantity of cold water from a little glass jug. She said in an absent voice.

"Oh, yes, he is coming back. That is why Morgan has gone. It does seem so unnatural, doesn't it? She stopped stirring and looked vaguely at Sarah. "I begged him to wait, but he wouldn't. I sometimes feel if they could only meet—but neither of them will hear of it. So unnatural, when you think that they are twins."

Sarah really couldn't bring herself to agree that a desire to avoid Mr. Morgan Cattermole had anything unnatural about it. Her own relief was intense. She ate her bacon and egg with a good appetite, and managed to refrain from making a face over the health tea. It had a horrid flavour of cabbage-water. One point about Wilson's and Joanna's diets was that their bacon coupons were available for the rest of the household, and that meant bacon three times a week instead of only twice.

Sarah was considering this in a spirit of cheerfulness, when the door opened and Wilson Cattermole walked in. It was really surprising how glad she was to see him. He might be a fussy old maid and the most tedious of bores, but in contrast with Morgan he was an angel of light. As she rang for his cereal and poured him out a pallid cup of health tea she really felt quite affectionately towards him.

"I hope," he said, looking at Joanna and lowering his voice, "I hope, my dear, that Morgan has left?"

Joanna threw him a glance of reproach.

"Half an hour ago," she said—"and with only a boiled egg and a slice of toast."

Wilson Cattermole looked down his nose.

"Neither you nor I require as much. I fail to see why Morgan should be commiserated on that account."

"I *begged* him to stay," she said in an agitated voice—"I really *begged* him."

"I am thankful to find that he has enough sense to refuse so ill-judged a request." Wilson's tone was such an acid one that Thompson's entrance at this moment appeared opportune.

By the time that she had laid out a packet of cereal and supplied him with a soup-plate and a dessert-spoon he had thrown off his ill temper. As the door closed, he said almost eagerly,

"Pray do not let us talk about Morgan. My dear, I beg your pardon—I was wrong. But as you know, the subject is one which is better not discussed between us. Let us speak of other things. I have had a most interesting time—a really most interesting time. And you will never guess whom I have met. No, no—you really will never guess, but I will give you each three guesses all the same. Now, Miss Sarah, you shall begin. What do you say?"

Without knowing in the least why she did so, Sarah took the first name that came into her head. It was a toss-up between Joseph Cassidy and Peter Brown, and the Reverend Peter won.

She said, "Mr. Brown," and saw quite an excited colour come up into Wilson's face.

He stared at her incredulously.

"Why, so it was! But how in the world did you guess? Come, come, Miss Sarah, you will have to tell me that."

Sarah laughed. She was feeling all easy and relaxed again.

"I expect it was the letters, and your ringing up about them last night. The name just came into my mind—I don't really know why."

"Sarah is psychic," said Joanna in a far-away voice. "I have always said so."

"Well, she is quite right. Really, Joanna, it was a most remarkable thing. After posting his letter to me he felt impelled to come up to town. You see, the manifestations have begun again, and he is sure that if we were to go down there at once we should get some very remarkable results, so he decided to follow up his letter in person, and actually arrived at the corner of this road as I was leaving the house. It was our first meeting, but seeing me come out of number twelve, he addressed me and enquired if I was Mr. Wilson Cattermole. A very interesting coincidence. Or perhaps not a coincidence—I hardly know." He rubbed the bridge of his nose and frowned in a dubious manner.

Sarah set down her empty cup.

"Mr. Cattermole, why did you ring up and ask whether I had posted Mr. Brown's letter—I mean, if you had already met him, it hardly seemed worth while."

The dubious expression disappeared. Mr. Cattermole smiled brightly.

"Ah, but you are forgetting Mr. Joseph Cassidy. My enquiry concerned his letter as well as that addressed to Mr. Brown. You must not forget Joseph Cassidy. And besides, I will let you into a secret. Mr. Brown was—well, quite doubting my assurance in the matter. When I told him that I had already replied to his somewhat voluminous letter he hesitated to believe me, maintaining that it could not have been done in the time. 'Very well then', I said, 'you shall hear me ring up the very efficient young lady who is my secretary. I will ask her whether she posted a letter to you, and you shall hear her reply.' So I asked my question and handed him the receiver so that he could listen to your answer—and I will do him the justice to say that he made me a very handsome apology. A delightful man, and with the true scientific spirit. And now we must discuss our arrangements. I thought as it is so cold that we should make a point of getting the journey over before lunch."

Joanna Cattermole leaned forward and said, *"We?"*

"My dear, I felt sure that you would be interested. Mr. Brown has very kindly invited us to be his guests. I am most anxious to have the fullest possible notes of any phenomena we may witness. Mr. Brown extended a most pressing invitation to yourself and to Miss Sarah. Indeed, as I said to him, 'Miss Marlowe's presence is not only necessary from a secretarial point of view, but she will also be quite an invaluable witness, since she is, I believe, rather a sceptic about psychic phenomena and I am always hoping to convert her.'"

"Do you mean that we are to go down to Morden Edge this morning?" Sarah tried to keep a tone of dismay out of her voice. She was not certain if she had succeeded, but Wilson continued to smile.

"I have ordered the car," he said, "and I will give you half an hour to get ready. The distance must be about forty miles. Fortunately we have used practically no petrol this month, so we have plenty in hand.

I have communicated with Wickham, and he informs me that the tank is quite full.

"I thought Wickham was ill," said Joanna, a little fretfully.

Wilson turned his smile upon her.

"My dear, he is a healthy young man, and healthy young men do not remain ill indefinitely—they recover. Wickham has most fortunately recovered, and he will be here with the car in half an hour's time, so I suggest that you inform the maids and set about your preparations. Miss Sarah will, I am sure, assist you." He turned to Sarah. "My sister is always rather upset at the idea of a journey, but I am sure she will find herself more than repaid by a most interesting experience. I would suggest taking plenty of warm garments, as sitting up in an empty house is likely to be a chilly business. I should perhaps have said an empty wing, since Mr. Brown inhabits the modern part of the house himself and he assures me that it is provided with every comfort. Still, warm rugs, warm wraps—these I should certainly recommend, but otherwise you need not trouble about dress. Our host is a bachelor and devoted to the simple life."

Joanna got up. There was a vague, distressed look upon her face.

"Such very short notice," she said, and put a hand to her head. "How long shall we be away?"

"Oh, no more than a day or two, I suppose," said Wilson Cattermole.

Chapter Eleven

GETTING JOANNA READY to start on a journey was a task to absorb all Sarah's energies. Previous experience had left her no illusions on this score. The procedure was always the same. Miss Cattermole drifted aimlessly about the room, pulling things out of drawers and cupboards. When the bed, the chairs, the couch, and even the floor was littered, she would begin to wring her hands and declare that she could not possibly get packed in time. By dint of tact, hard work, firmness, and the will to win, Sarah and Thompson managed to separate the necessary from the superfluous, pack the former, and restore the latter to cupboard, drawer, and shelf. By the time the process was complete Joanna was tearfully certain that everything she most required had been left behind.

"Planchette—I must have my planchette!"

"It's at the bottom of your case, miss."

"Oh, Thompson, are you sure?"

"I put it there, miss."

"Oh, Sarah—my little black spencer!"

"You said you would wear it, Miss Cattermole—under your fur coat."

"Oh dear—so I did! But my mother's sapphire ring—I can't go without that—I never go anywhere without that! And I know I had it on last night."

"You've got it on now, miss," said Thompson in a restrained voice.

"Oh, so I have! And I had better take the blue rug, because blue is the right colour for the next three days—colours are so important. And my lapis lazuli chain, and the blue slippers, and that very warm scarf I got in the sales—"

"You go and pack, Miss Marlowe—I'll finish her." Thompson spoke in an undertone. "You haven't above five minutes."

Sarah slipped from the room and ran upstairs. A plaintive wail from Joanna followed her.

"Oh, but I must have my lapis lazuli chain! It is a talisman."

Sarah banged her door and began throwing things into a suit-case. Sponge-bag, slippers, dressing-gown, pyjamas—*What am I going to do about the packet?*—cami-knickers, bust-bodice, another pair of pyjamas—*what am I going to do about Henry?*—two pairs of stockings, shoes, brush and comb, hand-glass—*what am I going to do about the police?*—handkerchiefs and a warm pullover…. The answer to all the questions was, "I don't know and I haven't got time to think."

Afterwards, of course, she was able to think of quite a number of things she might have done. Whether any of them would have affected the course of events is another matter. What she did do was the best she could set her mind to in the time. She took a sheet of paper and scrawled upon it with a blunt-nosed pencil which was all she could find, "Going ghost-hunting at five seconds' notice. Telephone out of order. *Must see you urgently.* Address C/o Rev. Peter Brown, Maltings, Morden Edge. Sarah."

As she doubled the paper and stuffed it into an envelope, the gong sounded from the dining-room floor. She wrote Henry's name and address, found a stamp in her purse, and called down over the banisters, "I'm just coming". Then she went back and deliberately tidied up her face. Employer or no employer, gong or no gong, she was not going to start out for the day looking as if she had come out of a rag-bag.

When she had put on her fur coat and the brown pillbox hat which she had worn to travel up from Craylea she looked at herself in the glass with a trace of anxiety. It was so very much a London hat, with a stiff four-inch petersham fitting close about the head like a coronet and the crown filled in with velvet—extravagantly smart, extravagantly becoming, but most emphatically not the right hat for ghost-hunting in a country village. The question was, would that occur to anyone else? She thought not. Joanna was too vague, and as to Wilson Cattermole and the Reverend Peter Brown—well, men just didn't notice that sort of thing—at least not the kind of men who were members of psychical societies. Curiously enough, she did wonder about Wickham. But it got no farther than that—she was a good deal more concerned with the set of her pill-box. That sort of thing had to be immaculate, and she thought she detected a wrinkle. Well, whatever happened she must wear it. She rummaged for an eye-veil, noted that it made the hat look more unsuitable than ever, and as the gong sounded a second time she collected gloves, handbag and suit-case and ran downstairs.

It was an enormous relief to find that the gong had been sounding for Joanna as well as for her. Mr. Cattermole was pacing the hall, watch in hand, his own suit-case already disposed of in the boot. He wore an expression of pained restraint, and Sarah thought it best to hurry past him without speaking.

The hall door stood open. Wickham, a tall, elegantly built young man in a dark chauffeur's uniform, stood ready at the kerb. As he took her case, she noticed how pale he was.

"Good-morning, Wickham. Are you all right again? I was so sorry to hear you had been ill."

He gave her the briefest of replies.

"I am quite well again, thank you."

And with that Wilson Cattermole had come down the steps.

"Is my sister nearly ready, do you know, Miss Sarah? I cannot think what is keeping her. Dear me, it is really extremely cold. Are you quite sure, Wickham, that you are sufficiently recovered to drive in such cold weather?"

The chauffeur's rather impassive features did not change at all, but there was a faint something which suggested to Miss Marlowe that if he had not been on duty and very conscious of the fact, he might have frowned. She had seen him frown once or twice when he was not aware that she was watching him. For some reason these occasions had pleased and amused her. When a young man who ordinarily presents a particularly blank countenance to the world suddenly lapses into a display of temper, there is undoubtedly something amusing about the exhibition. It had occurred to her to wonder what Wickham was like when he wasn't on duty. Social contacts were funny things. She and he had been fellow employees for four months, and she knew less about him than she knew about the paperboy, who had given her full particulars about his fight with Bill Hampton from the green-grocer's round the corner and had also confided a cherished determination to learn the saxophone and graduate into a dance band.

When Joanna had been collected and they were slipping through the grey streets, Sarah found herself wondering about Wickham's ambitions. It had occurred to her once or twice that they might have come down in the dust. Something in the way he had looked when the duty mask had slipped. Something Joanna had said—but then Joanna was always so vague.

She slid her hand into the pocket of her fur coat and felt the edge of the letter she had written to Henry Templar. All that really mattered about Wickham at this moment was that she must get him to post Henry's letter.

The car was a Vauxhall limousine, and she was sitting in the comfortable back seat between Wilson and Joanna. She turned a little and said in her sweetest voice,

"Oh, Mr. Cattermole, would it be a trouble—might we stop at a pillar-box? There's a letter I would like to have posted."

Wilson beamed.

"But of course, Miss Sarah." He bent to the speaking tube. "The next pillar-box, Wickham."

When they drew up Sarah handed over her letter. They had stopped some ten yards short of the box. She watched Wickham go towards it, and thought, "He's not hurrying himself." All at once a seething impatience rose up in her. Here she was, tied down between Wilson and Joanna with a rug across her legs, when she might have been running to push her letter through the slit and hear it fall on the top of all the other safe, posted letters.

At this moment Wilson gave a smothered exclamation.

"Dear me—I had quite forgotten I have a letter too! How very stupid!"

With surprising energy he flung open the door, jumped out, and ran after Wickham, calling him back. Sarah watched them meet and talk for a moment. Wilson's hand went out. Then he turned and came back to the car, whilst the chauffeur went on to the letter-box. Still with that odd impatience, Sarah saw him pass round to the farther side. Now his hand went up, and now it fell again.

She sat back with a sigh of relief. Her letter to Henry was in the post, and she had nothing to do but wait and hunt ghosts until he came.

Chapter Twelve

"IT IS GETTING COLDER every moment," said Joanna Cattermole in a complaining voice. "I think it would have been better if we had gone down by train. Wick-ham looks very pale. Do you think he is really fit to drive? Influenza is such a horrid thing."

"He assures me that he is. I can do no more than ask him." Wilson's tone was rather dry. "I hope I am not such a barbarous employer that he would imagine himself bound to prevaricate. And as to his being pale, he never has very much colour. After all, two years in prison would remove the tan from his skin, and as he was only released in September he has not had much opportunity of regaining it."

Sarah had not meant to speak, but a painful stab of incredulity and pity brought words to her lips.

"In prison? Wickham?"

Wilson shook his head with an effect of self-reproach.

"Dear me—now I shouldn't have said that, should I? But I am sure, Miss Sarah, that it will be safe with you. I really had forgotten that I was not alone with my sister. Very wrong of me. Yes, the poor fellow was sent to me by one of those excellent societies which undertake the after care of discharged prisoners. But of course I did not intend that anyone except my sister and myself should be aware of his unfortunate past. He was involved in a bank robbery with violence. I believe he might consider himself lucky to have escaped with so light a sentence. It was either three years or two—I am not really sure which. I fear that he was led away by his unfortunate political opinions. He was, I regret to say, a member of a very extreme group of Communists, but, as I said to the secretary of the society at the time that I engaged him, 'Every man has a right to his opinions as long as they do not lead him into conflict with the law, and every man has a right to a second chance. I am sure that after his late unhappy experience he will do his best to avail himself of the chance I am prepared to offer him.'"

Sarah sat there wedged in, and had to listen. There was a great deal more, and she had to listen to all of it—Wilson's views on the Penal System, on Prison Reform, on Communism, on the Rights of Man—"As you know, I myself am a liberal"—with excursions into Free Trade, Raw Materials, and the Colonial Problem.

Joanna had fallen asleep, but tedious as Wilson might be, Sarah had never been more wide awake. The glass screen might be soundproof—she hoped with all her heart it was—but she felt a blatant indecency in the discussion of a man on the other side of it. She could see him in profile, the line of brow, cheek and chin. Suppose he could hear what was being said—suppose he had heard. The face should have been a sensitive one—it had a frozen look. She had seen him frown, but she had never seen him smile. Did two—or had it been three—years of prison blunt you so much that you didn't care, or did they drive thought and feeling inwards to rage and fester there?

Wilson came back to the point from which he had started.

"He was, I believe, at quite a well known public school. His father, I think, was in the army. A natural reaction from militarism, which I would be the last to condemn, may have been the beginning of his downfall. I myself, as you are doubtless aware, have been a lifelong pacifist—I was a conscientious objector during the last war...." He continued to talk.

It was about half an hour later that the car showed the first signs of trouble. After a mile or two of lumpy running, Wickham pulled up by the side of the road and opened the bonnet. Presently he came round to the window and announced that he would like to get the car to a garage.

"There'll be one at Hedgeley."

"Dear me—how very unfortunate! And how far is it to Hedgeley?"

"A couple of miles."

"Is there an hotel there?"

"Of sorts," said Wickham laconically.

"I said we ought to have come by train," said Joanna. "And it is going to snow—I feel quite sure that it is going to snow."

They were detained at Hedgeley long enough to reduce I Miss Cattermole to a state of nervous depression, and her brother to the limit of his self-control. The hotel was of the cheap commercial kind. The food was definitely bad. The fire in the coffee-room smoked and kept on going out. There was nothing to read. When Sarah suggested going out to get a paper, there seemed to be a number of reasons why she should not do so. The nearest paper shop was half a mile down the street. The car might be ready at any moment. The morning papers would be sold out and the evening papers not yet in. And finally, "I must really ask you not to leave my sister—she is in a sadly nervous state."

Sarah, whose inclination had been of the slightest, gave way, and was rewarded by a mild half promise that Wilson would look out for a paper-boy.

If he looked, it was in vain. No paper was forthcoming. Sarah, who was divided between boredom, curiosity, and a quite strong reluctance to read any more about Emily Case, began to wonder why there had been no papers at breakfast. As a rule there were three, but this morning none except yesterday's *Times*. She wondered whether Morgan had taken them. She wondered whether they contained too faithful a description of Sarah Marlowe.

The day grew steadily colder. At intervals of half an hour Wilson crossed the street to the garage and came back with discouraging reports.

"They can't find out what is wrong"... "Wick-ham says it may be the coil" ... "No, my dear, they cannot say how long they will be. We must just possess our souls in patience." ...

It was not until five o'clock that Wickham came across to say that the car was in running order. It was quite dark as they took the road, running on through the town and out upon a tree-bordered highway.

Presently they turned right-handed, and then turned again. Two right-hand turns take you back in the direction from which you have come, and a third brings you to the road you have just left. Prolonged boredom makes you either very dull or very observant. It had the latter effect upon Sarah. She said in a tone of surprise,

"Why, we are back on the Hedgeley road!"

"We might be on any road in this dreadful darkness," said Joanna in her most complaining voice. "I am sure I cannot think how Wickham manages to drive with those wretched black-out lights."

"Wickham is an extremely good driver," said Wilson complacently. "You need not be in the least nervous, my dear."

"But why are we going back?" said Sarah.

"What makes you think we are going back, Miss Sarah?"

She turned a puzzled face upon him.

"We are coming into Hedgeley again."

In the darkness she wondered whether Wilson was smiling. His voice sounded as if he were.

"One place looks exactly like another in the blackout, and I am sure you can trust Wickham not to lose his way."

Sarah said no more. She leaned back and stared out into the darkness. They were driving back, right through Hedgeley, between the garage and the hotel, past the church with the pointed spire. She could not see these things, but she knew that they were there. She knew that they drove right through the town and out at the other side.

Presently they took a turning which brought them by an uphill road to open ground. There were no trees or hedgerows any more, only a black moor in the darkness under a freezing sky.

Chapter Thirteen

ABOUT A QUARTER of an hour after Mr. Cattermole's Vauxhall had driven away from his front door Henry Templar walked up the steps and rang the bell. It was an unconventional hour, and Henry had been bred to a regard for the social conventions. If Sarah had been in her own home, it would still have been a little marked, but since she was Mr. Cattermole's employee, to walk in at half past nine in the morning and demand an interview was an uncomfortably conspicuous act, and one to which only a sense of extreme urgency could have compelled him.

His conversation with Sarah on the telephone the previous evening had exasperated and alarmed him. He had not known her for seven years without being aware of the lengths to which her warm heart, her generosity, and her obstinacy were capable of taking her. If she thought getting involved with the police was going to throw her out of a job and interfere with her supporting Miss Tinkler, then she was liable to compromise herself to almost any extent in a pig-headed attempt to dodge the law. When you came down to brass tacks, the thing that made women so difficult to deal with was that fundamentally they had no respect for the law. He supposed it was because they had only recently had any voice in the law-making business, and before that for generations of women the man-made and man-wielded law was a thing to be borne, suffered under, dodged, flouted, or broken.

During the watches of the night Henry considered very seriously the consequences which Sarah would be inviting if she persisted in withholding vital information from the police. He composed speeches and marshalled arguments, but he had extremely little hope that they would cause Sarah to see the error of her ways. In the whole time that he had known her he could not remember an occasion on which he had induced her to change her mind. Not when it had really mattered. And her answer when pressed had always amounted to this—"What's the good of arguing, when that's how I feel?"

There it was—if you were a woman you didn't reason; you felt. The irrational nature of the female sex really came home to him for the first time. Along with his serious consideration of the consequences which Sarah might be bringing upon herself, he began to be almost as deeply concerned about those in which he might himself be involved if he were to allow his feelings to precipitate him into matrimony. Because there was no disguising the fact that Sarah was a dangerously impulsive person. It was part of her charm. But—

During those sleepless hours Sarah's charm presented itself to Henry under the time-honoured guise of flowers decking the edge of a precipice. And Henry had no natural bent towards precipices.

At 7.0 a.m. he dialled Mr. Cattermole's number, and received no reply. At 7.15, at 7.30, and 7.45 he repeated the performance, with the same result. At eight o'clock he was informed that the line was out of order. He then rose, shaved, dressed, and breakfasted. By this time it was nine o'clock. He decided that by walking to Bank Street he would get some fresh air and exercise and catch Sarah before she started her morning's work. He could allow himself a quarter of an hour.

Thompson answered the bell, and the minute she opened the door Henry had a premonition. Something was going to go wrong with his neat timetable. Something had in fact already gone wrong. Thompson, prim and tidy in lilac print and an apron which crackled with starch, shook her head reprovingly. She too prized the conventions, and to come asking for a young lady when it wasn't hardly breakfast-time wasn't at all the thing—not in the class of house she was accustomed to.

"Oh, no, sir—they've just left."

"Left?" said Henry in a stupefied tone.

"Gone away for the week-end," said Thompson, as one explaining things to a dull-witted child.

"And there he stood," she told Mrs. Perkins afterwards in the kitchen. "Looked as if he couldn't hardly believe it, and frowned something shocking. And then he said, 'Are you sure?' and I said, 'Yes, sir.' And he said, 'Where have they gone? I suppose you can give me the address?' and I said, 'Indeed I can't!'"

Mrs. Perkins heaved a sigh.

"Sounds as if he'd got it bad," she said—"doesn't it?"

"I don't know about that." Thompson's voice was sharp.

Mrs. Perkins shook her head.

"Ah, no—you wouldn't. You mark my words, Lizzie, they've had a tiff—that's what it is. You mark my words!"

"That was him on the 'phone last night. I heard her say 'Henry' as I come past with my tray—'Henry, I can't', she said. And I thought to myself, 'You just go on saying that and it'll be a bit of all right.' And what it was he was wanting her to do, well, it isn't for me to say, but from what I've come across, they're all alike, men are, and all any of them want is to have things their own way, so I just hope she goes on saying can't to him."

Mrs. Perkins made a vaguely sympathetic sound.

"Ah well, dear, you're bitter—and no wonder, the way you were treated. But there's all sorts. You depend upon it, they've had a quarrel, and he come here on the way to his office in the hopes of making it up. A bit of a facer for him, poor fellow, to find them all gone off and no address, which I can't say I hold with myself. Suppose we was to be murdered in our beds, or the house burnt down—it stands to reason we ought to know where we could get word to Mr. Cattermole. We *did* ought to know where he is, and that's a fact."

"He doesn't want to be bothered," said Thompson—"and I don't blame him."

Henry Templar proceeded to his office, and in due course went out to lunch at his club, where he was joined by a friend of the name of Blenkinsop.

Mr. Blenkinsop, who was a year or two older than Henry, was the secretary of an Under-Secretary. It being Saturday, there was time for conversation as well as food. Mr. Blenkinsop was discreet, but not so discreet with Henry as he would have been with most other people.

Henry was never quite sure how the murder of Emily Case came up, but all in a minute there it was, and Blenkinsop was saying,

"The inquest's on Monday, I see, but they'll ask for an adjournment. There's something behind it, you know."

Henry said, "Is there?" and hoped that he said it in his usual tone.

Blenkinsop nodded.

"Oh, obviously. I wonder who the girl was."

"What girl?"

"The girl who was with her in the waiting-room of course. There's something there. Why doesn't she come forward?"

"People don't like getting mixed up in a murder case."

"Silly of her," said Blenkinsop briskly. "That morbid shrinking from publicity only results in attracting it. Nobody would have noticed her if she had come forward at once. Now everyone wants to know who she is."

It was perfectly true. Henry's annoyance with Sarah deepened. If she had taken his advice—Women never did take advice. They asked for it, but when they got it they chucked it away and did what they had all along made up their minds to do. He nodded and said gloomily,

"Girls don't reason. I expect she panicked."

Blenkinsop went on talking about Emily Case. It wasn't any use trying to deflect him, because when he wanted to talk about anything he talked about it. All you could do was to abstract your mind and wonder whether the club Stilton had definitely deteriorated, or whether it was merely your own palate.

Presently Blenkinsop appeared to have talked himself out. Putting sugar into his coffee, he produced a name like a rabbit from a hat.

"Blechmann—did you ever hear of anyone called Blechmann?"

Henry said, "No," and then wasn't sure. "Ought I to have heard of him?"

"I don't know—I just wanted to see if there was any reaction."

Henry said, "I don't think so—" There was just a trace of doubt in his voice. "What's it all about anyhow?"

Blenkinsop put his elbows on the table and leaned across it.

"Look here," he said, "do you remember when we were at Interlaken in July?"

"How do you mean, do I remember? Of course I remember."

"Well, what I really mean is, do you remember old Bloch?"

"Of course I remember him."

Blenkinsop edged nearer.

"Well, that gets us started. What do you remember about him?"

"Look here," said Henry, "I want to know what all this is about."

Blenkinsop gave an impatient sigh.

"I'll tell you in a minute, but I want you to say your piece first. Suppose it was a matter of life and death, and you had to make a statement—suppose you had to describe old Bloch—just what exactly would you say?"

"In a statement to the police?"

"If you like to put it that way."

"Is this a statement for the police?"

Blenkinsop's shoulder jerked.

"It might be. Go on—what would you say?"

Henry looked at him and considered. Something was certainly up. Blenkinsop had the air of a terrier at a rat hole—stubbly reddish hair bristling, small grey eyes alert and bright. He said,

"Well, he passed as a Dutchman—but as you're taking so much interest in him, he may have hailed from over the Rhine."

"I don't want speculation—only what you yourself observed."

Henry nodded.

"All right. As far as I came across him—and that wasn't any more than you did—he was just what he purported to be, an amiable middle-aged professor of entomology who had spent a good deal of his time in the Dutch East Indies. I suppose you don't want me to describe him?"

"Yes, I do. Go on."

"Sounds silly to me. You saw just as much of him as I did. Well, I should put him down at fifty-one or fifty-two—about five-foot-eleven—thickset and heavy—large, pale, flattish face—good teeth—deep voice—strong, very ugly hands.... I think that's about all."

"Hair? Eyes? Colouring?" Blenkinsop jerked the words at him one at a time.

"Well, I said he was pale—what more do you want? Eyes nondescript—hazel to grey—nothing you'd notice much anyway. Hair grey and rather long—but it was a wig, you know."

Blenkinsop took him up with energy.

"I know? How should I know? I didn't anyway. But what's more to the point is, how did *you* know?"

Henry laughed, partly at all this much ado about nothing, and partly at the recollection of old Bloch's head emerging egg-like from the bushes. He said,

"I know because I saw him without it. He tripped up and went head first down a bit of a slope into some bushes and came up bald as the back of your hand."

"You never told me."

"Well, as a matter of fact he asked me not to give him away. He was horribly put out and begged me not to mention it—said he'd lost his hair in Java, and that it was impossible for a man of science to keep his end up, especially with students, who he assured me were a race of devils, if they had any excuse for regarding him as an object of ridicule."

Blenkinsop said abruptly,

"Had he any eyelashes?"

"No—I don't think so. He wouldn't have if he'd lost all his hair like that."

"Blechmann was bald—no hair at all—no eyebrows, no eyelashes."

"So are dozens of other people," said Henry. "Anyhow, who's Blechmann? Your turn now—I'm through."

Blenkinsop drank his coffee at a gulp and pushed the cup away.

"Well, here you are. A man in the Foreign Office asked me if I wasn't at Interlaken in July, and when I said I was, he wanted everything I could tell him about Bloch. It seems they think he was Blechmann."

"I'd take more interest if I knew who Blechmann was."

"Well, that's just what they would like to know. Ostensibly he's a Belgian from the Eupen district, and actually he's a German agent, and a very clever one at that. He can pass as Belgian, Dutch, Swiss, or English. At the moment—look here, Henry, this is very hush-hush—they think he's over here, and they'd very much like to get their hands on him. The idea is that he's come over on Fifth Column business, to organize what you might call an extensive news-agency for transmitting weather reports and other information useful to the enemy."

"Why do they think he's Bloch?"

"I don't know, but they do. Your story about the wig rather bears it out. And here's something I didn't tell you. When I was in Paris in October I saw a man ahead of me in the street whom I took for Bloch. The light was bad, and I only had the back view to go by—a kind of silhouette, if you know what I mean. But I thought it was Bloch— something about the set of the head and the heavy shoulders—and when I caught him up it was a Frenchman with a little pointed beard and a flourishing moustache. *But he hadn't any eyelashes.* Now what my man wanted to know was this. Was there anything about Bloch which he couldn't disguise—besides the lack of eyelashes? And when I said I couldn't think of anything, he asked me who I had with me at Interlaken, and said I'd better find out whether you'd noticed anything I hadn't."

Henry was frowning. He said,

"His hands—I'd know them anywhere—beastly, ugly hands— thick through—fingers like a bunch of bananas. I'd know them anywhere. But look here, I should have thought he'd stick out a mile over here, because though his English was perfectly fluent, he'd any amount of accent."

"I'll tell you something," said Blenkinsop. He pushed his face right into Henry's. "I said he was ostensibly a Belgian from Eupen, but he isn't one really. My man says they're practically sure he's English, and that's what makes him so dangerous. He used to call himself Paul Black when he was over here. That is to say, they can't prove it, but they're morally convinced that Black, and Bloch, and Blechmann are all the same man, and that that man was English born."

"And what do they think he's calling himself now?"

"They haven't the faintest idea," said Blenkinsop.

Chapter Fourteen

IN THE KITCHEN of no. 12 Bank Street Mrs. Perkins and Thompson had finished their midday meal and were enjoying a nice cup of tea. The old-fashioned range gave out a warm, glowing heat, and a savoury smell of rabbit curry hung in the air. When the sound of the telephone bell made itself heard it was received without enthusiasm.

"If it was me I'd let it ring," said Mrs. Perkins comfortably.

But Thompson got out of her chair with a jerk.

"If I don't go, it'll be Miss Cattermole to say she's left something. Such a to-do we had getting her off—worse than ever, though you wouldn't think she could be. And if I do go, as like as not it'll be Mr. Templar or some such, going on about that address. And if I haven't got it I can't give it to him—well, can I?"

But when she took up the receiver and put it to her ear, it wasn't Henry Templar. It was Mr. Cattermole all right, and a good deal sharper and more to the point than he sometimes was.

"Is that you, Thompson?"

"Yes, sir."

"Well, will you please listen. I have come away without some papers which I had promised to post to a friend. That is to say, Miss Marlowe was to have sent them off for me yesterday, and she seems to have forgotten to do so. Can you hear me all right?"

"Oh, yes, sir."

"From what she tells me, I am afraid that the papers have been mislaid. I cannot understand how it has happened—she is usually so careful. But there it is, and I have had to ring up my friend and let him know. He is naturally a good deal put out, and as he attaches considerable importance to having the papers today, he suggested that he should come round to my house and look for them."

"I could do that, sir." There was a note of offence in Thompson's voice.

"To be sure—to be sure. But you might not know when you had found them. No, Mr. Green had better come round—in fact I have already accepted his kind offer. This is just to tell you that he has my authority, and that you can allow him to make a thorough search. It is most unfortunate that Miss Marlowe should have no idea what she did with the papers, so you must just allow Mr. Green to go on looking until he finds them. Is that quite clear?"

"Yes, sir—quite clear. Is it your wish that I should stay in the room with the gentleman while he does his looking?"

"Oh, no, that will not be necessary—not in the least. He will ring and let you know when he is finished."

"Did you say the name was Green, sir?"

"Yes, Green—Mr. Frederick Green. That will be all."

Thompson went back to the kitchen with a grievance.

"I suppose I can find anything as well as a Mr. Never-heard-of-him-before Green! And if it was my house, I wouldn't want a strange gentleman here there and everywhere, turning things inside out. Queer goings on, that's what I call it."

Mrs. Perkins drained the teapot into her cup.

"Well, queer he is, and no getting from it. And what you want to worry yourself for, Lizzie, I can't think. Saves you a lot of trouble, this Mr. Green coming and looking instead of you, and all the rooms as cold as ice. If it was me, I'd be thankful I could stay in the warm and get on with that comforter you're supposed to be knitting for your cousin Hetty's eldest that you told me might be called up any minute now. You'll get a nice piece done over the week-end if you set to it. I'm in my fourth sock for my niece Ethel's husband, and I reckon to get the two pair done in time to take them round tomorrow afternoon."

Mr. Green arrived at a quarter to three—a small, brisk gentleman in a blue serge suit and a bowler hat. Behind horn-rimmed spectacles his eyes were very sharp indeed. He wore a black overcoat and carried an umbrella and a brown attaché case. Thompson disapproved of his shoes.

She came back into the kitchen and told Mrs. Perkins that he was the right one for the job and no mistake about it. "Nosey Parker written all over him—read anyone's letters as soon as look at them. If Miss Marlowe's got any lying about that she wouldn't want read, well, I'm sorry for her. But I've got my orders—he's to go where he likes and poke his nose wherever he pleases, and no one to keep an eye on him.

But I tell you this—orders or no orders, he doesn't go into my room without I'm there."

It was not the first time that Mr. Green had searched a house. He knew all the likely places in which to look for papers which somebody wanted to hide, and all the unlikely places too. He ran those sharp eyes of his over mattresses and pillows to see whether there was any sign that one or the other had been unpicked. An inch or two of different cotton, a seam sewn by hand instead of on a machine, and he would have had it unripped before you could say knife. Had the dust under the edge of a carpet been disturbed? Was there anything fastened to the under side of any table, chair, bedstead, or other article of furniture? And so forth and so on. He made a very thorough job of it. Short of taking down the wall-paper and taking up the floor, he went through the house with a tooth-comb, working methodically from the top to the bottom.

At a very early stage in the proceedings he encountered the oiled-silk packet, and immediately noticed, as Sarah had noticed, that two inches of the stitching featured an ordinary white cotton instead of the prevailing linen thread. At this evidence of carelessness he made a clicking sound with his tongue against the roof of his mouth. Having been instructed by their employer that the packet now contained nothing of interest, some agents would have left it at that, but not Mr. Green. He reopened the packet and discovered that the envelope inside contained nothing more exciting than some strips of newspaper. He took the trouble to sew the oiled silk up again, and to use the linen thread which he had noticed in Miss Marlowe's dressing-table drawer, although according to his information it was extremely unlikely that she would ever see the packet again.

At the end of two hours he had satisfied himself that the lists were not in the house. Under the disapproving gaze of Thompson he had gone rapidly through her room and that of Mrs. Perkins, after which he retired to the study and rang up Hedgeley 673.

The ring produced the hall-porter of the George, and the hall-porter produced Mr. Cattermole.

"That you?... Green speaking. Well, I've been right through everything, and they're not here.... Sure? Of course I'm sure! It's my job, isn't it? You don't ask your cook whether she can fry a rasher. They're not here, and you may take it that's final."

He rang off, put on his black overcoat and his bowler hat, picked up his brown attaché case and his umbrella, and walked out of the house.

At the sound of the closing door Thompson looked up gloomily from her knitting.

"Mr. Nosey Parker Green!" she said, and dropped a stitch.

Chapter Fifteen

SARAH'S FIRST IMPRESSION of Maltings was also to be her most lasting one. Solitude, darkness, and cold. A gloom in which all detail was lost obscured the approach, but so narrow and rough a track could only exist in a lonely and unfrequented locality.

The house, when they reached it, was no more than a spreading blur. They came into a sparsely lighted hall which even after the bitter outside cold struck dank and chill. It was of some size, with stone flags under foot and a gaping black hearth rising to a great chimney. At the far end the stair ran up to the bedroom floor. The place was plainly old, and as plainly ill kept and in need of repair, the air stale with a mingled smell of mould, tobacco smoke, and a suggestion of spilled oil. What light there was came from an old-fashioned paraffin lamp fastened to the wall.

The Reverend Peter Brown came bustling to meet them—a large, untidy man, all hair and beard and spectacles, in baggy clerical clothes and carpet slippers. He shook hands, exclaiming at the cold, at his pleasure in their arrival, and ushered them past a closed door on either side into what he termed "my den".

Sarah was wishing that she had not taken off her glove. The clasp of Mr. Brown's hand affected her unpleasantly. She wasn't quite sure what there was about it, but she did not like the contact—something smooth and damp. Smooth—that was odd, because he had such a lot of hair everywhere else. But there was no hair on his hands.

The den was as untidy as Mr. Brown himself. There was a very dirty carpet on the floor, frowsy curtains, a littered writing-table, a bottle of whisky, and a thick tumbler like a tooth-glass. But at least the room was warm. A hot fire burned in the dirty grate.

Here, under the light of a lamp with a ground-glass globe, Mr. Brown looked larger and shaggier than ever. His grizzled hair came down to his bushy eyebrows, and the eyebrows straggled into his spectacles in what Sarah felt must be a most uncomfortable manner. As for his beard—and she had always hated men with beards—it started somewhere on a level with his ears, and after covering the greater part of his cheeks and the whole of his upper lip and chin came well down over the middle of his waistcoat. Like the hair of his head it was grizzled and curly. From its depths glimpses of strong, white teeth could be seen when he smiled. He smiled a good deal.

"Well now"—the Reverend Peter beamed upon them—"this is really very delightful indeed! But perhaps the ladies would like to see their rooms. I am afraid, Miss Cattermole, that you will find us very primitive after London. A most interesting old house, but no modern conveniences—we have to pump our water, and hot water has to be carried up in cans. However, as I always say, the men who made England what she is today were born and bred in just such surroundings as these, and if we cannot put up with them for once in a while—well, I maintain we prove that we are degenerate, and not that the conditions are insupportable." He had a rich, resonant voice and rolled out his sentences as if he were addressing a congregation.

Joanna put up her hand to her floating hair.

"Oh, if I might, Mr. Brown! It has been such a long, cold journey."

Cold—it was the cold that dominated everything. The bare boards of the upper landing seemed to give it off. Once they might have shone with beeswax, but now, dull and dented, they echoed as drearily as if the house around them were quite uninhabited.

Four doors opened upon the landing. The dark mouth of a passage showed on the right.

Mr. Brown did the honours with effusion. He carried a lamp, and allowed its yellow light to mitigate the darkness of each room in turn.

"Miss Cattermole, I have put you here. I do hope you will find the arrangements adequate. There are a pair of candles on the dressing-table—oh, thank you, Miss Marlowe, that is so very kind. Well now, here we are. And you are just a little further along. I think you have the matches—if you will be so good. Ah—that is quite an illumination! And the room beyond is the best we can do towards providing a bathroom—I do hope that you will find it adequate. Now, Mr. Cattermole, you and I are across the landing. And there is a room for your chauffeur just down that passage. I hope you have no objection. Mr. and Mrs. Grimsby, my married couple, occupy a room next the kitchen, the only one available down there, and I hardly liked to put him in the old part of the house—the manifestations can be very alarming."

"The old part?" said Joanna fretfully. "All this looks old enough."

Mr. Brown shook his head.

"This part is only seventeenth-century. It has always been called the new wing. The really interesting part is a good deal older. It has not been occupied for at least a hundred years, and portions of it are not very safe, so we always keep the connecting doors locked. There is one on the ground floor, and one up here at the end of that passage. But your man need not be nervous—there are never any manifestations on this side."

When she was alone with Sarah, Joanna sat down and burst into tears.

"I would never have come if I had known what it was going to be like—and I ought to have known, because I was warned. I woke up this morning with the most distinct impression of someone saying 'No'. And it was a warning. When Wilson came bursting in with this ridiculous plan and said we were all going down to Maltings I ought to have remembered about the voice and said no, because it was a message and a warning. I shall probably get pneumonia."

"Dear Miss Cattermole!"

The hectic colour brightened in Joanna's cheeks.

"Sarah, can you look me in the face and say you honestly believe that these beds have ever been aired since the house was built? And we came off in such a hurry that I didn't bring my scales or any of the health foods."

"Hot bricks," said Sarah in a firm, soothing voice. "I'll get hold of Wickham."

"Hot bricks?"

"Wrapped in flannel and put into the bed. Much better than hot water bottles, and you can have dozens."

They descended to a kind of tea-supper in an awful room with chocolate lincrusta on the walls and an oleograph of Mr. Gladstone over the mantelpiece.

The food was surprisingly good. Whatever Mrs. Grimsby's other shortcomings were, she could cook. There was tea, and there was whisky, and there was beer. There were scones of heavenly lightness. There was the kind of omelette you do not expect to find in the English country. There were sausage-rolls which melted in the mouth. There was angel-cake, and homemade macaroons, and a queer dark red jelly which Sarah thought was quince. And they were all very, very good. Sarah felt very much better when she had eaten them. The idea of having to confront ghosts on a cold and empty stomach had been getting her down, but Mrs. Grimsby's high tea had a fortifying effect. She could have wished Joanna the same support, but milk and water and about a teaspoonful of omelette was as far as Miss Cattermole would venture. Wilson, with the air of a man who braves the worst, actually partook of sausage-roll and angel-cake and washed them down with copious draughts of weak tea.

Mr. Brown showed himself to have a hearty appetite. He also displayed a remarkable capacity for talking and eating at the same time. Sarah thought her employer piqued by their host's monopoly of the conversation, his efforts to enter it and, having entered, to maintain his position being rendered ineffectual by the superior resonance of the Reverend Peter's voice—a robust organ, and with great reserves of power. He had only to boom a little louder, and Wilson's feeble twitterings were swallowed up.

On the whole this was an agreeable change. She had plenty of Wilson at home, and the Reverend Peter, though profuse, was not uninteresting. In spite of his uncouth appearance, he spoke like a man of culture and breeding. He had evidently travelled widely, and was engaged upon a monumental work dealing with folk lore in its connection with psychic phenomena.

"It is an aspect which has been largely overlooked. The vampire stories have of course attracted an undue amount of attention, but that, I think, can be put down more to the spectacular success of Mr. Bram Stoker's blood-curdling romance *Dracula* than to any spirit of scientific enquiry."

"Very true—very true indeed. These works of fiction—"

"Completely obscure the realities of the situation," continued Mr. Brown. "That is what I was just about to observe."

Joanna turned bright apprehensive eyes upon him.

"Oh, Mr. Brown—*not* vampires! If you don't mind—so disturbing! I really don't think—I remember reading *Dracula* when I was a girl, and I woke up in the middle of the night clutching my throat. I had screamed so loud that I had waked up everyone in the house, and my dear father took the book away and put it on the kitchen fire."

Mr. Brown laughed heartily.

"Then we will certainly not talk about vampires, for I am most anxious that you should sleep well after your very trying journey."

Sarah wondered whether this would be a good moment to mention bricks. The beds were sure to be damp, and even if they were not, Joanna was so firmly convinced they were that she was all set to worry herself into having a chill. But before she could speak Mr. Brown had started again about folk-lore.

"More widely spread but far less widely known are the stories in which some man or woman forms an association or a marriage with a non-human partner. There is usually a condition attached to the continuance of the association. In one story the woman disappears when her husband has broken a vow never to speak roughly to her in company. In perhaps the most famous of the tales Melusine, who married the Comte Guy de Lusignan, exacted from him the promise that once a year when a certain day came round he would most strictly respect her privacy and make no attempt to enter her chamber. They lived together happily for a considerable time, and she bore him several children—this, by the way, is a common feature of these stories—but at length his curiosity got the better of his good faith. He gave out that he was going hunting, but actually he returned in secret and through the keyhole or some other small aperture looked into his wife's room. There he saw the beautiful Melusine bathing herself. But she was only a woman as far as the waist. The rest of her shape was that of a brightly coloured serpent. The Count in his horror uttered some cry or oath, whereupon he saw his wife's face change horribly and become convulsed with rage. After which she spread dragon's wings and sailed out of the window, never to be seen again. That also is a common feature of these legends—the person disappears—and is never seen again."

Mr. Brown's fine voice invested this climax with a thrill of genuine horror.

Sarah murmured to herself, "*Grimm's Fairy Tales—*" But that "never seen again" had sent a shiver down her spine. She brought her mind back firmly to the question of hot bricks for Joanna's bed, and managed to keep it there while Mr. Brown discoursed about Tobit and the Angel, the Hound of the Pandava brothers, and Hans Andersen's Travelling Companion, which he declared had its counterpart in nearly every European country.

As he spoke, Sarah pursued her own thoughts. A question which had preoccupied her at intervals recurred strongly. Where, all this time, was the male half of the Reverend Peter's married couple? He had spoken of the Grimsbys, and whilst Mrs. Grimsby was represented by her omelette, her quince jelly, her angel-cake, and sausage-rolls, Grimsby had so far not been in evidence at all. And it was probably to Grimsby that she should address a demand for hot bricks.

One part of her mind continued to concern itself with this problem, whilst the rest gave a surface attention to Mr. Brown's further remarks about disappearing partners. He had brought them down to the present day with the rather intriguing story of a girl whose husband disappeared with a loud clang in an octagon turret room at midnight on Hallowe'en before a move was made to the other room.

Joanna shivered as they crossed the hall.

"I think perhaps if you would be so good, Sarah—just my blue chiffon scarf. I have left a candle burning."

As Sarah came out of the bedroom with the scarf in her hand she saw Wickham at the entrance to the passage on the other side of the landing. It startled her to see him standing there. He was in his chauffeur's uniform, but bare-headed. His shoulder leaned against the wall.

Her first thought was, "What is he doing here?" I Then she remembered Mr. Brown saying that he had given him a room at the end of the passage.

She crossed the landing, and saw him straighten up and make as though to turn away. She was in her travelling-suit, all dark, all brown, from her dark shining hair to her dark brown shoes. The blue scarf, a bright wispy thing interwoven with silver, struck an alien note. But Sarah was not thinking about colour-schemes. She was a persevering girl, and in Wickham she saw a solution of the great brick problem. She called softly but insistently, and when he turned she plunged directly into the business.

"Oh, Wickham—the beds are damp, and Miss Cattermole says she will get pneumonia. Do you think the man here—Grimsby, isn't that his name?—well, do you think he could produce some hot bricks—you know, baked in the oven—and then we can wrap them up and move them about until the bed is comparatively dry. It's the only thing I can think of. And do you think you can find Grimsby and get him going? I haven't set eyes on him myself, and I don't like to go into the kitchen."

Wickham preserved an impassive front. His last view of Grimsby blind to the world did not encourage the supposition that he could be got going this side of tomorrow. What he said was,

"I'll see what I can do."

After which he turned rather abruptly and walked away down the passage.

Sarah ran downstairs with the scarf in her hand. She ran because she really didn't want to go down at all, and the best way of doing what you don't want to do is to do it quickly. Cold as the hall was, she would rather have stayed even there than go back into Mr. Brown's den. She didn't know when she had taken such a dislike to a room.

The air was heavy and hot as she opened the door. The smell of the kerosene lamp and the smell of Mr. Brown's pipe lay upon it in layers. No one took any notice of her. She pushed the door to behind her. The hasp did not catch. She had to turn round and shake the handle before she could make it stay shut. Mr. Brown was saying,

"De-materialization is not the only way in which a person can disappear. I have known some other ways myself." He laughed as he spoke.

The room was hot. Sarah came from the icy cold of the unwarmed house. And once again she felt a creeping shiver run down her spine.

Chapter Sixteen

WHEN THE EVENING was over and Sarah looked back upon it she wondered why she had minded it so much. There was nothing that she could take hold of. Mr. Brown was an interesting and assiduous host. Mrs. Grimsby's coffee had all the virtues which coffee should have but so very seldom achieves. Above all—and for this she really did feel grateful—no one suggested that they should repair to the haunted wing. Yet in spite of all this she had felt, and indeed was still feeling, most uncomfortably like a dog who is about to put his nose in the air and howl.

Mercifully, Joanna cut the evening short by at least an hour of its orthodox time. It was no more than half past nine when she shivered, yawned behind the hand which wore her mother's sapphire ring, and said that she thought she would like to go to bed.

Sarah accompanied her with enthusiasm, and Mr. Brown, in his character of attentive host, came up to make sure that they had all they required. He stood in the doorway of Miss Cattermole's room and frowned at the small, shrunk fire.

"But you have no coal! That's very remiss of Grimsby—very remiss indeed. But I believe the poor fellow is indisposed. Perhaps your man.... Oh, no, my dear Miss Cattermole, you must certainly keep a good fire. The weather is most inclement, and it is some time since this room was used. I will just take the scuttle and get your man—what is his name?—ah, yes, Wickham—to fill it and make up the fire

for you. I really should not sleep if I thought that you might be cold."
He went off with the scuttle.

Sarah slipped her hand under the bedclothes and felt a delicious warmth. Wickham had managed to produce the hot bricks. There they were, four of them, wrapped in newspaper, with an old-fashioned copper warming-pan to keep them company.

Joanna gazed at them in an uninterested way.

"Yes—very nice," she said. And then, in a voice that had gone away to a whisper, "Why did we come?"

"The bed can't possibly be damp now."

Sarah's tone was cheerful, but her spirits sank. If Joanna was going to have an attack of gloom, it really would be the last straw. If it had not been for the cold, she would have begun getting Miss Cattermole out of her clothes and into a good warm bed, but with the probability of Wickham arriving at any moment there was nothing for it but to wait. She said,

"Do you know, I've never seen a warming-pan in a bed before—only hanging on walls."

"Why did we come?" said Joanna again. Her eyes were fixed and staring. "You ought to have said no. He couldn't have made you come. This house is full of evil. Don't you feel it?"

"It's full of damp," said Sarah in a practical voice. "And I should think there were cockroaches in the kitchen. I don't believe the house has had a good spring-cleaning for at least fifty years—that's the feeling it gives me."

Joanna had been looking, not at Sarah, but at some point above and behind her. Now suddenly her stare shifted and broke. Tears rushed into her eyes. She put a groping hand on Sarah's arm.

"Don't talk like that! You—"

Feet crossing the landing, and a knock on the half-open door—

With relief Sarah drew away.

"Come in!" she said, and pulled the door wide to let in Wickham and the coals.

He made up the fire carefully and went out. She heard him go along to her room and come out again.

The break had changed Joanna's mood. She was restless, irritable, eager to be alone.

When Sarah left her and emerged upon the landing she saw to her surprise that Wickham was still there. She had heard him come out of her room, but he had done no more than that. A heavy baluster guarded the well of the stairs. Like them it was of oak and dark with age. Wickham was leaning against the corner post, bent forward with outstretched hands grasping the rail on either side. In the dim light the effect was startling in the extreme. It was the attitude of a man who has been flung by a wave upon some piece of wreckage to which he most desperately clings.

Sarah repressed an exclamation, shut Joanna's door behind her, and ran to him.

His head was bent. The hand she touched was clammy. Even in the half light she could see the sweat upon his face.

"What is it?" Her voice was low and insistent. The arm she held was rigid.

And all in that moment she heard a door open upon the hall below, letting out a rush of voices and the sound of feet. They rang on the cold air.... Footsteps now on the stone flags—and the voices nearer—

She said, "They're coming up," and Wickham stirred, lifting his head and drawing a long breath that was just not a groan. Next moment as the voices rose towards them, plainly coming nearer, he straightened up and, whether by his own volition or hers, she did not really know, reeled back across the half dozen feet which separated them from her open door. It was certainly Sarah who pulled him in and shut the door upon them. Her heart thudded. She had the wildest sense of danger escaped.

When he had sunk down upon a sagging wide-lapped chair, she turned the key in the lock and ran to dip a towel in the ewer and come back with it cold and wet. He lay in a helpless sprawled attitude, shoulders slipping, one hand trailing on the floor. She thought he had fainted, but when the icy water touched his face he jerked away from it and opened his eyes.

Two candles burned on the dressing-table. He must have lighted them himself, for she had left the room in darkness. They made a soft yellow glow, very quiet and steady. By this light their eyes met. His were clouded. A veil had been dropped, and a veil withdrawn. The cold pride which had ruled there was hidden. Something anguished and helpless looked out.

It was only for a moment, and then the cloud was gone. A controlled alertness took its place. He said on what was only just a breath, "Water—" and when she brought it to him in a heavy old-fashioned tumbler he was ready to hold out a hand for it. When he had drunk, the faintness seemed to have passed. He drew himself up in the chair, looked about him, and said, still in that soundless voice,

"Why did you bring me here?"

She put the glass down and came back with a sparkle in her eyes. "Did I bring you?"

"Well, I'm here. I don't remember very much about it, I'm afraid. I must apologize. I've been having influenza."

Sarah frowned.

"You shouldn't have carried those coals. Where's Grimsby?" She spoke as he had done, with the least sound that would carry the words.

For the first time, she saw his face relax.

"Blind," he said.

Her frown deepened.

"You shouldn't have done it. Are you all right again?"

He nodded.

"If you don't mind seeing that the coast is clear, I'll be off."

"Are you sure you're all right?"

"Quite. Just look out and see if there's anyone about."

As Sarah unlocked the door she wondered at the impulse which had made her lock it. The whole thing was quite beyond reason. She had found Wickham fainting, and instead of feeling relief at the approach of help she had experienced an irrational but quite overwhelming terror.

She looked out and found the landing bare. As she turned back towards the room, Wickham was beside her, one hand on the jamb as if he needed it to steady him. He was so close that she had to look up to see his face. It was still dreadfully pale. The corner of his lip lifted in a twitching smile.

"The stock compromising situation," he murmured, and was gone.

She shut the door immediately. But she stayed there with her hand upon it. When a long minute had gone by she drew it open again and looked out—faint yellow light—an empty landing—the passage running away into the dark. From where she stood she could have seen almost to the end of it if there had been a light there, but there was no light. Only as she waited she heard the faint sound of a closing latch. With the sound a weight seemed to lift. She shut her own door locked it, and went over to the bed. Fatigue had come over her—a longing to lie down and sleep.

But when she turned the bedclothes back she felt all at once as if a finger had been laid upon some spring of tears and laughter. Joanna's bed had been pranked out with four hot bricks and a warming-pan. Since there was no warming-pan for Sarah, she had been given six bricks, all neatly wrapped in Mrs. Grimsby's clean kitchen paper. Newspapers were good enough for Miss Cattermole, but Sarah Marlowe's bricks went very fine in white. She could have cried, and she could have laughed.

And then she was angry, with a little quick anger which hurt. What business had he to give her more bricks than Joanna, and to wrap them in white paper? And what business had he to go toiling up and down the stairs with bricks and coals until he fainted? She hadn't asked him for bricks for herself anyhow. And why couldn't someone throw a bucket or two of cold water over that drunken beast Grimsby and make him do his own coal-carrying?

Her anger focussed itself upon Grimsby in a very satisfying manner. When a man has just fainted in your service, you cannot get any satisfaction out of being angry with him. Grimsby was the most convenient scapegoat.

As she undressed she began to think about Henry Templar. He would have got her letter by now—oh, yes without fail—and he would certainly come down with the least possible delay. If he could get leave off he might be down by the middle of the morning. He would get leave if he asked for it. But would he ask? Sometimes she thought he would, and sometimes she thought he wouldn't, because of course he would have to say why. Henry mightn't mind that—but then on the other hand he might. He would have to go to his chief and say, "Look here, I know the girl whom the police want to interview about the Case murder, and if you'll give me the day off, I think I can persuade her to come back and talk to them." Well, would Henry say that, or wouldn't he? Because unless he did, he couldn't possibly get down here till pretty late in the evening.

She had reached the pyjama stage without being able to make up her mind what Henry was likely to do. She dropped her shoes by the dressing-table, peeled off her stockings, and went over towards the bed with the candle in her hand. As she passed the chair in which Wickham had sunk down, her naked foot touched something wet—a wet, cold spot on the carpet—a wet, sticky spot.

Instantly everything in her startled. She had dipped her towel in water. She told herself that it had dripped upon the floor. But she had stood on the other side of the chair and leaned to him from there. It couldn't possibly have dripped on this side.

She stayed where she was with the candle in her hand for about a minute, and then very slowly she drew back. The carpet was dark with age, the colours sunk and changed—blue gone away into grey, and crimson into rust. There was a small wet patch where Wickham's hand had hung trailing down. Her foot had touched this spot.

She held the candle steady and, stooping, touched the smeared patch with the tip of her finger.

The stain was blood.

Chapter Seventeen

SARAH LAY IN BED. She had put out the candle but the room was not dark. The fire which Wickham had made up was burning clear. She could see the shape of the chair in which he had leaned back fainting. She could not see the patch which his blood had made upon the carpet, but she knew that it was there. She had been shivering with cold when she got into bed, but she was warmer now. She kept the bricks close to her, and was glad of them.

What was she going to do?

She had at present no idea at all.

The obvious course she had not even debated. For some reason, or rather for no reason at all, she could neither go to Wilson Cattermole who was Wickham's employer, nor to Mr. Brown who was their host, and say, "Look here, this man is ill. He has some wound, some injury. He nearly fainted on my hands just now." Every time she thought of doing this—and she had thought of doing it—a deep, irresistible reluctance blocked the way. It was beyond argument. It was bound up with the unexplained impulse which had made her lock the door upon Wickham and herself.

And so what?

One of two things. She could do something, or she could just do nothing at all—turn over and go to sleep and leave to-morrow to take care of itself.

Put into words, the second possibility lost any appearance of being possible. It was not in Sarah to go peacefully to sleep when someone might, for all she knew, be bleeding to death just down the passage. She might argue the improbability of this terrifying suspicion as vehemently as she pleased, but there was only one way of disposing of it, and that was to go and see for herself. It was so simple that in ordinary circumstances there would have been no need to think about it twice. The trouble was that the circumstances were not ordinary. They loomed, they teemed with possibilities, they threatened and commanded. If she put a foot wrong, all this looming and teeming and threatening might close in upon her and precipitate disaster, and the fact that she had no idea what form this disaster might take only added to her misgiving.

Anyhow she could do nothing until the house was still. She had heard Wilson and Mr. Brown come up some twenty minutes ago, but it would not be safe to count on their remaining in the rooms they had entered. For all she knew, they might have planned a midnight excursion into the haunted wing. It was cold enough to put even the most determined ghost-hunter off, but—you never could tell.

She waited half an hour and lit the candle.

By this time she had her plan. First she would clean up the bloodstain on the floor and make sure there were no others, and then she would satisfy herself that that wretched young man was not bleeding to death.

Something like panic overtook her at the thought. He had been gone the best part of an hour, and a good deal of bleeding to death could be done in the time. She spoke sharply to herself on the subject of exaggerated phrases. "You say bleeding to death, but of course that's nonsense. What you mean is that he may have a cut that ought to be properly tied up."

The towel she had wetted hung on the old-fashioned wooden horse. She used it to rub out the stain on the carpet. There was a smear on the arm of the chair, and a dark patch on the wood of the jamb where he had leaned when she opened the door. When she had got all the stains out she had the towel on her hands, and a nasty messy sight it was. It is quite astonishing how far a little blood will go.

She undid her door and looked out. The light still burned on the landing, but the lower hall was dark. The improvised bathroom was no more than a dozen feet away. She reached it in triumph and locked herself in. There was no fixed bath, but there was a hip-bath, a sink, and a cold-water tap. There was also a bar of yellow soap. Bloodstains are quite amenable when they are fresh, and cold water gets them out better than hot.

She made the return journey. Having hung the towel over the horse again, she considered the next stage of the adventure. The landing was a wide one some twenty feet across, with the well of the stairs coming up into it. She would have to skirt the well and pass the Reverend Peter's door to reach the passage. Once round the corner, she would be out of sight even if anyone did open a door and look out, the only room which commanded a view of the passage being her own. The trouble was that she dared not take a candle, and she did not really know which was Wickham's door. The passage was a long one. There were doors on either side. All she had to help her was the impression that Mr. Brown had indicated a room at the far end. He had apologized for putting Wickham on this floor at all. She thought his sense of decorum would have placed him at as great a distance from his employers as possible.

Well, it was no good thinking too much about it. She put on the blue dressing-gown over her pyjamas and reached the mouth of the passage without drawing a second breath. Once she was round the corner there was an illusory sense of safety. She was shut in between these long, straight walls, and with every step the half light from the landing grew fainter, and dusk shaded into darkness.

A dozen feet down the passage there was a door on the right. She opened it cautiously and felt a cold draught come up in her face. She could see nothing at all, but the place did not feel like a room. She guessed at a stair. There was a smell of damp, and soot, and food. She thought the stair must go down to the kitchen premises.

She drew back, shut the door again, and went on. There were three more doors. She slid her hand along the wall, feeling first on one side of the passage and then on the other. The last door was on the left. Her fingers touched the jamb. She thought she had come to the end of the passage, and feeling before her with both hands now, she came upon a wall that blocked her way. There was a locked door in it. This, then, was the way into the haunted wing. The door felt heavy and old, with a great bolt set in it beside the lock.

She drew back, and went to the door on the left. All these doors had smooth wooden handles. The knob was icy cold against her palm as she turned it softly and let the door swing in. She must have pushed it, for it slipped from her hand and went on moving until she could see the whole room.

She stood on the threshold and looked in. There was a clutter of furniture, all dark and dimly seen by the light of a half-burned candle. The candle was on a chair by the side of the bed. It stood so low that all the shadows were thrown upwards. The flame moved in the draught, and all the tall, dark shadows moved and wavered too.

Sarah came in and shut the door softly behind her. Wickham was lying across the bed. He was in shirt and breeches. There had been some attempt to drag the bedclothes across him, but they had fallen back and he was for the most part uncovered. But he was asleep. He lay on his back, his left hand at his breast, the other arm thrown wide.

Sarah stood there and wondered how old he was, and why he had robbed a bank, and how he had got his wound. For a wound there certainly was. The left side of his shirt was stained with blood beneath his hand, and under it she could see the shape of a bandage.

How silly of him not to undress properly and cover himself up. He must have been most desperately tired to fall asleep like this. A bitter air came in from behind the dark curtain which screened an open window. She thought it was just as well that she had come. He didn't seem to be bleeding now, so she need not wake him up, but she could at least cover him.

She bent over the bed, and saw her own shadow run up the wall to a fantastic height. It wasn't going to be so easy to cover him properly. His right foot had caught in the bedclothes and was holding them down. She had to free them gently an inch at a time, taking some of his weight with her other hand. Odd how heavy a man's foot could be. The words "a dead weight" passed through her mind and left a shudder behind them.

But he wasn't dead. He was only asleep—deeply, dreamlessly asleep.

She began to draw the bedclothes over him—the sheet, a heavy cotton twill; three blankets, very thin and yellow; and a wadded quilt covered with an old sprigged chintz. As she settled the quilt she heard his breathing change, and with no more warning than that a hand shot up and took her by the wrist. His eyes opened, looked into hers, and were at once sharply awake.

"What are you doing here?"

Sarah was feeling pleased with herself. Until you have been in an emergency you cannot possibly know how you will behave. She might have screamed, and she hadn't screamed—she hadn't even gasped. She said in a cool, soft voice,

"I was covering you up."

"Why?"

"Because you were uncovered."

She saw him frown, and zigzagging into her mind came the idea that he frowned because he might very easily have laughed. She said severely,

"You really shouldn't lie there under an open window with nothing over that wound."

"Wound, Miss Marlowe?"

"Yes, wound. I'm not asking you where you got it or how you got it—I daresay it won't bear asking about. But if you come and bleed all over my carpet and then just fling yourself down and go to sleep in a bloodstained shirt—well, it isn't any good saying you haven't got a wound, is it?"

He pulled himself up against the head of the bed. He did not wince, because he did not allow himself to wince, but as far as deceiving Miss Sarah Marlowe went the effort was wasted.

"Look here," she said, "I think you're being stupid. Is that thing properly bandaged?"

"It is."

"Sure?"

"It has had the best surgical attention. I'm sorry I bled on the carpet. What have you done about it?"

"I washed it. It wouldn't have shown anyhow. You could have a murder on any of these carpets without its showing."

"Perhaps that's why they're here." The words were light, but the tone was not a light one. His eyes looked straight into hers, and another of those nasty shivers ran down her spine. He said, still in that menacing voice, "You had better get back. Let's hope no one sees you."

Miss Marlowe's colour rose brightly.

"I came because for all I knew you might have been bleeding to death."

"Thank you—it was most kind. But I don't bleed to death as easily as all that."

"And I suppose you'd have liked it if I had gone to Mr. Brown or Mr. Cattermole?"

He smiled, and suddenly his face flashed into charm.

"I shouldn't have liked it at all."

"Perhaps you would like me to go and tell them now?"

"I should dislike it damnably."

"Then don't say that sort of thing to me again!"

She turned towards the door, and had taken a step or two, when she heard a faint shuffling sound. It was so faint that only the quickest of hearing would have caught it at all. It was the sound of someone coming down the passage in a loose pair of carpet slippers.

The colour that had been in her cheeks went out of them as quickly and suddenly as a blown-out flame. She stood staring at the door, and felt the cold that was in the room close in against her heart. Wickham's voice came from behind her in the most peremptory whisper she had ever heard in her life.

"Cupboard door there on your left! Get in!"

She had not noticed it before, but she saw it now—a narrow strip of a door papered over, with a handle of yellow glass. The paper was cracked all down the line of the hinges and marked with deep brown stains where the rust had struck through and spread.

The shuffling sound was in the passage outside. As Sarah turned the yellow glass handle it ceased. She stepped over a wooden sill into a dark, stuffy place and shut herself in. At the last moment, when she could still see a crack of light along the edge of the jamb, she heard the shuffling sound again, only this time it was nearer. It was so much nearer that it was in the room which she had barely left. She pulled on the knob she was holding till the bright crack was gone. Through the panel of the cupboard door she heard the Reverend Peter Brown say,

"I just thought I'd have a word with you. He's stuck to me like a leech all the evening."

Chapter Eighteen

SARAH LET GO of the knob and stepped back. She heard Wickham say something, but she could not catch the words. It went through her mind to wonder whether this was because he did not want her to hear what he had to say to the Reverend Peter Brown. She could hear no more now than the sound of the two voices, like a duet in grand opera between the baritone and the bass. The only difference was that in opera it really did not matter whether you heard the words or not, because they did not seem to mean very much anyway, but here it might make all the difference between safety and danger.

She wondered how long Mr. Brown would stay, and whether he had seen the bloodstains on Wickham's shirt. He needn't have if Wickham had been clever and had remembered to keep the sheet well up on that side.

As she stood, she could feel a heavy coat hanging against her on the left. She thought it was Wickham's greatcoat. There were other clothes in the narrow space. They were hanging from wooden pegs fastened into the back of the cupboard, which was so shallow that there was only just room for her to stand between the pegs and the door. On the other hand, shallow as it was, it seemed to stretch away on either side of her. She began to move to her right. She could think of no reason why Mr. Brown should open the door, but if he did, she would be right there behind it, waiting to be seen. She thought she would feel a great deal safer if she could get away from it.

When she had gone a yard she stopped and turned round to face the pegs. They were full of women's clothes, very long and bulky, with billowing skirts. There was a silk—she had to take great care not to set it rustling. There were lines of velvet ribbon on it for a trimming. Sarah wondered what colour it might be. Tinkler knew someone who could tell colours in the dark. She thought this would be black, or a deep old-fashioned violet. There was a sort of pelisse affair on the next peg. It smelled of old fur, old camphor, old peppermint. It was dusty and rough to the touch—

All at once she felt crowded in. There was not enough room for her and for these old belongings of people who were dead and gone. The garments that had clothed them were dead too, and should have had decent burial instead of hanging here in a Bluebeard's cupboard smelling of moth and decay. Perhaps it was this smell, perhaps there really was not enough air—Sarah did not know—but a most dreadful conviction came over her that she was going to faint. There was a numbness in her head and limbs, and a shower of bright sparks before her eyes. With a horrified perception that to faint here would be the ultimate disaster, she caught with both hands at two of the wooden pegs. Whatever happened, she mustn't make a noise, she mustn't fall. The sparks went up in a dizzy rush. Her knees buckled under her, bringing her weight upon the pegs. She had a giddy sense of slipping forward. And then all at once there was cold air blowing in her face—ice-cold air, keen with frost.

It blew the sparks away. Her knees stiffened and her head cleared. She was still holding the pegs, but they were not straight in front of her any longer. They were tilting away from her at a sharp angle, so that her right hand was out at the full stretch of that arm. She took an involuntary step forward with her right foot and drew in another long breath of the cold air. The last of the giddiness left her, and she realized that she had opened a door in the back of the cupboard. Her weight coming on the pegs must have released the catch. She held them still, the wind blew in her face, the door was ajar. The sleeve of one of the dead garments hanging on it moved in the draught and brushed her cheek. With a shudder she let go of the pegs, pushed the door wide, and stepped over the threshold on to a boarded floor.

It was the most blessed relief to be clear of the cupboard. She closed the door behind her lightly, pulling a fold of the nearest garment between it and the jamb, so that she could be sure of getting back again if it should turn out that there was no better way. Then she looked about her with an uneasy sense of adventure. It was not quite dark. She could see the walls of a room, and a window facing her, the tracery of its latticed panes very black against the faint diffused light which was coming from the sky. It was not strong enough for moonlight, but it was the kind of light which filters through the clouds when the moon is veiled. By this light she could see that the room was a small one, and that it was perfectly empty—naked floor, bare walls, window uncurtained to the night, with a great smashed hole high up in the right-hand corner. It looked as if a stone as big as a cannon-ball had been hurled through it. Even at that moment Sarah wondered who could have thrown anything large enough to make that hole. The night air poured through it, bitterly cold.

There was a door in the right-hand wall. When she came to it Sarah found it ajar. It opened upon a passage, and all at once it came to her that this was a prolongation of the passage down which she had come to find Wickham's room—there had been a wall across it with a locked and bolted door. The empty room through which she had just come backed on to Wickham's room. She was now in the passage beyond the locked and bolted door. She was, to put it exactly, in the haunted wing. She experienced a decided reluctance to remain there. She did not believe in ghosts, but it is a great deal easier not to believe in them when you are not alone at midnight in a haunted house.

She felt her way to the wall and made sure of the heavy door. Yes, there it was, just as she had felt it from the other side, only here the bolt was drawn back.

It was quite dark in the passage except for a faint greyness where she had left the door of the empty room half open behind her. It was stuffy too, with a smell of mildew and unstirred dust. She had a sudden longing to be back in her own room with a fire burning and a warm bed waiting for her full of comforting hot bricks done up in kitchen paper. Only an insensate lunatic would have come prowling about this horrible house without so much as a sixpenny torch just in case a bank-robber who had never spoken a civil sentence to her in his life might want bandaging. And heaven knew why. It was a hundred to one that he had been up to his old games, because after all, you didn't get stabbed for nothing. Or shot.

Sarah's conscience, or her heart, experienced a sharp prick of remorse. "However he got shot or stabbed, he was getting on all right until he carried coals and bricks for you. And only an inhuman monster would have stayed in a warm room and gone to sleep without finding out just how badly he had hurt himself—" It is a hard choice between an insensate lunatic and an inhuman monster, but perhaps better to be demented than depraved.

The immediate question was how long would she have to remain here freezing and mouldering. Mr. Brown might stay talking to Wickham for hours. It seemed odd that he should have wanted to talk to him at all. If they were strangers.... It came to Sarah with the extreme of certainty that they were not strangers. There had been a most familiar and accustomed accent about the Reverend Peter's "I wanted a word with you." If Wilson Cattermole had really never met Mr. Brown in the flesh until last night, that familiarity raised a host of questions.

Sarah put these questions out of her mind with vigour. Everything was quite bad enough without looking for trouble, and anyhow Henry would be here tomorrow. The only question she really had to deal with at the moment was how to get back to her room. The way she had come was blocked by the Reverend Peter. The passage was blocked by a bolted door. If there was a third way, she had better set about finding it.

Slowly and without enthusiasm she began to move forward, feeling her way along the right-hand wall.

Chapter Nineteen

SHE HAD NOT GONE more than a dozen steps, when the passage turned right-handed. She had the feeling that it was narrower, and the ceiling lower down overhead. There was not the very faintest glimmer of light, and presently she found out why. Her hand groping, touched a window jamb and, moving on, came upon boards where there should have been glass.

She stood there leaning against the sill and tried to get her bearings. If there were boarded-up windows all along this passage, then there would be no way back to her room from here. Because windows on this side meant that the haunted wing ran parallel with the rest of the house but separated from it. The passage with the bolted door linked the two wings. But it must be their only link. These windows must look into some court or yard. It was no use going on.

And yet before she went back she would like to know just a little more about this place. If there were windows on this side of the passage, there might be doors on the other. She crossed over, and found one facing her under the shape of an arch so low that her hand, feeling before her, actually touched the keystone. The door itself had no handle, but an iron latch rough with rust. She had the impulse to lift it, and a reluctance which pulled her back. In the end the impulse won. The door moved, creaked, and swung in. She had to stoop to look into the room. It was small and not quite dark, because one of the boards at the pointed window had slipped and let in a narrow panel of that grey, filtered light. It was very cold. There was a weight on the air. It was very still.

And then all at once there was a sound—like a faint rustling—like a silk dress moving over the rough boards a long way off at the end of the passage. Such a small, harmless sound to turn your hands to ice and set your heart thumping.

It took her all she knew to shut the door. She must shut it, or they would know that someone had been here. It creaked again as she pulled it to, and from the end of the passage there came again the sound of the rustle of silk. Sarah told herself that she mustn't run. If she ran, blind panic would overtake her. She must get back, but she mustn't run. The cupboard loomed up as a haven of refuge. She turned the corner, and as she did so, like Lot's wife she looked back.

There was something there.

She did not wait. A cold drop went trickling down her spine, and she ran as she told herself she must not run, with a blind panic driving her. It was so blind that she struck against the bolted door and bruised herself. It was touch and go whether she screamed and beat upon it in a frenzy. With the last shreds of her courage she choked back the scream and leaned for a moment against the oak. Then with a very great effort she turned.

There was someone, quite close to her, quite silent. In the vague dimness which came through the door which she had left open she could just see a shadow in the darkness—quite near, quite horribly near. She made a sound too faint to be a cry.

John Wickham's voice said, "Sarah!"

For the second time that evening she came near to fainting. Afterwards she told herself that it was the sudden rush of a relief so great that it gave the measure of her fear. She might really have fainted if she had not remembered that if Wickham had to take her weight, it would be much worse than a scuttle of coals and his wound would almost certainly begin to bleed again.

She kept her feet, felt an arm about her waist, and was somewhat vaguely aware that she was being hurried along. A door shut, and once more the cold outside air was blowing in her face. She drew a long sobbing breath and heard Wickham say, "Hold up!" His arm was still at her waist. She said with as much indignation as she could muster,

"I am."

"Not very noticeably—but you've got to. You'd no business to come here at all, and you've got to get back to your room."

Anger is a brisk restorative. Sarah was surprised by her own rage, but it enabled her to dispense with any further support than that of the wall. She went back a step, leaned against it, took another good deep breath, and said with spirit,

"How could I help coming here? You didn't expect me to wait and meet Mr. Brown?"

"No. I think I indicated the cupboard as an alternative. It was a perfectly good cupboard. Why didn't you stay there?"

"And suppose Mr. Brown had opened the door?"

"He didn't."

"He might have. And besides, there wasn't any air—only a sort of concentrated fog of moth and mould and camphor, and I thought I was going to faint, and if there'd been a heavy thud in the cupboard, Mr. Brown *would* have opened the door."

He said in rather a curious voice,

"How did you find the spring?"

She was herself again now, and she thought, "How did *he* find it?" And then she remembered that she hadn't quite closed the secret door. She had pulled a fold of one of those horrible dresses out through it too, so as to be sure of finding her way back. But all the same she didn't think it was that. She thought that he had known about the spring, and she thought that he had not meant her to know that he knew. This went at racing speed. She said quickly,

"I caught at the pegs. They gave, and I found there was a door. I came in here because of the air."

She had slipped into excusing herself. Her anger flared again. Why should she account to him for what she did?

"Then why didn't you stay here?"

"Why should I? I wanted to find a way back to my room. You mayn't have noticed it, but it's fairly cold."

His voice changed. There had been something in it which made her feel that she was being laughed at. That something went. He said,

"Yes, you must get back at once. But before you go I want to know what you've been doing. You went down the passage—didn't you? How far did you go?"

The anger went out of her. She was cold again.

"Round the bend and a little way along—not very far really."

"See anything?"

"I—don't—know."

"And what do you mean by that?"

She repeated the words she had just used.

"I—don't—know. I looked back—there was something—I don't know what it was. There was a rustling—like silk—"

"You didn't see anyone?"

"No."

"You may thank your lucky stars for that. Now look here, this place is dangerous. This part of the house—it's dangerous. You're not to come into it—do you hear me? You've found a way in, but you're not to use it again. It's not kept locked up for nothing, and you're to keep clear of it. If you had met what you might have met tonight, or seen what you might have seen—well, people can die of fright, you know, as well as from several other very unpleasant causes. You keep quiet and stick to Miss Cattermole! And now you had better go back to your room!"

The really frightening thing about this speech was that it didn't make Sarah angry. It ought to have, and it didn't. So far from firing up, she couldn't raise a spark. She went meekly back through the cupboard into Wickham's room.

The candle was on the mantelpiece now. After the dark passages and the dusk of the place from which she had come, the light from this one bending flame seemed searchingly bright. They could see one another, and what Sarah saw increased the weight upon her spirits. He had slipped his coat on. The bloodstained shirt was hidden. Over the dark collar his face had a pale and frowning look.

What he saw was a girl in a blue dressing-gown who had just run as big a risk as she was ever likely to encounter short of death. There was dust on her hands, and dust on the hem of her gown. There was a dusty smear on her cheek. Her hair hung loose upon her shoulders, and her eyes were wide and dark with something—he did not quite know what. He hoped with all his heart that it was fear, because if she was afraid she would keep quiet, and if she didn't keep quiet there was going to be plenty of reason why she should be afraid.

He went to the door, opened it, and went out. Sarah stood where he had left her.

Presently he came back.

"The coast's clear. Go quickly! I mustn't come with you."

She took a step or two and turned back.

"What are you going to do about that wound? You'll want a fresh bandage."

"I've got one."

"Can you do it yourself?"

"I'm an expert." Quite suddenly he laughed. *"Das ewig Weibliche!"*

"What do you mean?"

"No German? Pity. It won't translate. 'The eternal feminine' is rotten—mere *ersatz*—an inferior substitute."

Something happened between them—anger like the thrust of a knife to cut the mockery from his look and voice. And quick on that the feeling that the knife had slipped and only cut herself.

He held the door for her ceremoniously and watched her out of sight—first a dark shadow moving as soundlessly as a real shadow, then the blue of her dressing-gown in the lamp-light on the landing, and last of all the movement of a door on the other side of the well of the stairs. It opened, and it shut.

The curtain was down on the first act. John Wickham went back into his room, and wondered about the rest of the play.

Chapter Twenty

IT WAS A LONG TIME before Sarah slept. Her thoughts were restless and driven, like the shadow dance of leaves when the wind is high. They seemed like that to her—shadow thoughts driven here and there by an unseen wind, and she could only guess at what had cast the shadows. There were many things to be guessed at, but as soon as she tried to hold a thought and follow it back to its source, it eluded her and was gone again. Her body was so tired and her brain so restless that she felt as if she would never sleep. Yet in the end she did sleep, and woke to hear rain beating on the window, and slept again.

When the morning came with its reluctant light, she thought she must have been mistaken about the rain. If it had been bitterly cold the night before, it was still colder now. It could not possibly have rained with the air as cold as this. She got up and went to shut the casement window, which she had set a handsbreadth open after putting out her candle and drawing the curtain back. To her surprise the casement would not move. It was frozen to the sill. She had to use all her strength to break the ice and free it.

She looked out upon the strangest sight. The rain had been no dream. It must have come from some high place of warmer air and frozen as it fell. She looked over the sill and saw the ivy on the side of the house frozen where it clung, each leaf in a mould of ice which followed every vein and was perfectly transparent. There had been no snow—only wherever she looked clear glassy ice, covering the ground below, the five-barred gate at its farther side, a jutting slant of the roof. The bare boughs of an oak thrown up against a lowering sky, its interlacing branches, its tracery of twigs, were all seen through a sheathing of ice. The dark hedgerow looked for all the world as if each shoot, each spray, were enclosed in glass. A few late berries still clinging to a thorn were like fruits in jelly. The rough grass at the hedge foot stood up in frozen spears. Ice everywhere, and the breath of it on the air.

She drew back with a shudder and shut the window. Her heart was like lead. If this queer rain had been anything but a local shower, the roads must be impassable. And if the roads were impassable, how was Henry going to get down? She began to realize how much she had been counting on him.

As soon as she was dressed and had made her bed she went in to Joanna and found her nervous and fretful. Such luxuries as early morning tea did not apparently exist at Maltings, and Miss Cattermole did like her cup of tea in bed. Of course it ought to be her own special health tea, and it was entirely owing to the inconsiderate way in which she had been hustled that this had been forgotten.

"I have never known Wilson so inconsiderate. And where was the hurry after all? We didn't get here any sooner. And as far as I can see, we need never have come here at all. In fact we never should have come. If I had not been so hurried, if I had been given the slightest time for reflection, I should have said quite firmly, 'No, Wilson—I must really beg to be excused. You can of course do exactly as you like, and if you want to go to Land's End, or John o' Groat's, or the Malay Archipelago in this very unsuitable weather, you can of course do so, and I should not dream of trying to prevent you, but Sarah and I will stay *here*."

"I'm afraid that is just what we shall have to do," said Sarah.

Miss Cattermole managed to look exactly like an exasperated ant.

"And when I say *here*, of course I don't mean here at all—I think you really might know that. I ought to have told Wilson at once that I would not come down here. If I had had time to read the paper before I came away I should have known better than to give way to him. Morgan took all the papers when he went, which isn't like him at all, because he knows I always begin the day by looking at what 'Janitor' has to say in his *'Advice from the Stars'*, and if I had had the opportunity of reading it before we started I should never, never have come. Nothing could be more unfortunate. Just listen to this!" She produced from under the eiderdown a dishevelled sheet of newspaper and read in a trembling and indignant voice, "'Any journey undertaken today is not likely to add to your health and happiness. There are dark clouds ahead. It would be better not to undertake any new enterprise. Purple will be your most fortunate colour for the next few days.'" She pushed the paper away so vehemently that it fell on the floor. "*Purple*—and I have brought nothing but blue! I shall tell Wilson that I must insist on returning today!"

Sarah picked up the paper. It bore yesterday's date.

"How did you get hold of it?"

"The bricks," said Joanna—"very nice and comforting. I don't know what I should have done without them, but of course they did not stay hot, so when I lit my candle—at about six I think it was, and I had been awake for some time—I turned them out. And when I found they were all wrapped up in yesterday's *Daily Flash* I took it off to look for the Advice column, and I've been feeling most upset ever since. I shall insist on going back to town immediately after breakfast."

Sarah discovered that she had some curiously mixed feelings. It might have been self-control that enabled her to say in quite a cheerful voice,

"There's about an inch of ice all over everything this morning. I shouldn't think we'd be able to move a yard."

Chapter Twenty-One

SARAH COLLECTED all the pieces of newspaper and carried them away to her own room. She left the bricks neatly piled on the hearth, and she thought she could stuff the *Daily Flash* carelessly into the grate when she had finished reading what it had got to say about the murder of Emily Case. She could not really disguise from herself the suspicion that the reason why Mr. Morgan Cattermole had walked out of the house before breakfast yesterday, taking all the papers with him, had something to do with a desire that Sarah Marlowe should not learn that the police were anxious to interview her. So much had happened in the last twenty-four hours that now for the first time she really allowed this suspicion to take definite shape in her mind. It had been there all the time of course, as moisture is in the air before it condenses into rain.

She laid out the sheets of newspaper, and found what she was looking for on what had been the middle page. It was quite a short paragraph. It said,

> The police are anxious to interview a young woman who spent about three quarters of an hour in the first-class ladies' waiting-room at Cray Bridge between 5.15 and 6 p.m. on the evening of Thursday, January 26th.

There followed an alarmingly accurate description of Miss Sarah Marlowe. No one who knew that she had been travelling up from

Craylea on Thursday evening could possibly have failed to identify her with the young woman whom the police desired to interview, and no one who read the rest of the paper could fail to link this desire with the murder of Emily Case.

The paper seemed quite full of the murder of Emily Case. There were photographs of her, mostly quite unrecognizable, of the sister with whom she had been going to stay, of the sister's cottage, of the railway station at Ledlington, of the compartment in which the murder had taken place, and of Mr. Snagg, the porter who had discovered the body.

With every line that Sarah read the shadow of Emily Case, whom she had seen once and with whom she had exchanged a few brief sentences, seemed to grow longer and darker.

She sat there, and acknowledged tardily that Henry had been right—she ought to have gone straight to the police and given them the oiled-silk packet. She had a tolerably clear idea that if she had taken this course she would not at this moment be marooned in a disagreeably isolated house, cut off from the world, the police, and Henry Templar by impassable and ice-bound roads.

If the roads were impassable it was no good expecting Henry to arrive and rescue her, and if Henry didn't arrive, what was she going to do? She had not the very slightest idea. Of course she was probably frightening herself about nothing at all. Morgan Cattermole was almost certainly a bad lot. Even his brother and sister barely disguised the fact that he was a black sheep. That being so, it was not difficult to guess who had opened the oiled-silk packet while she was out of her room last night. But to open it he would have had to look for it, and to look for it would mean that he had known it to be in her possession. And how could anyone know that?

Sarah thought about the footsteps on the foggy platform. Anyone walking up and down there might have looked through the chink where the blind had slipped and seen Emily Case and Sarah Marlowe. She remembered how Emily's head had turned and her eyes had watched that crack whilst the footsteps receded in the dark. The man who had followed Emily Case and murdered her for the packet which she had put in Sarah's bag might have guessed at its being worth his while to trace the girl who had been closeted for nearly an hour with his victim.

But it couldn't have been Morgan Cattermole. A voice said softly and coldly, "And why not?" She had no answer to this. Only if he had traced her he was much cleverer than the police, who had not managed to do so. There was certainly something very suspicious about his sudden arrival and the tampering with the oiled-silk packet.

But, Morgan gone, why should Wilson Cattermole transport them all to this inaccessible place? It might be the merest coincidence, or it might not. She could look back over the four months she had worked for him and find as many instances of a sudden whim translated into action. No, she really could not find it in her heart to suspect Wilson. The Reverend Peter Brown was another matter. Since Wilson and he had never met before, how and when had he known John Wickham? The longer she thought about it, the more the tone of that casual "I wanted a word with you" declared not only a previous but an intimate acquaintance.

If it was Wickham who had followed her.... The thought struck a spark from her mind, and went out as a spark goes out in the dark. Bundling the sheets of newspaper together, she went back into Miss Cattermole's room and stuffed them down into the grate upon the still warm ashes. If they were to burn, so much the better, but whether they burned or not, they would not be fit to use again, She might therefore hope for fresh wrappings on the bricks tonight.

Joanna, in a robe-like garment of peacock blue, was putting on her string of lapis lazuli beads and mourning because they were not purple and she could so easily have brought her Aunt Phoebe's amethysts.

"It all comes of being in a hurry—one always does the wrong thing."

As she followed her downstairs Sarah wondered whether she had done the wrong thing about the papers from the oiled-silk packet. If it came to that, she wondered if any of the people through whose hands the papers had passed had done the right thing. They had all been in a hurry because they had had to be in a hurry. The young man in the train had been in a hurry when he gave them to Emily Case—and perhaps he was dead, and perhaps he wasn't. Emily Case had been in a hurry when she put them into Sarah's bag—and she was certainly dead. Sarah Marlowe had been in a hurry when she had ripped open the packet and taken out the folded envelope with all those names and addresses in it. She had been in a hurry when she took them out and when she put the envelope back again with some nice plain foolscap inside it. And very appropriate too. It had given her a good deal of pleasure ever since to imagine Morgan Cattermole's feelings when he opened the envelope. And the best part of the joke was that he wouldn't be certain, and nobody else could be certain, that she had changed the papers. The young man in the train might have changed them—or Emily Case—or Sarah Marlowe. But nobody could be sure that it was Sarah Marlowe, and nobody—*nobody* except Sarah knew where those names and addresses were now. The oiled-silk packet was under her pyjamas in the middle drawer in London, and what was inside it now was Morgan Cattermole's affair. He had thought he was fooling her, but she had fooled him first, and by now he must know that he had been fooled.

Sarah thought, "If he turns up here, I shall have to look out for squalls." And with that they were in the dining-room, and everyone was saying good-morning and beginning to talk about the weather. "No getting out today, I'm afraid." ... "Oh, yes, dreadfully cold"... "I remember in '94" ... "Grimsby says there's an inch of ice on the roads"... "Not a chance of the Sunday papers, I'm afraid."...

Sarah realized with a shock that it was Sunday. She had been thinking of Henry going to his office and not being able to get away until the evening, and all the time it was Sunday and he could have got away as early as he liked if it hadn't been for the ice on the roads.

"Grimsby says it's very bad indeed," said Mr. Brown. "He tried to get across the yard to the coal-shed, but he couldn't keep his feet. He is putting down ashes now, I believe."

In the light of what Wickham had said, Sarah wondered whether it was fair to blame the ice for the fact that Grimsby found it difficult to keep his feet this morning. She felt rather curious about the Grimsbys, and anxious to see them.

As she was crossing the hall after breakfast she had at least part of her wish. Grimsby came out of a green baize door behind the dining-room and went across to the Reverend Peter's den with a scuttle of coals. It was a very large scuttle, well piled up, and he carried it as if it had been a basket of eggs. He wasn't very tall, but he looked as strong as a bull, with an immense chest and long arms, a dark empurpled face, and black hair growing low on his forehead. His looks were not improved by a nose with a badly broken bridge and small, bloodshot eyes. Sarah thought, "He's dangerous. I wonder what he's like when he's drunk."

He looked at her sideways as he went past. It was the look of a vicious animal—sullen, with a spark of violence. If he had been a dog, there would have been a growl in his throat and his hackles would have been up. Sarah felt she would have been happier if he had been on a chain in the yard.

She went on up the stairs, and saw Wickham in the open doorway of Miss Cattermole's room. He had a pile of bricks on his arm, and when he saw her he went back a step.

"I'm just taking these away. Will you be wanting them again tonight?"

Sarah said, "Yes please," and then, "But you oughtn't to carry them. Make Grimsby do it. After all, it's his job."

He actually laughed.

"Have you seen him? I think I make a better chambermaid."

"You oughtn't to carry them."

"This arm's all right."

"Are you all right this morning—really?"

He nodded.

Quite suddenly, without the slightest intention and to her own surprise, Sarah said,

"Is it true—you were in prison?"

He balanced the bricks thoughtfully. His colour was much better today. She noticed that, because she was looking to see whether it changed. It didn't, nor did his voice. He said,

"Oh, yes. Mr. Cattermole told you yesterday in the car, didn't he? He has made up his mind that you can't hear through the glass, but of course you can. I heard him telling you."

It was Sarah whose colour rose in a burning flush.

"Why?" she said.

John Wickham smiled quite pleasantly.

"Why does one rob banks? To get money. Pure case of demand and supply. Unfortunately I didn't get away with it, so I'm a little disenchanted with the ways of crime. Would you like to reform me?" He laughed and went past her and across the landing.

Tears of pure rage stung in Sarah's eyes. At least she told herself that there was nothing in her heart but anger. If they were once out of this place she need never speak to him again. That was one thought. There were others.

She began to tidy the room. Miss Cattermole had an unusual talent for untidiness. She could impart a dishevelled air to any room in the least possible space of time. The things she had worn the evening before were strewn up and down the length and breadth of this one. It was certainly not a secretary's job—and Mr. Cattermole's secretary at that—to collect these widely diffused garments and dispose of them in drawers and cupboards. But on the other hand, it didn't seem to be anyone else's business either, and Joanna certainly wouldn't do it.

When everything had been put away she went back to her own room. The door which she had left shut was wide open. Wickham was very busy collecting the bricks which she had left piled up beside the hearth. It occurred to her to wonder how long he had been there, and whether he had been waiting for her. She came just inside the door and stood there, expecting him to go.

He came towards her slowly with the bricks piled up on his arm. Without lowering her voice Sarah said,

"You need not trouble—I shan't want them tonight."

"Oh, I think you will—and it isn't any trouble at all."

Sarah made no answer.

Just before he came level with her he dropped his voice and said,

"You asked me something just now, and I answered you. If I ask you something, will you answer me?"

"I don't know. What is it?"

"You go down to Craylea when you have a holiday, don't you? Were you there this week?"

She moved a little farther from the door, and he followed her.

"Suppose I was?"

"When were you there? What day did you come back? Thursday—was it Thursday?"

"Why do you want to know?"

She saw his face change.

"Because I do—because it's important. Do you want me to ask Mr. Cattermole?"

Sarah felt shaken where she should have been angry. She was so sure she ought to be angry that she achieved a cold, rebuking look as she said,

"I think you are behaving very strangely."

He took no more notice of that than if she had been a child.

"Did you come back on Thursday?"

"Yes, I did."

"By way of Cray Bridge?"

"There isn't any other way."

"What train?"

A bright sparkle came into Sarah's eyes. She said, a little too sweetly,

"The 5.17 from Cray Bridge."

The sparkle met an answering one.

"Sure about that?"

"Quite sure."

"You left Cray Bridge at 5.17?"

"That's not what I said."

"Then you didn't leave at 5.17. When did you leave?"

The sparkle died.

She said in an uncertain voice,

"There was a fog."

"When did you leave Cray Bridge?"

"Why do you want to know?"

"I've got to know, and if you don't answer me, well, that's answer enough. I think you didn't leave until six o'clock."

She walked away past him to the window and stood there looking out. She heard him come up behind her, but she did not turn. He said very quick and low at her ear,

"Did she give it to you? For God's sake tell me if she gave it to you! Are you such a fool as to think that you can play a lone hand like this?"

She said in a slow, bewildered voice, "I don't know what you mean—" because that is what Sarah Marlowe would have said if she really had not known, and that is how she would have said it.

Well, it wasn't any use, because he came back at her with a contemptuous "You know perfectly well! What have you done with it?"

She found that she didn't know what to say. She couldn't keep her anger. She couldn't act well enough to take him in.

He spoke with a fresh urgency.

"Sarah—for God's sake tell me! It's not safe—you're not safe. I tell you I've got to know!"

And then, before she could answer, there came Joanna's voice, calling plaintively from the stairs.

"Sarah—Sarah—where are you? They say the roads are dreadful and we can't possibly get away. They say it's dangerous."

Wickham turned and went out with his load of bricks. His voice came back to Sarah from the landing,

"No, I'm afraid you can't go, madam. Mr. Cattermole is quite right—it would be dangerous."

Chapter Twenty-Two

THE WORD WAS TO RING in Sarah's ears through all the long, cold day—*dangerous*. It was dangerous to stay here, and it would be dangerous to try and get away. One kind of danger or another—what did it matter? She had some fear, but it is hard to rid oneself of the generations who have lived safely. They stand guard about your thought and set danger a long way off. It is something you have heard of, read about—not something that comes into your own life to break it up.

When she had the hall to herself she opened the front door and went out. But when she had taken two steps she knew that if she took another it would bring her down. There was a sheet of ice over everything, and it was ten times more slippery than the common ice of a frozen pond, because ice frozen on water is level, but this followed the contours not only of the ground but of every stick and pebble upon it. There was no place where you could steady your foot. She wanted to turn round and go back, but she couldn't. One movement out of the straight and she would be down. She would have to step backwards. But as sure as she picked up one foot the other would go from under her.

"My dear Miss Marlowe!" said Mr. Brown. His voice came from behind her, full of concern. "My dear Miss Marlowe!" His hand came out and grasped her above the elbow—a very strong hand.

She took her step back. She was thankful for the support. As Mr. Brown shut the door, he told her just how dangerous this kind of ice could be.

"You mustn't dream of putting a foot outside until we've got some ashes down. Miss Cattermole was telling me that she would be obliged to return to London. I am afraid I disappointed her by saying that it was quite out of the question. The gain is of course mine. Anything which gives me the pleasure of your company for a little longer is certainly a blessing in disguise. We must try and make the time pass as pleasantly as possible. There are books in my den, and of course Mr. Cattermole will be anxious to pursue his investigations. We shall have to wait until the late evening—I have told him that. The manifestations do not ordinarily begin before ten o'clock, but we may look forward, I hope, to an interesting evening. He tells me you are something of a sceptic. Perhaps we shall have the pleasure of converting you."

What do you say to an enthusiast who wants to convert you? Sarah said nothing, merely smiled and made her way to what she supposed was the drawing-room of the house, a pale intact specimen of Victorian gentility. Vases in symmetrical pairs, a faded floral carpet, stiff sofa and chairs covered in a tapestry which suggested mildew, and on the walls a sky-blue paper with satin stripes now rapidly turning grey, and a fine period collection of photogravures representing the more popular works of Landseer and Millais. There was a *Soul's Awakening* over the mantelpiece, flanked by a *Monarch of the Glen* and a *Dignity and Impudence*. There were many, many others. A fire had been lighted, but was doing very little to raise the temperature.

Miss Cattermole complained that the atmosphere was inimical.

"We cannot get away from this place. I shall be ill. I am very sensitive to atmosphere. And the cold—"

"Horrible, isn't it!" said Sarah. "But the fire is really cheering up a bit now."

"Oh, it's not that. You're not sensitive, so of course you don't feel it. There's a horrible cold feeling about this house which has nothing to do with the weather. Wilson won't tell me what happened here, but I know it was something dreadful. He says he wants me to have an open mind, but I wish very much that we had never come near the place."

It was when she next crossed the hall that Sarah had her first glimpse of Mrs. Grimsby. It was quite literally only a glimpse. The baize door to the kitchen premises stood ajar, not by accident but of design. Four fingers showed on it to the knuckles, and a little higher up a face looked through the gap. The fingers red and steamy as if they had just come out of hot water, the face round, and flat, and white as a well floured scone; untidy grizzled hair; no-coloured eyes—these were the things which Sarah saw before the door swung to. She felt distaste, repulsion, and had to remind herself of Mrs. Grimsby's virtues as a cook—"And anyhow it's taken a weight off my mind, because I was feeling dreadful about anyone being married to Grimsby, and now I needn't."

The excellent meals provided by Mrs. Grimsby were, in fact, the only bright spots in a cold and tedious day. Sarah searched the bookshelves in vain for anything which she could feel she really wanted to read. There were the complete works of Robert Browning, Wordsworth, Tennyson, and Southey. There were a great many books of sermons by divines who had obviously been popular in the early part of Queen Victoria's reign. There were a number of novels of the same period, published in three volumes of which one usually seemed to be missing. There were a number of biographies of people whose names meant nothing to her. She was reduced at last to a choice between a work of fiction entitled *A Sister's Sacrifice* and Vol. I of *The Pillars of the House* by Charlotte M. Yonge. Actually she found this a most enthralling work. What ingeniously ordered lives this vast Victorian family led. How small a happening could rouse and hold one's interest. Felix's birthday tip from his godfather, and the burning question of how much of it should go into the family exchequer, and whether he would be justified in blueing part of it on a picnic—with a wagonette—for the entire family, Papa, Mamma, and ten brothers and sisters. When Papa expired and Mamma had twins the same day, thus bringing the family up to thirteen, and Felix and Wilmet had to support them all, the contest between Miss Yonge's ingenuity and Sarah's scepticism became excitingly acute. In the end she gave Charlotte best. It might have been done, she could even believe that it had been done, and though not in sight of the end of Vol. I, she contemplated turning out all the shelves till she tracked down Vol. II.

In the early afternoon the sky darkened and snow began to fall. By the time the curtains were drawn the ice was already covered. She thought, "If it's not too deep, the snow will help us to get away." Like an echo there came a restless movement from Joanna, and the words, "If it snows, we ought to be able to get away tomorrow."

Miss Cattermole had got out her planchette. She was sitting up to a small gimcrack table, her hands poised above the board, a sheet of foolscap laid ready to take a message down. From either side of the mantelpiece a candle in an overloaded Dresden candlestick threw a soft glow upon her and upon the table. She had been sitting like that for a good half hour, but the little heart-shaped board had not moved at all and the paper lay blank beneath it.

Quite suddenly and silently Miss Cattermole began to cry. The tears just brimmed over and rolled down. Then in a faint, despairing voice she said,

"I want to go home. Oh dear, I do so want to go home."

Sarah did her best to be consoling. The bright thought had suddenly struck her that Henry might after all get down tonight. As soon as the ice was covered the roads would be driveable, and as soon as Henry *could* come he *would*. She hadn't the slightest doubt about that. The glow which this conviction imparted enabled her to be very brisk indeed with Joanna, who presently showed signs of being assuaged and departed upstairs to remove the disfiguring traces of emotion.

She had not been gone more than half a minute, when Wickham came in with logs for the fire. It was an entrance too prompt not to arouse the suspicion that he had been waiting for just such an opportunity. On his knees before the hearth with a log in his hand he would present a most innocently convincing picture of faithful service should anyone open the door. Sarah, in the sofa corner no more than a yard away with *The Pillars of the House* laid open on her knee, was any girl with any book on a snowy Sunday afternoon.

Without preliminaries he began where he had left off about six hours ago.

"What have you done with it?"

She kept her hand on her book and looked past him into the fire.

"I don't know what you mean."

She might not be looking at him, but she knew what kind of a look he had for her—a black, angry one, and a voice edged with anger as he said,

"You're not a fool—don't talk like one! And don't talk to me as if I was one either! No one who knows that you came up from Cray Bridge on Thursday evening can possibly mistake the porter's description of the girl who was in the waiting-room with Emily Case, even without the initials on the suit-case. It was you to anyone who knows you. Did she give you the packet?"

Sarah's hand closed so hard upon the book that the edge of it made a long red furrow across her palm. She said in a voice of creditable calm,

"What do you mean? What packet?"

"Four by three, done up in green oiled silk, and you very well know it. She gave it to you, didn't she? What have you done with it?"

All the colour went out of Sarah's face, and all the colour went out of her mind. There were left two possibilities, starkly black and white. To say what he had just said, it must either have been John Wickham who had given Emily Case the packet, or else it was John Wickham who had done murder to take it from her, and done it in vain. For a moment she saw these two possibilities as separate ideas. Then with a rush they merged and were one. She said,

"Did you give it to her?"

"What did she tell you?"

"Was it you? She said he had been stabbed—and he gave her the packet—was it you?"

He made some impatient movement which might have meant "Yes" and broke into a hurry of words.

"What have you done with it? It's about as safe as dynamite—I suppose you know that by now?"

She said in a small, dry whisper,

"Did you kill her—to get it back?" And as soon as she had said it she was afraid.

He dropped the log he was holding and turned on her.

"What a mind! Didn't you hear me tell you not to talk like a fool? You're trying to have it both ways. If I gave it to her, she'd have given it back to me, wouldn't she? She was anxious enough to get rid of it or she wouldn't have given it to you. Why should I kill her? Talk sense if you can!"

She felt quite weak with relief. Of course that was true. Poor old Emily would have simply tumbled over herself to give him the packet if it was really he who had pushed it into her hand and said "They mustn't get it." But suppose he was one of *them*. Presumably *they* knew about the packet too, or they wouldn't have tried to kill two people to get it.

She said, "Did you give it to her?" and got a furious "Yes, I did!"

"What did you say?"

"I don't know—I was just about all in. Something like 'Don't let them get it.' I know that's what I had on my mind, so I suppose I tried to say it."

Sarah saw him as if from a long way off. She could have put out her hand and touched him, but she felt as if he was a long way off. She couldn't see his thoughts, or whether she could trust him or not. Something hurt her at her heart. It was like being pulled two ways at once. There was that feeling of being a long way off, and yet it would be the easiest thing in the world to put out her hand and touch him. A warm current of something that wasn't fear flowed over her. Her hand relaxed. She became aware that she had bruised it. She heard him say with the utmost urgency,

"What did you do with the packet?"

She was afterwards ashamed of the meekness with which she said,

"I put it in a drawer under my pyjamas."

"You didn't go to the police?"

She shook her head.

"No."

"They wouldn't have got you down here if you had. Why did you come?"

"I didn't know. We've often been to places like this before, ghost-hunting. It's part of my job."

He frowned at that.

"You've no business in a job like this—you'd better get out of it as quickly as you can. Did you leave the packet in your drawer?"

Sarah considered, and decided that it couldn't possibly do any harm to be frank. Since Morgan Cattermole must know all there was to know about the packet she had left in the drawer, she didn't see why Wickham shouldn't know too. If he was on Morgan's side, it didn't matter, and if he wasn't on Morgan's side, it didn't matter either. And she wanted to tell him—very much. She was not naturally secretive, and it would be the greatest possible relief to tell someone what she had done. She smiled suddenly and said in a different voice,

"Well, I did—and I didn't. I put it there, but when I was out of my room last night someone must have taken it away and opened it."

"What!"

He had turned almost as pale as when she had seen him faint. His eyes closed for a moment under dark, straining brows.

She said, "Don't! It's all right—he didn't get anything—I'd taken the papers out."

She could feel the relief which brought his colour back. It was almost as if it were her own.

"What did you do with them?"

She looked at him and said in a laughing voice,

"I'll tell you exactly what I did. I took the papers out of the envelope and put them away in a safe place, and then I filled the envelope with foolscap and sewed it up in the oiled silk again. But when I came back to my room the sewing on the packet wasn't mine."

"You're sure about that?"

She laughed.

"Oh, quite. I sewed it up with linen thread just like it had been sewn before, but Mr. Morgan Cattermole had sewn it up with ordinary white cotton."

"*Morgan* Cattermole?"

"Oh, yes—it couldn't have been anyone else. He had opened the packet and sewed it up again all in a hurry whilst I was soothing Joanna after a nightmare. I expect he took out my envelope and put in one of his own, but I didn't unpick his stitches to see. I just left the packet there under my pyjamas."

Wickham was staring at her with a most arresting look of surprise. He said,

"Who is Morgan Cattermole?"

"Don't you know?"

It was odd to remember that she had ever thought his face impassive. Between fire and candle-light it now registered the extreme of angry impatience.

"Go on—tell me about him—quick! We haven't got all night. I'm taking a risk as it is."

She felt the shock of something she didn't understand. It sobered her.

"He's Mr. Cattermole's twin. A bad hat. Wilson won't meet him. He's been abroad, but he turned up last night. Miss Cattermole adores him."

"What's he like?"

"Like his brother outside, only hair brushed down, and frightful vulgar clothes. He's a howling cad all over—vulgar, hearty, loud—everything that Mr. Cattermole is not. I don't wonder they don't get on. They say he's been abroad, but I shouldn't wonder if he'd been—"

She bit off the end of the sentence just in time—or was it in time? A most burning blush ran up to the very roots of her hair as Wickham said,

"Why don't you go on?" His eyes looked right into hers. "You wouldn't wonder if he'd been in prison—that's what you were going to say, wasn't it? You needn't mind about my feelings—criminals are not sensitive. But let's get back to Morgan. What makes you think he's been in prison?"

She looked away with relief. Something in his eyes, something in his look, hurt her more than she would have believed that she could be hurt. And it was strange, because he had smiled, and it was then that she had felt as if she must cry out with the pain. She said in a hurry,

"Oh, I don't know—he's an awful person—I just thought—"

And there was the scarlet burning her face again. She heard him laugh.

"You keep putting your foot in it—don't you? But the blushes are all yours—I'm quite shameless. What makes you think that Morgan opened the packet?"

"There wasn't anyone else. There were only five people in the house. I don't see Mrs. Perkins or Thompson coming up out of the basement in the middle of the night on the chance of my being out of my room."

He said, "I don't suppose there was much chance about it."

She had thought about that, and it was a thought to turn away from. She hurried on.

"But Mrs. Perkins, and Thompson—it's nonsense. Why should they? I just don't believe it. And I was with Miss Cattermole, so it couldn't be her. And that leaves Morgan."

"Where was his room?"

"On the same floor as hers. He could have heard her come up to my room and fetch me down."

"Or he could have sent her."

He saw her wince, but he saw too that the idea was not a new one. She said with trouble in her voice,

"She wouldn't want to hurt anyone, but—she adores him—I can't think why."

With startling suddenness he laid a hand upon her knee.

"What did you do with the papers?"

Cold and heat ran over her. They were back again where they had started.

She said, "They're safe," and felt the grip of his hand.

"They're not safe for you—they're damned dangerous. Let me have them and I'll get you out of here."

"I can't."

"You've got to. Don't you know when you're in a jam? I'll get you out if you'll trust me."

She looked at him, and heard her own voice say,

"Why should I trust you?"

He laughed.

"Because you've got to. Give me the papers, and we'll have a shot at getting away."

She shook her head.

"Sarah, don't be a fool! If you left those papers in the house, it's a hundred to one they've found them. Morgan Cattermole would only have to walk in and say he'd left some private papers behind him and he'd get the run of the house—wouldn't he? Or what was to prevent Wilson ringing up yesterday afternoon from Hedgeley while I was putting in time over the car, and telling Thompson to search your room or any other room? She'd have done it, wouldn't she? And we were there quite long enough for him to ring up again and find out what sort of luck she'd had. And if they think you read the papers, and that you know enough to take in what you read, then they can't afford to let you go. *Now* will you tell me whether you left the papers in the house?"

She shook her head.

He took his hand off her knee and drew back to frown at her.

"All right, don't tell me—I'll chance it blind. Are you coming?"

"Where?"

"Hedgeley first—put the car in a garage and go on up to town by train. I don't want to be pinched for a car thief, but you'd never get to Hedgeley on your feet—it's all of seven miles. Will you come?"

The thing hung in the balance between them. Afterwards she was amazed to think how nearly she had said yes. It was inconceivable, but at that moment under some compulsion which she did not understand she came very near indeed to saying yes. If it had not been for her letter to Henry Templar and the fact that she now expected him to arrive at any moment, John Wickham might have tipped the scales in the way he wanted. Some things would have happened differently, and some would never have happened.

He said, "Come—*Sarah!*" and Sarah said nothing at all.

His eyes smiled under frowning brows. He put out a hand towards her. When it touched her she knew that she would say yes. But before it could reach her the handle rattled and the door began to move. In a flash John Wickham was leaning over the fire with a log of wood in his hand.

Joanna Cattermole came into the room with an old fringed shawl about her.

"So terribly cold in the passages," she said. "Oh, thank you, Wickham! Those logs will be very nice. We must keep up a good fire here. Perhaps you will just draw the curtains. There is something about snow that makes one feel very low-spirited."

The moment had passed. No, something more than that—it had never been.

Wickham trimmed the fire, banked it with coal, and stacked the other logs where they would not catch. He went to and fro with his neat dark uniform and his handsome, expressionless face, fastening the old-fashioned shutters, drawing the curtains across them, bringing in a lamp with a ground-glass globe. When he had finished he went silently away and shut the door.

The impossibility of that moment in which she had so nearly said yes impressed itself more and more deeply upon Miss Marlowe.

Chapter Twenty-Three

THE EVENING WORE slowly on. The two men remained closeted in Mr. Brown's den. Sarah hoped earnestly that they were finding the day as interminable as she was. She could not even set the clock back sixty years and pursue the fortunes of the Underwood family, because Miss

Cattermole wanted to talk, and of all things in the world, what did she want to talk about but dearest Morgan?

"He was such a clever little boy. And so pretty too, with his fair hair done in ringlets and a white sailor suit for Sundays. My dear mother was so proud of her twins. I was three years older, though I don't suppose anyone would think so now. And I was called after my father's sister Jane, only my mother thought it such a very ugly name that she turned it into Joanna for me. And Aunt Jane must have been annoyed, because though she didn't say anything about it at the time, when she died, which was not till thirty years later, it came out that she had left all her money to found scholarships for girls who had been baptized Jane. So it all went out of the family, and my father was terribly put about. Names are so very difficult, don't you think? My mother was a Miss Wilson, so of course it was quite all right for her to give the name to one of the twins. It used to vex her terribly if anyone turned it into Willie, but of course they did. People will do that sort of thing. I remember being called Jo at school, and how angry it made her. But Morgan was called after my father's great friend Samuel Morgan. They were quite like brothers, and my mother said if she was asked to have a child called Samuel she had only one answer to give and that was no, so they called him Morgan. It wasn't any use arguing with my mother, because she never changed her mind, and if she said anything, that was the way it had to be—even my father knew that. Such a strong, determined character, but he always let my mother have her way. It felt so strange, you know, my dear, when they were gone, because I had always lived at home and had no say in anything, and if Wilson had not let me come and live with him, I really don't know what I should have done. You see, I have always had someone to tell me what to do, and it is very difficult to get into new ways when you are as old as I am."

Sarah felt a sudden compunction. Under the foolish, fitful, elderly ways there was this child who had never been allowed to grow up. She patted the thin elderly hand and said,

"Yes, I know—I was only twelve when my father and mother died."

"I never get any messages from them—don't you think that is strange? But you don't believe in the messages, do you? Morgan doesn't believe in them either—he never did. Dear Morgan—it was such a pleasure to see him again. He has such high spirits—so full of fun. Why, when he was a little boy—you wouldn't believe the tricks he used to play on everyone, and never the least bit afraid, not even of my father, though the rest of us were, dreadfully. I remember his balancing a very heavy dictionary on the top of the study door so that it came down on my father's head. He was quite bald, and the edge of the book cut him right across the scalp. Oh dear—he was so angry, and the more Morgan laughed, the angrier he was. It was just his high spirits, but of course my father might have been very seriously hurt. And another time when Aunt Jane was staying with us he set a booby-trap for her with a jug of cold water—one of those very large china jugs with a big flowery pattern all over it—and besides quite soaking Aunt Jane—she was in bed for two days afterwards—the jug was broken to bits, and as it was part of a double set which belonged to the spare room, my mother was dreadfully put out, and Morgan was most severely punished. Nothing would stop him playing practical jokes—so high-spirited, and such a sense of humour."

Things are seldom so bad that they mightn't be worse. Sarah took comfort from the thought that she had never had to be a visitor in the home of Mr. and Mrs. Cattermole in the playful days of Morgan's childhood. No wonder Aunt Jane had left her money to found scholarships.

"Now Wilson," said Joanna—" Wilson was always such a studious little boy—"

As if he had heard his name, Mr. Cattermole came into the room with the Reverend Peter Brown behind him.

Presently Sarah slipped away and went upstairs. It was bitterly cold there, but she wanted to be alone, and she wanted to think. It had been snowing now for at least four hours, and there was still no sign of Henry Templar. Of course he might not have noticed the snow at once—you don't take all that notice of the weather in London. On a gloomy afternoon with the lights on, the snow might have been coming down for an hour or two before he gave it a thought, and even then it might not occur to him at once that it would make the ice-bound roads passable again. He might be at a cinema or a concert, or he might be at his club. With the roads as they were it would take him a good two hours to do the forty miles, and if he didn't get off till after dark it might take him a good deal longer than that. It was now getting on for seven o'clock, and the snow had started before three.

She stamped her foot on the top step, and heard Wickham say, "What's that for?"

The voice startled her. She hated dusky landings with wall-lamps which only gave just enough light to see how dark it was. She looked about for Wickham and couldn't find him. Then he came out of Mr. Cattermole's room and right up to her, and dropped his hands on her shoulders.

"Are you coming?"

She said, "How can I?"

"Quite easily. Look pale at dinner and don't eat—say you've got a headache and go to bed. When the others have pushed off to their séance in the haunted wing, get up and go down to the drawing-room. I'll meet you there and take you out to the car. It's as simple as mud."

It was beautifully simple. It was quite impossible. Called upon to give a reason to herself for this impossibility, she found a useful set of conventions ready to her hand. She couldn't leave her job at a moment's notice and on what amounted to no provocation at all. She couldn't run away and leave Joanna who had been kind to her. She couldn't run away when she had asked Henry to come down and he might be here at any moment.

She lifted her eyes to the face she could only just see. It was very near her own. His hands were hard upon her. And all at once she wanted quite dreadfully to go with him. The house frightened her, the Grimsbys frightened her. It was the sort of house where anything might happen—things you didn't believe in. There was a feeling of things like this asleep in the dark, ready to stir, and uncoil themselves, and pounce out of their hidden secret place. It came, and was gone again between one caught breath and the next. If it had lasted any longer, her hands would have gone up to catch at his, and the words which trembled in her mind would have come tumbling from her lips—"Take me away—take me anywhere you like! Oh, for God's sake take me away!"

Thank goodness she had come back to her senses in time. She drew a long breath and said,

"I'm afraid it can't be done. I couldn't just go off like that."

"Why couldn't you?"

"I couldn't leave Miss Cattermole—or my job—there's no real reason—"

He said in a harsher whisper than she would have thought possible,

"If you're counting on Henry Templar, you needn't. He won't come."

"What do you mean?"

She tried to step back, but he held her.

"I said you weren't a fool, but you're new to this game. Did you really think he'd let you post a letter?"

Something ran through her like ice. It numbed her.

"But I saw you post it."

"No, you didn't. He got out of the car and came after me with a letter of his own—I expect he had it all ready just in case. And that's what you saw me post."

Her throat felt quite stiff, and her lips too. She had to try twice before she could get them to say,

"But my letter—what happened to my letter?"

That harsh, exasperated whisper so near her, and his bands so heavy.

"Sarah, you *are* a fool! He took it back of course—said it was a mistake and you didn't want it posted after all. He had his back to the car, and he just put it in his pocket and gave me his own letter instead. So it's no good counting on Henry Templar, who isn't within forty miles of knowing where you've got to."

"Is that true?"

"Gospel."

She said very low, "Let me go—I must think—I don't know what to do. Please let me go."

"In a moment. But we've got to get this fixed."

"I've got to think."

"All right, you can have till dinner, but I must know then. If it's yes, keep your handkerchief in your hand when you come downstairs, and I'll meet you like I said. Better make it yes, Sarah."

He let go of her suddenly as a door opened below. She ran into her room in the dark and sat down on the bed. She felt as if she had run a long way. She was shaking, and the dark room shook round her. She had the most horrible feeling that the floor was tilting with her, and that presently she, and the bed, and all the other furniture would go sliding down into a black gulf and be swallowed up.

It didn't last for long. If it had, she would not have been able to keep herself from running after Wickham and begging him to take her away, and then she would never have been able to look herself in the face again.

She got up from the bed, felt her way to the dressing-table, and lighted the candles which stood one on either side of the tall mahogany looking-glass in white china candlesticks bordered with apple green. The candlesticks were part of a set. There was a tray, four china boxes, and a ring-stand like a little tree with jutting branches, all in the same shiny white and green.

Sarah looked between the candles and saw her own face pale against the dark background of the room. She stayed there looking at herself, as if this Sarah in the glass could tell her what to do, but it wasn't any good.

She went back to the bed and tried to think. If Henry wasn't coming, it altered everything. She had not really known how much she had been counting on him until she learned that he had never had her letter. Always at the back of her mind there had been the comfortable feeling that Henry knew where she was. Now nobody knew. She had just been whisked off the map and spirited away. She remembered how they had run through Hedgeley and out on the far side and then turned off into lanes and taken a roundabout way back again. She had thought it odd at the time, but now it wasn't odd any more. It was part of a plan. If the police were looking for Sarah Marlowe—and they very well might be by now—they would trace her to Hedgeley, and the porter at the George and the mechanics in the garage opposite would all be quite sure that they had driven right on through the town and out on the north-east side. It had been quite dark when they passed through the street coming back.

And right there and then Sarah felt how convenient that darkness was for people who wanted to cover their tracks. It was so convenient that she wondered if it had not been planned. Sarah Marlowe had to be got away from town before she could see a paper and communicate with the police. But she mustn't arrive at Maltings until it was too dark for anyone to see when and where the car left the road. In other words, a forty mile drive had to be made to last for eight or nine hours. Obviously something had to go wrong with the car, and obviously something had gone wrong. Where, then, was John Wickham in all this? Very difficult to suppose that he hadn't been in it at all. Almost impossible to believe that the exact amount of delay could have been forthcoming without his being in it up to the hilt. Then why turn round now and offer to get her away?

There was a horrifying answer to this. She had told him that she had removed the papers from the oiled-silk packet. She must have been mad. But she *had* told him, and he would guess that she hadn't left them in town. She hadn't told him that, but he would guess. Because of course her room and the whole of the house in town would be ransacked. She couldn't possibly have found a place where she could be sure that they would be safe. No, he would guess that she had them on her, and if he could get her to go away with him—Her thought broke off.

It was a good argument, but it wasn't a sound one. There was something wrong with it. It was extraordinarily difficult to believe that someone you had seen every day for months was a criminal. Even if you knew that he had been in prison.

She turned away from John Wickham and began to think about the Cattermoles and the Reverend Peter Brown. This was easier in one way and more difficult in another. It was easier because for some reason she was able to give them a more dispassionate consideration. They had not, so far at any rate, dripped blood upon her carpet or fainted on her hands. But all the same it was difficult to associate such an unusual thing as crime with a benevolent if fussy employer, or with a parson who was writing a book on folk-lore. If it hadn't been for the Grimsbys she couldn't have done it. But it was only too easy to believe that the Grimsbys were no better than they should be, and having got as far as that, it was hard to understand why a respectable parson should employ them—only of course he might be a really noble parson with an urge to give criminals a second chance. It really was very difficult indeed. Above and beyond all argument was the fact that John Wickham had been stabbed and Emily Case murdered for papers now in the possession of Sarah Marlowe, and that under Wilson Cattermole's roof Sarah Marlowe's room had been searched and an envelope, which was fortunately not the right one, had been taken from her drawer, probably by Wilson's brother. On the top of that, and in all probability upon finding out that the stolen envelope contained nothing but some blank pieces of foolscap, the telephone had gone out of order, the newspapers had disappeared, and Sarah had been whisked off the map.

These were facts. She contemplated them, and let herself feel instead of think. Much easier this way. Thought flowed strongly and deep. She wanted to get away. She never wanted to see Maltings again. She wanted to put miles between her and the Grimsbys. She didn't care how many banks John Wickham had robbed.

All at once she felt quite calm and settled in her mind. She put all her things into her suit-case and locked it, and then remembered that she was supposed to be going to bed with a headache. Perhaps better leave her pyjamas on the bed, and her dressing-gown and her slippers where they would catch an enquiring eye. It really wouldn't take her a minute to pack when they had all gone off to the haunted wing.

When she had washed in some icy cold water, she did her hair again and paid a good deal of attention to her face. But just as she thought it was looking rather nice she remembered about the headache, so the lipstick had to come off. She must have smudges under her eyes and be pale enough to make bed seem reasonable. When she had produced the required effect she made a face at it. Without colour and bloom she thought Sarah Marlowe a very plain Jane. But she did look ill.

She took her largest handkerchief, shook it out, and went downstairs, letting it hang conspicuously against her dark brown skirt.

Chapter Twenty-Four

Half way down the stairs Sarah paused. From where she stood she could see the drawing-room door slanting open. That meant the room was empty. She went back a step or two until she could see the door of Miss Cattermole's room—a dark closed door with a line of light at the foot where the passing steps of ten generations had worn the threshold down.

Joanna was obviously dressing. Sarah wondered whether she would consider black velvet or blue the correct attire for a séance in a haunted wing. She herself had nothing but what she stood up in, owing to the raging hurry in which Wilson had swept her from his house.

Though her head was not much above floor level, she could see the whole of the landing. The other two doors were open and the rooms behind them without fire or candle-light. The entrance to the passage which led to Wickham's room and the haunted wing came into the picture as a very black shadow like the dark mouth of a cave. Nobody moved, or breathed, or stirred in the darkness.

She went slowly on down the stairs into the hall. There was no one there. The drawing-room was empty, and the dining-room too.

She moved along the hall towards the den, not with any idea of joining Mr. Cattermole and the Reverend Peter, but because she wanted to know whether they were there or not. If they were, and she heard their voices, she would know from what direction to expect them. Then if Wickham came.... Absurd really, because she wasn't going to exchange a single word with him—why should she? She was only going to let him see the handkerchief in her hand. But all the same she just had the feeling that she would like to know where everyone was, and then if there were anything he wanted to say to her—But of course there wouldn't be. Why should there?

She was still some way from the door, when she heard the sound of voices. This surprised her a good deal, because the doors and walls at Maltings were all so heavy and thick. And then in a minute she discovered why she could hear so plainly. The door was not quite shut, and she remembered that the catch had sprung last night.

Well, there it was now, not really ajar but free of the catch—free to be pushed ajar if anyone wanted to listen to what was going on in the room.

All at once Sarah knew that this was what she was going to do. It was an opportunity with a capital O, and if she threw it away it would never come back again. Opportunity never knocks twice at any man's door. Where had she heard that? This was Opportunity's door, and she wasn't going to knock on it, she was going to give it the most attenuated ghost of a push—not enough to let a draught in or the lamplight out, but enough to allow Sarah Marlowe's very sharp ears to catch what was being said between host and guest.

Not a very nice thing to do, but then kidnapping and stabbing and murdering are not nice things. Tinkler would be shocked. Would she? Sarah wasn't really very sure. Her own conscience was entirely quiescent as she put the tip of her forefinger upon the panel above the latch and just moved the door. There was now a crack about a quarter of an inch wide between it and the jamb. She heard Mr. Brown say in his deep, booming voice,

"She's got them, and she's got them with her. Where else could they be?"

And hard on that John Wickham, very cool:

"You say she lunched with Templar. Suppose she gave him the papers then?"

There was a laugh Sarah knew, loud, hearty, and vulgar—Morgan Cattermole's laugh.

"Because we shouldn't be sitting here if she had—that's why. The police would have been on to her before you could say knife if she'd really spilled the beans. No, she's got the papers on her—that's what I say. They're not in her room in town or anywhere else in the house, and they're not in her room down here, so if she hasn't got 'em on her, where are they?"

Sarah felt quite dizzy with the shock. Morgan here—and closeted with Wickham who only an hour or two ago had professed entire ignorance of his existence!

"Dope in the coffee," said the Reverend Peter Brown cheerfully. "If you'd let me do it last night, she'd have been searched by now and none the wiser. Do it tonight, and we'll know where we are."

Wickham's voice again—such a quiet, pleasant voice:

"And what then? Suppose you get the papers—you don't know how much she's read or understood. I gather they're fairly compromising."

She heard Mr. Brown take a sucking pull at his pipe. He said,

"Not necessarily. She wouldn't make much of them."

"She'd connect them with Emily Case," said Morgan Cattermole. "That's the snag. It isn't the lists that matter, but what the Case woman may have said to her, and the fact that she's bound to link them up with the murder. No, I wouldn't dope her tonight. There's time enough for that. What we've got to do is to find out what she knows—make her talk. Scare her stiff, and she'll talk all right. That's the plan—rattle her, get her on the run, and then in comes Wickham to say his piece—'Let me take you away from this horrible place, my darling. Trust your John, and he will save you.' I tell you it's a cinch! Good as a play—what?" He broke into his uncontrolled laugh again.

All the blood in Sarah's body seemed to have gone cold and heavy in her veins. She did not think that she could move. But she must move. She must get away.

She heard the Reverend Peter say in a meditative tone,

"Yes—it might do the trick. What about it, young man—feel like taking it on? Can you do your stuff?"

John Wickham said, "Oh, easily."

She could tell from his voice that he was smiling. Of the three he was the nearest to the door. He was so near that there was not much more than the thickness of the panel between them. The thought sickened her to the very core of her heart. Her inability to move became an inability to stay. She turned from the door and groped her way along the wall to the drawing-room. She was so sick and faint that she felt as if she must fall. She mustn't fall.

She reached the drawing-room. She reached the sofa corner and sat down there.

A pale, prim room in the lamplight. A wood fire burning cheerfully. In the next room three men talking about a woman they had murdered and a girl they were going to betray.

The girl was Sarah Marlowe.

The handkerchief was still in her hand. She pushed it up her sleeve and out of sight.

Chapter Twenty-Five

SARAH HAD COME to the end of being able to think. It was too much effort. It hurt too much, and it wasn't worth while. It was as if everything she knew and lived by had sustained so severe a wrench that the planes had been broken up and all the channels along which thought had been wont to run were twisted and turned out of course. There was a picture in her mind of the wreckage of a house after a bomb explosion. It was something she had seen in a film, and it came back now, black and distinct—roof fallen in and walls at a crazy slant, a tangle of wires and pipes like torn muscles and broken bones, one whole floor wrenched from its place and sent driving down to batter the foundations. And over it all a film of smoke, and tongues of fire licking the ruins of what had been a home.

A horrible picture. It stayed there in her mind.

Joanna Cattermole came in trailing her black velvet, wrapped in her blue and silver scarf. Her light hair was floating wildly and there was colour in her cheeks. She shivered as she took the sofa corner by the fire, but the hand she laid on Sarah's was burning hot and dry.

"Just now," she said, "after you went upstairs—he came through. Such a lovely message! Mr. Brown came and sat down beside me. I am afraid he is rather a sceptic about planchette, but he was most kind, and as soon as he put his fingers on the board it began to move. It is like that sometimes, you know—a fresh person coming in. I believe one may be too intent too anxious to get results, instead of being merely the *vehicle*. Now Mr. Brown has of course no *personal* interest, and we got such a lovely message, and written so plainly that there couldn't be any mistake about it at all—not like some of the times when one has really just had to guess. Look—I have kept the paper to show you!"

She laid the sheet on Sarah's knee. In a bold legible scrawl were the words, "I only think of you—you are my guiding star." Joanna gazed at them in an ecstasy.

"So then I said, 'Who is it? Are you Nathaniel?' And look—there's the answer, 'Nat to you'! So then I thought I would ask him about the colours—whether it mattered my not having brought anything purple with me. I asked Mr. Brown if he thought I could, and he said, 'Why not—why not?'—really in the very kindest voice. So then I did. And look what he wrote!"

At the bottom of the sheet the same scrawl proclaimed, "Green's forsaken, yellow's forsworn, blue is the luckiest colour that's worn—all poppycock about purple."

"Such a *relief*," said Miss Joanna—"and so very, very kind of him to set my mind at rest. My dear, is anything wrong? You look pale. Or is it the light?"

Sarah said, "The light—it's a ghastly light."

She put up a hand and rubbed her cheeks until they burned. Then she remembered that she was to look pale, and have a headache and go to bed. But not now—oh, no, not now. Because that would all be part of the plot. It was part of the plot that she should be frightened, and that Wickham should pretend to save her. She heard Morgan's odious voice again, "Trust your John!" and Morgan's odious laugh. She heard John Wickham say, "Oh, easily," and she burned through and through with shame. She had come so very near to trusting him. The black picture of wreckage stood out—all black, all spoiled, all twisted.

The Reverend Peter Brown came in, large, shapeless, and untidy in the baggy old clothes which were his only wear. Wilson Cattermole followed him, hair brushed to a halo, hands newly washed and smelling of lavender soap. A black velvet smoking-jacket replaced the coat he had worn all day. Sarah watched to see Morgan follow him, but no one came.

The gong sounded, and they crossed the hall to the dining-room. But as soon as she sat down Joanna discovered the loss of her handkerchief.

"If you would be so kind, Sarah—I think just on the sofa where I was sitting—"

It was an accustomed errand. Joanna hardly ever managed to move from one room to another without leaving something behind her. Sarah, nearest the door, turned back almost before the request had been made. She was glad of the respite. She went back into the drawing-room, picked up the handkerchief from where it had fallen, and turned with it in her hand.

John Wickham stood just inside the door. His hand went out behind him and pushed it to. His eyes went from the handkerchief to her face. They smiled into hers. He said,

"You're coming—"

Sarah said nothing then. She crossed the room as if she had not seen him, her eyes wide and fixed, the colour burning in her cheeks, her lips dumb and stiff. He thought she looked as if she were walking in some remote and tragic dream. Not his dream—he had no part in it.

And then she stopped. He was between her and the door. She wouldn't touch him. Her hand just stirred and fell again to her side. The stiff lips moved and said from a long way off,

"Let me pass."

"Sarah—what's happened? You're coming?"

"No."

"But the handkerchief—"

"It is Miss Cattermole's. I'm not coming." The words had a slow distinctness which was not like natural speech.

There leapt into his mind the possibility that she had been drugged. He put a hand on her arm and felt her shudder and stiffen against his touch.

"Sarah—what is it? What's happened? Look here, I've got to get us both out of here tonight. I've run it as fine as I dare. There's a man coming down here tomorrow who'll know me—he's the fellow who stabbed me in the train. If he sees me, the game's up. And there's nothing to stay for if you've got the papers. Bring them down here as soon as they get going with their séance, and I'll get you away. You'll come?"

She said, "No," snatched at the handle, and got the door open. There was a moment when he kept his hold of her arm. Then his hand dropped and he stood aside.

Sarah ran from him across the hall.

Chapter Twenty-Six

IT WAS A DREADFUL MEAL. Fortunately, the others talked so much that no one would notice that Sarah Marlowe had nothing to say. Wilson Cattermole had begun the story of his quarrel with the Psychical Research Society, but he had to contend against his sister who was anxious to go over all the messages she had received from her smuggler, and against Mr. Brown who was quite determined to talk about were-wolves. As the Reverend Peter had very much the advantage in the matter of voice, he was able to boom the Cattermoles out of the conversation and reduce it to a monologue.

Sarah had never heard anyone talk about werewolves before. She still had that picture of a wrecked and blackened house before her eyes. As Mr. Brown talked, she began to see shadows moving in the fire-shot dusk—wolfish shadows, going soft-foot about some dreadful business. What was a were-wolf but a man with a wolf's savage treachery in his heart? She sat there and listened to the tale of men turned beast. But it wasn't your body turning into a beast's body which was the truth behind the tale. It was much more horrible, and quite true, that a man could go on looking like a man and yet have a wolf's savage, treacherous heart.

She took some food on her plate and ate a little of it. She refused coffee, because Mr. Brown might, after all, have taken his own way and drugged her cup. She would eat nothing except from the common dish and drink nothing except from the common jug. But if they wanted to drug her they would find a way of doing it. She was one against them all, and she had no chance.

By degrees the effect of the shock she had received began to wear off. She became less numb, less stiff. Painfully the power to think returned, and with the pain courage. She was one against all of them except perhaps Joanna, but she could still put up a fight. What she had overheard gave her an advantage, because she knew their plan. She was to be frightened into letting Wickham rescue her. They would count on her giving him the papers. She could hear his voice now, low and earnest, telling her to bring the papers with her. "Bring the papers, and I'll get you away." That had been his burden all along. And she would have brought them and gone with him if the Reverend Peter's door had had a stronger catch. She had been ready to go with him, as she had been—almost—to trust him with the papers. A little more, and the almost would have been quite. A bitter laughter came up in her, and she remembered that he had told her not to be a fool. Could anyone be more of a fool than Sarah Marlowe who had trusted John Wickham? Why, he hadn't even taken the trouble to pretend that he was honest. He had come to her a self-confessed thief without shame or remorse. Wolf in wolf's clothing—and she had trusted him. Why?

She looked back, and knew that she would have done it again. She had not known that it was possible to feel so much ashamed.

"Curious how the silver bullet motif crops up in these stories," said Mr. Brown. "None of the were-beasts can be killed by an ordinary bullet—that is common to all the stories in every country in the world. Sometimes holy water comes into it of course, but the silver bullet is a great favourite. It keeps on cropping up. Sometimes it is a button off a man's coat or a link off a woman's chain, and sometimes it is just a silver coin. Silver being white and bright may have something to do with it—the symbolism of good overcoming evil. Or because it was precious and different, and the sorcerer was not provided with a spell against it. Or because the silver coin was often marked with a cross or some other sacred emblem. And starting from this there may have arisen a confusion between the emblem and the silver, resulting in the idea that any silver bullet possessed the efficacy originally attributed to the bullet made from silver bearing the mark of the cross. There is a wide field for speculation in these borderlands of science and superstition, and I have found a peculiar fascination in wandering there."

"That," said Wilson Cattermole, "was precisely my thesis in an article which I wrote—let me see, it must have been fifteen years ago."

Sarah went back into her thoughts.

Now that she could think, she must make up her mind what she was going to do. The night lay before them all. They had a plan, and she had overheard part of it. She must make a plan too. It was rather like a game of hide-and-seek in the dark, because she must move cautiously for fear of blundering into some part of their plan, and they, most fortunately, would not be aware that she had a plan at all. At any moment a foot put wrong would mean disaster.

These are the occasions when courage either fails outright or rises to face the worst. Sarah's courage rose. Between now and tomorrow the issue would be decided. Her chance to get away was now, before they could put their plan into action.

She began to think what she could do. She could carry out part of the plan Wickham had suggested—say she had a headache and slip off to bed. Then instead of meeting him she could get out at the back—the den had a window which looked that way. Quite easy so far, but what next? Well, she would have to make her way to Hedgeley, and so long as they didn't find out that she was not in the house and come after her with a car, she thought she could do it. It must be all of seven miles and wicked going, but it would not be quite dark because of the snow, and she would have plenty of time—if they didn't find out that she was gone. That was one way. The drawback was that Wickham would still be about. He might even think she had changed her mind and was going to come with him after all.

For a moment her mind swung back and showed her, not Sarah Marlowe struggling over an endless icy waste towards a town she might never find, but Sarah Marlowe warm and comfortable in a car, covering those miles easily and safely. What was the good of thinking about things which had never been anything more than a mirage? John Wickham couldn't make her safe. He was one of the wolf pack, helping to hunt her down.

The other thing she could do was to fall in with their plan, go to their silly séance, and let them think they had frightened her. Then when the proceedings were over and everyone had gone to bed she could still get out of the window and make for Hedgeley.

No, it was too late. She couldn't risk it. This séance had been got up as a cover for something. She was quite sure about that, and she didn't know what the something was. She only knew that it smelled of danger. She just couldn't bring herself to risk it.

It would have to be the first plan.

As soon as she had made up her mind she felt curiously lightened. The pain left her. She took some more food, because if she had to walk to Hedgeley in this bitter cold, it wouldn't do to start chilled and empty.

"I am afraid I have monopolized the conversation." The Reverend Peter looked about him with an obvious desire to be contradicted. "But you are such good listeners, my dear people, and when I have an absorbing subject and attentive guests I am afraid I have a tendency to let my tongue run on."

Chapter Twenty-Seven

THEY HAD COFFEE in the drawing-room. Sarah refused her cup, and to her relief the refusal seemed to pass unnoticed. Then there was no plan to drug her tonight. The heat of the room and the relief from her most pressing fear made her feel relaxed and drowsy. Wilson Cattermole got in the story he had tried to tell at dinner. Joanna, unable to secure a wider attention talked about her messages to Sarah in a hurrying undertone.

When the clock struck nine there was a general move.

"There may not, of course, be any manifestations so early in the evening." Mr. Brown stood on the hearthrug with his pipe in his hand. "In fact I cannot guarantee that there will be any manifestations at all, but I think it will give everything the best chance if we repair now to the other wing. I have had a fire lighted, and I propose that we sit quietly by what light it may afford. It is very important that the right vibrations should be set up—there must be the correct psychic atmosphere. We must place ourselves *en rapport* with whatever it is that is causing the manifestations. There may be a desire to communicate, or there may not. I believe there is. But a desire to communicate is not the only factor. Giving and taking, cause and effect, are parts of a psychic whole. If I may borrow a phrase, it is for us to do what we can to ensure good reception. I propose that we take Miss Cattermole's planchette, and that we also adopt another method which sometimes gives excellent results by placing a slate and slate-pencil in a convenient position."

As he talked, Sarah woke right up. He had the sort of voice which made jargon sound impressive, but she was merely impressed with the fact that he still considered it necessary to impress her. This was a cheering thought. Rather a drop from the psychic whole to planchette and a slate-pencil, but only sceptics like Miss Marlowe worried about that sort of thing. She had an idea that he was inventing his jargon as he went along, and that amused her. It would be fun to catch him out.

The word convenient rang a little mocking bell in her mind. A slate and slate-pencil—the oldest of all the old cheating tricks! It angered her that he should think it good enough to serve. The only thing actually in doubt was whether the slate would be faked beforehand, or whether the Reverend Peter, or Wickham, or one of the Grimsbys was slick-fingered enough to do the faking there in the dark under her nose.

For a moment she was quite sorry that she would never know, because she was not going to be at the séance. She was going to be in bed with a headache, and a locked door with a tilted chair jammed against it under the handle. But later, when they were all in bed, she was going to slip out of the very window against which she was standing now and make her way to Hedgeley even if she had to crawl there on her hands and knees. Well, she would have to say her piece and slip away, and once she had got out of this room she need never see any of them again.

She addressed herself to Wilson Cattermole.

"Would you mind very much if I didn't come—if I went to bed?"

"Bed?" said Wilson. He peered at her in his shortsighted way.

Sarah said, "Yes." They were all looking at her now. She added, "I've got a headache," and thought how silly it sounded, because if you are a secretary and have come down to a haunted house with your employer on purpose to take notes of any phenomena there, it isn't really a very satisfying excuse to say you've got a headache and you want to go to bed. It had seemed all right as a plan in her head, but the minute they began to look at her she could see that it was not going to go down well. In fact it wasn't going to go down at all.

Wilson became the very image of an agitated ant.

"But, my dear Miss Sarah, you cannot really intend to desert me—us. I—we have been counting on you not only to take notes of the proceedings—a part for which no one else has the necessary qualifications—but also as an independent witness. There is such a sad spirit of scepticism abroad. You yourself are admittedly tainted with it, but in this case, and if it did not actually hamper the manifestations, that would be all to the good. The evidence of a sceptic in these matters is most valuable. But—dear me, Miss Sarah, you cannot actually mean—no, no, it is quite impossible—you did not really say that you wished to go to bed!"

Whatever she had said, the possibility of evading the séance, it was obvious, no longer existed. She could of course just swoon, in which case they would probably carry her up to bed and find some means of drugging her. They might very easily call John Wickham in to carry her. Wilson's brittle arms didn't look as if they could lift a child. John Wickham—An inward shudder took hold of her. She decided against the swoon and made a virtue of necessity.

"Oh, Mr. Cattermole, of course not, if you want me. I just had a headache—I'm afraid I was rather forgetting about the séance. I'm so sorry. Of course I'll come and take notes for you."

He eyed her in a bewildered manner.

"You forgot? But it is what we came down here for. I really fail to understand—"

Perhaps he wasn't in it. It was Morgan's voice she had heard, not his. But he had prevented her letter from reaching Henry Templar. No—that was John Wickham's story, put up to cover himself. Her letter could have gone into *his* pocket just as well as into Wilson's. She had only his word for it that it was Wilson who had kept it back. Then if Wilson Cattermole was innocent of this conspiracy, they were using him as a catspaw—Morgan Cattermole, the Reverend Peter, and Wickham who pretended that he did not even know of Morgan's existence.

Wilson ran his fingers through his hair.

"I really cannot understand how you can possibly have forgotten. Inexplicable—really inexplicable!"

"I'll go and get my pad."

"And a warm coat," said the Reverend Peter in a jovial voice. "The fire, I believe, is doing as well as can be expected, but you know what it is with an unused chimney. I hope you and Miss Cattermole will wrap up well."

"My fur coat," said Joanna—she followed Sarah out of the room— "and perhaps bedroom slippers—what do you think, my dear? They are lined with a special vegetarian health fleece, and they are certainly very warm. Of course the fur coat is quite against my principles, but I have had it a long time, and nothing I can do now would restore the minks to life. I haven't really the slightest idea what a mink is, and whenever I have asked anyone they have always said they hadn't either. And that does make it a great deal more impersonal, don't you think, because they may be a very destructive kind of animal, though that would not alter my convictions about wearing fur, and I should never buy another fur coat. So in a way I can't help hoping that it won't wear out for a long time. There's nothing so warm as fur, is there—and I do feel the cold so much, though I don't think I ever remember quite such bitter weather as this."

She was rather breathless when they arrived at the top of the stairs. She took Sarah's arm and drew her inside the bedroom door.

"I am not really sure about séances," she said. "That is to say, I think they are very nice in your own house or in a friend's house, but when it comes to haunted houses, it is all just a little disturbing, don't you think?" Her pale eyes gazed rather wildly past Sarah in the unromantic direction of the wash-stand, on which a battered hot water jug stood wrapped against the cold in a bath-towel. "I thought it was very brave of you to say you wanted to go to bed, and if you had, I would have gone too, because there is something about this séance that makes me feel very uncomfortable indeed, and it is not even as if I had my purple velvet—though Nathaniel did say that purple was all poppycock, didn't he, and of course that is very comforting. You must keep reminding me about that, my dear. Having passed over, he would know, wouldn't he?"

She slipped her arms into the fur coat which Sarah was holding for her and shivered a little.

"It is very warm and comfortable, but do you know, I met a woman—just before you came to us, I think it was—at one of Sybilla Havendale's parties. She was some kind of foreigner and I can't remember her name, but she was very psychic, and she said she could distinctly see the spirits of the minks which had been killed to make my coat following me round in a pack. It upset me a good deal, and I've only just begun to wear the coat again, but she didn't tell me what they looked like, and whenever I try to remember her name I can only remember that it sounded very foreign indeed."

The words went by Sarah Marlowe like wind blowing. She heard them, and they meant nothing. She said suddenly, in a voice which sounded as if it had been forced out of her,

"Is your other brother here?"

Joanna Cattermole turned round, the heavy old-fashioned coat hanging open over her trailing velvet dress, her hair flaring back from a face which had a frightened look.

"My brother! What do you mean?"

If Sarah could have taken her words back she would have done so, but they had escaped her. None of the words you speak can ever be as if you had not spoken them. She stiffened herself and said,

"Not Mr. Cattermole—your other brother. Is Mr. Morgan here?"

Joanna said, "Morgan—" in a wandering voice. Then she put a hand on Sarah's arm. "Oh, my dear, what makes you think of that? For do you know what I have been thinking all day—in fact ever since we came down here? You always say you are not psychic, but you must be, for you see we were both thinking about Morgan. I was wishing so very much that he was here, and thinking that if he were, I should not be feeling so uneasy. He always has such high spirits, and he does not believe in manifestations, or haunted houses, or anything like that—you remember how he laughed at my planchette—and just at the moment I feel that that would be very comforting. You see, it is not as if we knew what form the manifestations would take—Mr.

Brown has been so very non-committal—and if there is going to be anything violent or unpleasant, I shouldn't like it at all."

"Don't let's go," said Sarah in a whisper. "Let's go to bed. I'll tell Mr. Cattermole you are ill and I must stay with you."

Joanna's hand dropped from her arm.

"Oh, no—that wouldn't be true. And it would vex Wilson dreadfully. It wouldn't do at all. He is expecting you to take notes for him—you know he said so downstairs. He would be most dreadfully vexed."

"Would that matter?" said Sarah.

Joanna began to tremble.

"Oh, yes, my dear—oh, *yes*. You must *never* vex him—oh, no, never. And we mustn't keep him waiting either. Oh, no, my dear, it would never, never do. I will put my slippers on whilst you are getting your coat."

Chapter Twenty-Eight

THE DOOR INTO the haunted wing stood wide. As they all passed through it, Sarah remembered how she had come this way in the dark, feeling before her with her hand, and how cold the great iron bolt had struck against her palm. The bolt was shot back now. It showed black against the oak of the old door. The Grimsbys must do some work in the house after all. There was no rust upon the iron. The light from the lamp which the Reverend Peter was carrying showed that the bolt had been oiled.

They passed through, and the icy damp of vacant, unused rooms was heavy about them. The door swung to. Against this side of it Sarah had dashed herself, running from—what? She didn't know. She told herself that it was her own terror, and she remembered how she had wrenched round and seen a shadow stand black beside her in the dusk from an open door. And the shadow had been John Wickham. She felt her own relief again.

The lamplight seemed suddenly much brighter, perhaps because she was remembering the dark. On this side the bolt was rusted in its socket. It might have been a hundred years since it had been shot. The iron was corroded and pitted, the wood of the door showed rough. Everything looked as if at least a hundred years had passed since anyone had swept or dusted here.

And all at once Sarah was frightened. The dust lay thick. Her footprints must be plain to see—hers, and John Wickham's. And what were they going to make of that? She felt her heart waver and sink. If he was a traitor he had told them already. She looked along the passage and saw that any marks she might have made were indistinguishable. There were footprints enough to cover hers. The dust had been trampled by other feet.

They moved on round the corner which she had turned in the dark. She could see a line of boarded-up windows on the right, and on the left three doors. It must have been the first of these which she had opened. It stood a handsbreadth open now, low and arched, with the rough rusty latch which had scraped her hand.

There were two steps down into the room. Wilson had to hold the lamp whilst the Reverend Peter got his awkward size and bulk through the cramped opening. Coming down last, Sarah found out why her footprints had been trampled out. The room which she had half seen, half guessed at as quite bare and stark, had now been made ready for their company. There was a rug upon the floor, and a table for the lamp, and for Miss Cattermole's planchette and Mr. Brown's slate. A wood fire burned reluctantly upon the hearth, adding its own smell to the mould and damp which had for so long held possession here. Four chairs had been placed symmetrically about it. The boarded-up window no longer gave any glimpse of the sky. The slipped panel had been nailed back. If it was John Wickham who had done any of these things, he might, if he had so chosen, have trodden out her footprints, and that without any risk to himself.

The thought went through her mind like faint lightning. Only why should he? She didn't know. It didn't matter. It was the papers they wanted, and the papers they meant to have. It went through her again, but this time brightly and fiercely, that they would stick at nothing to get them.

Mr. Brown moved the table to a place between the chimney and the window. Then he took the lamp from Wilson Cattermole, set it down, and motioned them to their chairs.

"Miss Cattermole—perhaps you will come here, next to the table. I will divide you and Miss Marlowe, and my friend Cattermole will be on her other side. Either of us will then be in a position to indicate to her when she should take a note. But the chairs are wrongly arranged. We must not, I am afraid, sit round the fire. It is the door and the passage beyond it that we have to keep under observation. I think we can leave you in the chimney corner, Miss Cattermole, if you will just turn your chair a little so as to face the door. I shall have the pleasure of being next to you, and of course to Miss Marlowe. And your brother is, I am afraid, the farthest from the fire. Well now, as soon as we are settled I propose to turn the lamp as low as it will go without absolutely going out. I had intended to dispense with the lamp altogether and have nothing but firelight for our experiment, but as the fire is at present really giving no light at all, I think we must allow ourselves just a gleam from the lamp."

As he turned and stretched out a hand to the screw, Sarah looked about her. They were all facing the door now, with the boarded-up window behind them and the fireplace on their left. Except where the rug covered them the floor-boards were bare. The walls were covered to a height of about six feet with very old, dusty panelling. The fireplace was of a size disproportionate to that of the room. It had the air of a cave. A strong down-draught drove a fitful smoke about the room. The door into the corridor was shut and latched.

She saw these things in the lamplight. Then, with a turn of the screw, the flame dipped. There was an upward rush of darkness and the light failed. The last thing she saw was the enormous distorted shadow of the Reverend Peter's head and arm flung upwards across the panelling and the dirty plaster.

The lamp was not quite out. When she turned her head Sarah could see a faint blue glimmer at the base of the chimney. It seemed impossible that it should make any impression on the heavy darkness of the room, but by degrees she found herself beginning to see a little. The great shadowy fireplace was blacker than the walls. She could see the outline of Mr. Brown's big, untidy head, and beyond it something pale which was Joanna's hair. On her other side Wilson Cattermole was just a denser patch of gloom.

They sat still and in silence for a while. Of course no room with four people in it and a fire burning, or struggling to burn, is ever completely still. There is the movement of air drawn in and breath given out. You feel the beating of your own heart and the stir of your own pulse. You know that each one hears and feels these same things. We are so used to them that they do not interest us and we do not notice them. But when you sit in the dark and wait for something to happen, all these unregarded sounds come crowding into consciousness.

Sarah listened, and was aware of Joanna breathing quickly, of Mr. Brown moving first one foot and then the other with a slow sideways movement, and of Wilson Cattermole sitting so still that she wondered whether he was really there.

Against the background of these small uncounted sounds there came one that none of them could miss, the sharp rasp of a slate-pencil grating on slate. It is a quite unmistakable sound and unlike anything but itself. It came from the direction from which it might have been expected, the table on which the lamp was standing. To the right—that is, on Joanna's side—had been placed her planchette. To the left, immediately behind Mr. Brown, was the slate which he had suggested as a possible vehicle for messages. It appeared that a message was being delivered now.

Sarah turned her head and stared at the table, but she could see nothing. The lamp bulged below the level of the wick and cast its own shadow to deepen the general gloom. All that she could be sure of was that Mr. Brown had not turned round, and that he did not now appear to be moving at all.

The pencil drove furiously for what might have been the inside of a minute and then stopped. Then there was a small sharp sound as if it had been dropped impatiently. They heard it roll and catch against the wooden frame. Then silence again.

Mr. Brown reached behind him and turned up the lamp. In the sudden glow Sarah wondered whether she herself looked as startled as Joanna did, her eyes so wide that the ring of the iris showed clear, her lips parted in a soundless "Oh!"

Mr. Brown's hand came back with the slate in it.

"Well now, I thought there might be a message," he said.

Sarah found herself thinking, "Well now, I'm quite sure you did. And what's more, you put it there."

What could be easier than to lay the slate on the table, message down, and scratch on any little bit of slate with any little bit of pencil? She felt a sort of scornful pride at not being taken in.

He was looking at the slate and frowning.

"This is a very strange message. It doesn't seem—" He broke off and turned to Wilson Cattermole. "I really don't know what to make of it."

"If you were to read it—" Wilson's voice betrayed some impatience. And,

"Read it out!" cried Joanna fretfully.

The Reverend Peter read in a puzzled, hesitating manner, "*Can't get through—she won't let me—blood calling—*"

"That's a very strange message," said Wilson Cattermole on Sarah's other side.

Joanna put a hand to her mouth.

"What does it mean?"

"I don't know," said Mr. Brown. "I think we had better ask. Shall we see if we can get anything with the planchette? Perhaps you and I, Miss Cattermole—if that will satisfy your brother."

By turning half round and moving the table slightly forward so as to bring it between them they were able to rest their fingertips upon the board.

At Wilson's request Sarah wrote down the message from the slate upon her pad. Queer stuff—and Mr. Brown seemed puzzled over it—but of course that was acting.... She found herself clinging very hard to that. It was just a fake—a stupid, dangerous game—a dangerous criminal game. But even that was better than to believe in this frantic beating against a wall of oblivion, this trying to draw a curtain which couldn't be drawn. Horrible to believe in some creature which had once been human making an unavailing effort to get into touch with its own human kind. Thank God she didn't believe in any of it. But even to touch the fringe of someone else's belief made her shudder. She looked down at her pad and saw the words she had written on it—"*blood—calling—*" Oh, that was horrible!

She pulled round to watch the others, and saw that the planchette had begun to move—not writing yet, but trembling and jerking like a dog on a lead, in a hurry to be off. Their hands on it, Joanna's thin and trembling, Mr. Brown's thick and heavy—smooth—odd that there should be no hair on them. The light shining down—

Joanna spoke in an excited whisper.

"Quick! What shall we ask?"

"Who is it who won't let you come through?" Mr. Brown subdued his boom to a whisper.

The planchette was off almost before the words were out of his mouth. It wrote, and stopped. They lifted it and looked at the paper.

There was only one word on it.

The word was *"Emily"*.

"Write it down," said Wilson Cattermole at Sarah's ear.

"But that's what it said before," said Joanna.

"What!" Wilson's tone was sharp with something like dismay.

Joanna stared and nodded.

"Oh, yes, it is. When I was sitting with Morgan, the night you were away—something about *fog*, and *dark*, and *Emily*, and *where is it?* I thought it very strange at the time, because I don't know anyone called Emily. And Nathaniel couldn't get through either. I really don't like it at all. Who is Emily, and why does she try to interfere?"

Wilson Cattermole leaned over Sarah's shoulder and read from the pad on her knee. He had rubbed up his hair, and his voice had a worried sound.

"The message says, '*blood—calling*'. But—whose blood can it mean?"

"We had better ask," said Mr. Brown. He put his hands back on the board again. "Will you tell us whose blood is calling?"

Sarah felt a revulsion so strong that she could have screamed. If it was a game, it was a most profane and wicked game. If it was true that murdered blood cried out—there was a bit in the Bible about "thy brother's blood crying from the ground"... That was just a metaphor—it didn't mean what these people meant. It wasn't—it couldn't be Emily Case calling to Sarah Marlowe.

The planchette was moving. It rocked, slid an inch or two, rocked again, and stopped. Sarah watched the hands, clear in the yellow lamplight—Joanna's bloodless and attenuated, the Reverend Peter's square and heavy, with short bitten-down nails. They looked strong—horrifyingly strong. The nails were not very clean.

The board rocked again and the pencil began to write. When it had travelled a little way it stopped. Mr. Brown lifted his hands and drew the paper out. This time there were two words on it, and before he read them aloud Sarah knew what they were going to be "*Emily—blood—*".

Joanna Cattermole made a faint shocked exclamation.

"I don't understand! Who is Emily?"

"We had better ask," said the Reverend Peter.

They sat and waited for the board to move, but not a tremor shook it. It seemed as if a long time went by. Joanna took her hands away.

"It's no good," she said. "It is never any good going on when it stops like that. It's like holding on to the telephone when they've hung up at the other end."

To Sarah her tone suggested relief. She thought Miss Cattermole was not sorry to be cut off. Even knowing what she knew, she had felt her own nerves tingle. It was a wicked, unscrupulous game, played to frighten her, and even though she was forewarned, it had come near enough to doing what it had been meant to do. Just because they had sat in the dark, and because the Reverend Peter could play tricks with planchette, she had come within an ace of being shaken. She mustn't forget for a single instant that their game was to frighten her and send her running to John Wickham.

She came back from these thoughts to hear Wilson Cattermole say,

"I think we should turn down the light again. I did not come down here to take part in what I consider a futile attempt to obtain communications by means of planchette. I consider it a very unreliable vehicle. My sister is fully aware of my views on this point. I came down here to investigate certain manifestations which are said to take place in this room. You have never told me just what form these manifestations take, and I have purposely refrained from asking, as I wished to come to this séance with an unprejudiced mind. But in view of these unexplained and, if I may say so, extraneous communications, I feel entitled to ask whether they have any bearing on what is believed to have happened here."

Mr. Brown moved the table back into its original position and turned the light down again before he replied. He had the air of a man plunged in thought. His brows made a frowning line. His movements were slow and deliberate. When the darkness had brimmed up and they could no longer see one another he said in a low, grave voice,

"You are certainly entitled to an explanation, but I do not know that I can give you one. The communications we have just received have no bearing on what happened in this room a hundred and fifty years ago. As to what exactly did happen, that has never been cleared up. The dead body of a young woman dressed only in her shift was found beneath that window on a snowy January night. It was said that she had walked in her sleep and fallen, breaking her neck. Her name was Olivia Perrott, and she was the ward and kinswoman of Roger Perrott to whom the house belonged. It was said that he had wished to marry her, but that she preferred his brother Humphrey. They were betrothed and the wedding day fixed. The matter was never cleared up. Humphrey, who was absent on the night of the tragedy, never returned. His brother gave out that he was travelling abroad to mend his broken heart. But as time went on it began to be whispered that Humphrey did not come back because he was dead, and dead by his brother Roger's hand. When Roger broke his neck out hunting about a year later the property passed to a cousin, John Perrott, who shut up this side of the house. It has never been occupied since. Every now and then there have been hardy investigators who have offered to spend a night alone here. One of them was found dead on the very spot where Olivia Perrott fell. Another had a severe illness and was never the same man again. I have not myself spent a night in the room—I must confess that I was unwilling to do so without company—but I have heard—well—sounds." His voice went away into a deep whisper and ceased.

Sarah wondered whether the story was a true one, or whether he had made it up. It might be true. She felt a horrified pity for that long-ago Olivia and her murdered lover.

"And where does Emily come in?" said Wilson Cattermole.

"My dear friend—" the Reverend Peter was warmly explanatory— "don't you see, we have here an old tragedy producing disturbances in the psychic atmosphere. These are recurrent. They are especially pronounced at this time of year and in snowy weather. But if some newer disturbance were introduced—can't you see that this might cause a fading of the older manifestations? The force of the disturbance might be turned into the newer channel."

"Yes, yes, but has there been any fresh tragedy—that's the point."

"That is what we do not know. It need not necessarily have happened here. Any one of us four might provide the point of contact."

"How could we?" said Joanna Cattermole crossly. "I've never known anyone called Emily, and I don't suppose I ever shall! It isn't a name that anyone has, except that poor thing who got murdered the other day in a train—what was her name—Emily Case."

From the other side of the room, from the thick shadow beyond the jutting chimney-breast, there came a long, desolate sigh. Like a wavering echo a faint voice said,

"Emily Case—"

Chapter Twenty-Nine

SARAH FELT her spine creep. She could almost have sworn that something cold had touched it. It wasn't true—no part of this ghastly play was true. Mr. Brown had faked the message on the slate and played tricks with planchette. For all she knew, the words which he had read from the paper had already been there when they came into the room. It would be quite easy. All he need do was to turn the paper over as he took it up.

All this was in her mind before that wavering echo came. It stayed there. A cold drop might run down her back, but nothing was going to make her believe that whispering voice had anything to do with Emily

Case. She stiffened herself, and heard Joanna catch her breath and say, "Oh dear!"

"Who are you?" said the Reverend Peter Brown in a solemn voice.

The whisper came again, low on the edge of sound:

"Emily Case—"

"Oh dear! Why does she come to us?" Joanna's voice died away into a whisper.

Quite suddenly with no warning at all the low, heavy door of the room burst open with a crash. There was a sense of impact, of noise, and of force, which was startling in the extreme. The hinges creaked and strained. The latch struck the panelling. A cold air moved in the room.

Sarah stared in the direction of the sound. She could just make out the swinging, quivering door, the shape of the arched doorway against the unbroken darkness of the passage which lay beyond. Nothing moved there. The cold wind moved in the room, and all at once a high, desperate scream went up. The window rattled and shook behind them, and they all heard something fall.

Some thing, or some one. The sound was not loud. It did not seem as if it was in the room. If anyone had sat where they were sitting, Olivia Perrott's fall might have sounded just like that—Because there was snow on the ground.

Sarah set her teeth. "It isn't true! It isn't, *isn't* true!"

The silence came back. It was not complete at first. The door whined on its hinges. There was a faint, dry rustling from the dark passage—no more than a withered leaf would make moving in the draught upon the floor. It might have been a leaf, or a shred of paper—or the rustle of silk. Olivia Perrott might have worn silk for her wedding. Perhaps she had her wedding dress for a shroud. Emily Case had had no silk—

The rustle ceased. The door stopped swinging. The hinges quietened. Now the room was still. Only the soundless sound of pulse and heart-beats moving to the tune of the blood.

And then, out of that dark corner, a long sigh, and sighing words:

"Where is it? I gave it to you. Where is it?" And again that long trembling sigh.

Mr. Brown said, "Miss Cattermole—do you know what it wants? If you do, answer it."

Joanna took her breath with a gasp.

"Oh, I don't—I don't really—" The last word broke and failed.

"Cattermole?"

"I know nothing."

"Miss Marlowe?"

Sarah said, "Nothing," and thought, "That's a lie. And I don't mind if it is, because it's a trick, a trick, a trick."

The glimmer of light from the lamp shot suddenly into a momentary rocketing flame. The room was there for as long as a flash may take to flare and fail again. For that space there was someone in the corner by the chimney-breast—a neat, shabby little woman in a black serge coat with a grey opossum collar and a flat, depressed-looking hat slipping a little over to one side—Horribly, unbelievably, Emily Case.

The light went out—clean out this time. They were in the dark. It filled the room like water. It rose black from floor to ceiling. It stretched from them to the chimney corner where the little shabby woman had stood and held a handkerchief to her face—a little, shabby woman who looked like Emily Case.

Everything in Sarah rose up to deny what she had seen. Suggestion and a trick of the light, the shadow of the chimney-breast and her own imagination—

The voice came whispering out of the dark again:

"What have you done with the packet? I gave it to you. What have you done with it?"

Sarah said to herself, "What I ought to do is to walk into the corner and prove to myself that there isn't anything there. Or if there's someone, it's a trick. I ought to do that—I ought to do it at once."

And right there she was faced with a mutiny. She took hold of the arms of her chair and put her weight on them. She began to make the movement which would bring her to her feet, but her muscles refused it. They let her drop back again, slack and helpless. A wave of weakness passed over her. The whisper came again, dreadfully faint:

"I gave it to you. Oh, where is it?"

Wilson Cattermole put out his left hand and laid it on Sarah's wrist. She heard him say very quietly,

"Miss Sarah, she is speaking to you. Answer her if you can."

Well, what was she to say? The warm weakness flowed over her in a sickly wave. She said,

"I can't—"

It was very nearly true. She thought she was going to faint, and the idea terrified her. To lose consciousness here, in this horrible room— no, not whilst she had any fight left in her! She bit hard into the inside of her lip, and then, with the faintness just held back from swamping her, there came to her ears a gasping sigh and the sound of a fall. At once the chair next to hers was pushed back and Mr. Brown was saying in a concerned voice,

"Miss Cattermole has fainted. I'm afraid—Cattermole, can you find the door? I really think we should get her away from here. We ought to have a light, but I haven't any matches—I forgot them."

"I haven't any either." Wilson's agitated voice came from the middle of the room. He could be heard stumbling, and groping for the door. "Can you lift her? If I keep speaking, you'll get the direction. I'm in the doorway. Can you manage? We ought to have a torch. I thought—"

Sarah made another effort to rise. This time she got to her feet. To her dismay, she was not very steady on them. Her head swam and her sense of direction was confused. When she felt Mr. Brown go past her she followed him. One of her hands, groping, touched Joanna's trailing velvet and clung there.

They came like that to the door, and she remembered how low and narrow the opening was, and that there were two steps up to it. The Reverend Peter would never manage it with Joanna in his arms. She stood back to leave him room, and all in a moment the thing happened. A forward movement, a quick "Here—take her!", the clatter of feet on the bare wooden steps, and, loud and dreadful, the slam of the heavy door. She heard it, and she heard a bolt go grinding home. The door was so thick that no other sound came to her. She stood in the dark and listened, but there was no other sound.

She sank down on the bottom step and hid her face in her hands.

Chapter Thirty

At first nothing but the sense of darkness and fear. A mist of faintness, and as this receded, the fear rising in her, flooding upwards to the panic line. She sat there and fought to hold it back. Because once that line was reached, her control would go and anything might happen. Perhaps even what had happened to Olivia Perrott. She pressed her hands hard against her eyes, and then with a sudden desperate courage snatched them away and made herself look into the darkness. It was so deep, so dense, so complete, that the dropping of her hands and the lifting of her lids made no difference. Two lines which she had read somewhere came into her mind in a very uncomforting manner.

> Thy hand, great Anarch, lets the curtain fall
> And universal darkness covers all.

The sort of lines that would come into your head when you have just been locked into a haunted room. No, not locked, bolted—"Be accurate, Sarah. Don't go on thinking about Olivia Perrott and how dark it is, or about whispering voices, or Emily Case." Tricks—tricks—the whole lot of them—a bag of tricks to frighten Sarah Marlowe into giving up the oiled-silk packet. "Don't think about the packet—don't think about Emily Case. Don't think about Sarah Marlowe, or you'll begin to feel sorry for her, and the minute you begin to feel sorry for yourself you're done. Say the multiplication table. Say the Kings of England with their dates—William the Conqueror 1066 and all that. Say the names of the Underwood family out of *The Pillars of the House*—

Felix Chester Underwood. Felix because his parents were so happy when he was born and they didn't know they were going to have thirteen children on a curate's pay, and two lots of twins. And Chester after his godfather, Admiral Chester, who sent him a five-pound note for his birthday, and they spent a pound of it going for a picnic in a wagonette with a bottle of invalid port and a pie.

Wilmet Ursula and Alda Mary, the first lot of twins—

Something moved in the dark corner by the chimney-breast where it had moved before.

The thirteen Underwoods ignobly deserted Sarah, thinned away into the darkness, and left her alone with the thing that had moved. She stood up. It is an old, old instinct which gets you to your feet and sets your back against a wall and your face towards the enemy.

Sarah went up the two steps behind her and set her back against the bolted door. She was afraid, but she had herself in hand. She wouldn't run, or scream. She said in quite a loud, firm voice,

"Is there anyone there?"

She had braced herself to hear the whispering voice again, but it did not come—only that faint dry rustle as if a leaf was moving upon the boards—or the hem of a silk dress. As the sound of her own voice ceased and the rustle died and went out into the silence, she got a startling answer to her question. It came from behind her, right at her back. There was a rusty creak of the bolt. The door flung in and pushed her with it, so that she came down the steps at a run which took her half across the room. After the door the energetic entrance of John Wickham, calling her name.

"Sarah—are you there? Sarah! Where are you?"

"In the middle of next week," said Sarah.

And then she wasn't. She was in his arms, and thankful to be there. He might be a bank-robber and a traitor, but he was most solidly and convincingly human. He held her hard, and he kissed her harder still. And Sarah held on to him with both hands and kissed him back. It was a thoroughly demoralizing and humiliating performance. She was to blush for it afterwards, but at the time those human arms and those human kisses were heaven. She shook from head to foot and pressed against him in the dark.

"Take me away!"

When she had said it once she couldn't stop. It kept on saying itself.

"Take me away—take me away—take me away!"

He left off kissing her and dropped his hands on her shoulders.

"I'm going to—that's what I'm here for. Sarah, stop it! Do you hear—stop it at once! Someone will hear you. Stop it, I say!"

She stopped, but the words went on in her head.

He said, "That's better. We'll go right away. You ought to have come when I told you. You just played into their hands. Come along! Have you got the papers?"

The words froze her where she stood. The papers—oh, yes, the papers—that was what he had come for. That was the plan. They were to frighten her, and he was to come in and pretend to help her. Why, she had heard him boast of how easily he could take her in. Her mouth still felt his kisses. There was a pain that went through her like a sword. She stood quiet under his hands. She said quietly,

"I must go to my room."

"You can't—it's not safe, unless—are the papers there?"

It wouldn't matter how unsafe it was if the papers were there. He meant to have them. Well, there were two people playing this game. She said, still in that quiet voice,

"Yes, they are there. I'll get them."

For a moment he stayed like that, still holding her, and then he let go.

"All right, we'll chance it. Come along!"

And with that he had her by the arm and was hurrying her out under the arched doorway into the passage—and on....

They were in his room with the door ajar, listening. Her mind was in confusion. How much of this was according to plan? That was the worst of only hearing a part of it. "An actor in his time plays many parts." Was he playing one now, when he listened for sounds from the house, or now, when they had crept to the end of the passage and seen the landing empty before them? She didn't know. She only knew that she couldn't and wouldn't stay another hour in this house, and that at the very worst, with a choice of being murdered by Grimsby and Mr. Brown or by John Wickham, she would rather Wickham did it. And anyhow she didn't much care. Only she meant to save the papers if she could, because if she did she might come to feel that she had got back whatever it is you lose when you kiss someone whom you despise.

She got across the landing to her room and lighted a candle there. She must leave her suit-case—it didn't matter. She stood in front of the glass and put on the little pillbox hat with its stiffened veil. Her face was as white as paper and her eyes were burning bright. She put up a hand to her lips and felt them tremble. She thought, "I kissed him because I was frightened." Something laughed scornfully inside her and said, "What a liar you are! You kissed him because you wanted to. You have wanted to for a long time, and now you'll go on wanting."

She stamped her foot and said, "I won't!" and ran out of the room and across the landing without caring whether anyone saw her. She had blown out the candle and picked up her handbag. She came running down the passage to the door of Wickham's room.

He pulled her in and said quick and sharp.

"Clever girl—have you got them?"

Sarah said, "Yes."

Chapter Thirty-One

THERE WAS A LIGHT in the room, a candle set on the mantelshelf. They looked at each other. Sarah said,

"And now what?"

"Down the back stairs and out into the yard—if we can make it."

"Why shouldn't we make it?"

"We have to pass the kitchen door. It's always open."

She shook her head impatiently.

"Some other way then."

"Do you fancy the front stairs? I don't."

"Isn't there a way down through there—where we've just come from? There must be."

Wickham laughed.

"There is. The door at the bottom is locked and Grimsby keeps the key. It's the back stairs or nothing. Don't worry—I'll get you out."

The words came and went between them quick and low. And hard on that the sound they had heard in this same room the night before—a heavy step in the passage. At the first sound of it Sarah ran past him to the window. The idea of being shut in the cupboard filled her with horror. To be bundled in there with all those stuffy dresses, caught there perhaps, and dragged out if Wickham gave her away—no, and no, and *no*!

She ran to the window and got behind the curtains. They were old and heavy—serge lined with something smooth and cold to the touch. They were the colour of badly cooked spinach. She stood behind them and thanked heaven the window was shut. Even so, the cold from the glass beat against her back. She could feel it right through her fur coat, and the smell of the serge, a really horrible smell of dust and dye, came up in her throat and nose and made her want to sneeze. If she did, it wouldn't need Wickham to give her away. She pinched her nose hard.

And then she stopped wanting to sneeze. Mr. Brown was in the room, and at the sound of his voice she forgot everything except that she must hear what he was going to say.

He came in, and he shut the door, and he said in the voice that would sound hearty however he kept it down or whatever abominable thing he was saying,

"Where the devil have you been?"

Wickham said, "I didn't know you'd be wanting me."

The Reverend Peter went on.

"Well, I'm wanting you now. The girl's in there, locked up in the haunted room, and if she isn't screaming her head off, it'll be because she's passed out. So there's your chance. I'll show you the way and clear off, then you cut in and play the rescuing hero. If you don't get her arms round your neck, I'm a Dutchman. The whole thing went with a bang, and there won't be much stuffing left in her. Promise to get her away and she'll eat out of your hand. Come along with you!"

Anger rushed through Sarah with so much heat that she quite stopped feeling the draught at her back. And the fiercest glow came from the shaming fact that she had done exactly what that revolting parson had expected her to do—and worse. She had not only thrown her arms round John Wickham's neck, but she had clung to him and kissed him. It was one of those incredible things which make you feel you are in some horrible dream, and that presently you will wake up and find that it has never happened.

She heard Wickham laugh, and she heard them go out of the room together and shut the door. There was no time to be angry—she had got to do something. He would be back in a minute. What was she going to do? If she could get down the back stairs to the car, would she be able to get it out and away? It was a very slender chance, but it was the only one, and she must take it now—at once. But when she opened the door a cautious inch the door into the haunted wing was standing wide and she could hear their voices—Wickham's and Mr. Brown's. However dimly the landing on her right was lit, they could not fail to see her cross the passage if they were looking this way. She would be a black shadow against the glow from the landing.

She stood there listening. Mr. Brown would not stay. He was bound to leave Wickham and come back by himself, because the very essence of the plot was that Wickham should appear to be acting on his own. You can't make any plausible show of rescuing a distressed damsel if the villains of the piece are all queued up outside putting their eyes on sticks to see how you get on. No—Mr. Brown would have to come back and keep well out of sight, and Wickham would have to give him time to do it. So there was Sarah Marlowe's slender chance. She would have just so much time as John Wickham's prudence should dictate to get down the stairs and out to the garage. The back door might be locked or the garage door, and the keys in Wickham's pocket for all she knew. She did not even know where the garage was, but take it or leave it, there was her chance.

She stood there with her ear to the crack of the door and listened to the reverberations of the Reverend Peter's voice. She heard him say,

"No hurry, my boy—no hurry. Let her cool her heels—she'll be all the better pleased to see you." His laugh came booming down the passage. "But don't forget it, it's the packet you're out for, not kisses. We've got to get those papers."

Sarah drew back. Could one play the same trick twice? She had fobbed Morgan Cattermole off with a spoof packet—well, why shouldn't the same trick serve again? There was no harm in trying.

She turned and threw a hurried glance about the room. There was no sign of any writing materials. You don't, after all, supply your chauffeur with a davenport. The one solitary object which suggested paper was one of the Penguin books thrown down on the chair by the side of the bed. It sprawled face downwards, and the light of the candle above it picked out the black and white and green of the paper cover. If there wasn't anything better, that would have to do.

Almost before this thought had taken shape she was tearing out a handful of the pages and racking her brains for something to put them in.

It was as she turned that she saw the chest of drawers and remembered that the drawers would probably be lined with paper. She had the top left-hand drawer out in a flash and had snatched the lining from under John Wickham's handkerchiefs and collars. Then back to the door again, and the distant murmur of John Wickham's voice answering Mr. Brown. They were still there then, and she had time—

She folded the pages to the size of the sheets which she had taken from Emily Case's packet. She doubled the lining-paper and wrapped them in it. Pinched flat along the edges and tied up in a handkerchief, it would look not so much unlike the packet they wanted. She had a coloured silk handkerchief about her neck, a gay affair of bronze, and green, and coral-red. It was large enough to take the packet and, knotted firmly, it really had a quite authentic look.

She pushed the whole contraption down inside her jumper, where it gave her a bulging Victorian bust and was most uncomfortable. However, since this was the immemorial way of concealing a secret document, she felt the discomfort to be well worth while.

Up to this moment she had been so busy thinking, planning, and acting that she had not had time to feel. Now, when the acting and planning were for the moment over and she had perforce to stand by the door and listen for the pause which would tell her that Mr. Brown had torn himself from his audience and would be coming back, the tide of feeling flowed in again.

There would be a pause, and then his footsteps coming this way and passing on. As soon as he had reached the landing she must slip across to the stair—

They were still talking—no, not they, just Mr. Brown. Wickham wouldn't want to talk. He would want to get rid of the Reverend Peter and come back. But just why had he not given her away? He had only to say, "Oh, but she isn't in the haunted room—she's here behind the curtain." Why hadn't he done that? The painful tide of feeling rose. She thought she knew that answer. If he had given her away then and there he could never hope to take her in again. But now, in a minute or two, he would come back and pretend again—pretend to be her friend, pretend to be her lover, cheat her into giving him the papers.

She could hear his voice now. Perhaps that was what they were talking about—settling between them just how she was to be tricked. It hurt so much that she turned physically giddy and found herself clinging to the jamb, her forehead bent against it, her hands bruising themselves in an agonized grip.

And right on that the footsteps she was waiting for. They came without warning, because she had missed the pause which should have warned her. They were on the threshold of the door between the two wings, no more than a yard from where she stood against the jamb of Wickham's door. And the door was ajar—three inches—four— with Sarah Marlowe so close to the gap that anyone who passed might see her hands, her cheek, the dark line of her fur coat, between him and the candle-light beyond.

There was no time to think. Her right hand loosed the jamb and went out to bring the door to. Now there was no gap. But had she been quick enough? If she had not, if he had seen the door move, she would only have made discovery certain instead of leaving it to chance. Her heart beat hard against her side. She lifted her head to meet whatever might come. And heard the steps go past.

She made herself count ten before she slid the door open again and looked out. To the left the black and empty passage of the haunted wing. To the right Mr. Brown in silhouette against the landing light. She watched him turn the corner and pass out of sight.

Then she ran down the passage towards the light and opened the door at the head of the back stairs.

Chapter Thirty-Two

SARAH DREW THE DOOR noiselessly to behind her. The cold draught which had met her failed, but the stuffy smell which it had brought remained—a smell of dirt, and mouldering wood, and cabbage-water, and burned fat. Mrs. Grimsby might be a first-class cook, but on the strength of that smell Sarah was prepared to bet her last shoe-button that she kept her kitchen like a pigsty.

And the kitchen door was always open—John Wickham had said so. "Well, get on with it, Sarah, or he'll catch you up. Open or shut, you've got to get past that door. Get on with it!"

She got on with it. There were about twelve steps, rather steep. They went straight down without a break and came into a flagged passage, very uneven under foot. The kitchen door stood wide a yard or so to the left, and a little farther on there was the end of the passage, and the door which would give her her chance.

No use stopping to think. Light came from the kitchen door—light and the sound of voices. A man—that would be Grimsby. And a woman—no, two women—Mrs. Grimsby and—who? "What does it matter who any of them are? Get on with it!"

She went down the passage quick and light. She wouldn't let herself run. The warmth of the kitchen came out and struck her as she went past, and just for a moment she knew how cold she was, and felt a starved longing for the fire. And then she was at the door, and no room left in her mind for anything except "Don't, don't, *don't* let it be locked!"

It wasn't locked. The handle turned easily and the door swung in without a sound. When she had shut it behind her, her heart lifted. For the first time she began to think that the chance she had had to take was a chance that was going to come off.

She moved away from the door and discovered that she would have to move very carefully if she was to keep her feet. The place was just a glither of ice. But another step or two took her into snow. It came up over her shoes and worked down inside them, wetting and chilling her, but she could keep her feet, and it was not deep enough to be hampering.

She was in a courtyard formed by the two wings of the house and the connecting block through which the long passage ran. The kitchen premises were on her right, the haunted wing on her left. If she went forward she would get clear of the house and perhaps be able to see where the garage lay. It was not so dark out here as it had been in the passage. There must be a moon behind all that cloud, because there was light coming from it. She could see the walls of the house standing up black against the snow, which seemed to give out a faint, cold light of its own.

She went forward, but something puzzled her. The smooth, vague whiteness should have stretched on indefinitely, but it didn't. It was cut by a black vertical shadow. Her heart began to sink and turn cold inside her, because it wasn't a shadow, it was a wall. She came upon it and touched it with her outstretched hands. It was a rough stone wall closing the courtyard in. It ran from wing to wing almost level with the front of the house, and it rose at least two feet above her head.

But there must be a gate or a door. No one would enclose a place like this and not leave any way of getting in and out of it. She moved along the wall, feeling with her right hand. There was ice on the stone, as hard as glass. Her fingers burned on it.

Suddenly she saw the gap. There was a gate, and it stood open about a foot. She could see the opening, because the snow showed through it like a white stripe against the darkness of the wall. Wickham must have set the door open, because this was the way he had been going to bring her out. The ice and snow had been dug from about the gate-post so that the gate should open enough to let them through. She shut it behind her, because shutting it made her feel safer. She did not know that there was a bolt on this outer side or she would have shot that too. She was to know later. Now she never thought about it—just pushed the gate and went on in the snow round the end of the haunted wing.

She felt sure that the garage must be somewhere in this direction. She had a vague impression of the car driving on this way after it had set them down at the front door. It was only an impression, but she thought the old stabling of the house would have to be on this side. The windows of her room and of Joanna's room looked the other way, and there was no sign of stabling to be seen from them. No—the stables must be somewhere here.

She turned the corner of the wing, and knew that she had been right. A faint light shone ahead—the merest glimmer from a door that was not quite shut. She could distinguish a dark huddle of buildings across another yard. Barns, cowsheds, stabling, were what she guessed at. And, about midway, that welcome glimmer of light.

She hurried as much as she could, and found the car in the old coach-house, with the door swinging loose and a stable lantern alight on a shelf in the corner amongst old tins and bottles. The snow had been cleared here too, and the door swung wide without any trouble. If Wickham had done all this he would surely have seen to it that the gate to the road was open.

She stood for a moment and wondered what he had meant to do. He had cleared the snow and left this lantern burning as if he really meant to drive out of this horrible place with her and take her away. But why? She had told him that she had the papers. She could hear his voice again, quick and eager, "Clever girl—have you got them?" And she had said "Yes." So there wasn't any need for him to take her away. When Mr. Brown came in on them he had only to say, "She's there—behind the curtain." There wasn't any need to go on with the pretence that he loved her and wanted to get her away. There wasn't any need for him to pretend that she was still shut up in the haunted room. Her thoughts were puzzled and confused. There was a weight on her, and she felt it heavy to bear. Only there was no time to stand here thinking—

The car was a Vauxhall limousine. She had driven it before. Once on a fine October day on a long, straight road over a Surrey heath, with the colour fading out of the heather and the bracken brightening into bronze and gold. It came back to her in a brilliant flashing picture, as if a hole had been broken in the dark and she was looking through it. How vivid memory could be. For a moment the picture was more here than the dim coach-house and this cold twilight of the snow.

As she slipped into the driving-seat she had to wrench her mind from the feeling that Joanna was behind, with her hat slipping over one ear, and Wickham here on her left. "Oh, of course, my dear—if you would like to drive, I am sure.... Oh, yes, Wickham, Miss Marlowe will drive for a little. But you will be very careful, won't you?" That was when she had first begun to wonder about John Wickham—whether he had always been a chauffeur, and if not, how he came to be driving Wilson Cattermole's car.

It was Sarah Marlowe who was driving it now. A smooth, easy start. Wickham must have warmed her up—no cold engine ever started like that with the thermometer down to goodness knew where.

Out of the coach-house and across the yard, putting on pace but not too much, because she had to feel her way. She couldn't risk the lights.

She would have to risk them. She couldn't possibly round the house and clear the gate like this—and after all, if anyone did see them, what could they do now? Because she was off.

The light ran out over the snow—hooded to comply with the black-out regulations, but to eyes that had been a long time in the dark astonishingly bright.

As they slid past the courtyard, a man wrenched at the gate which Sarah had pushed to, and got it open. She saw him out of the tail of her eye. He came running over the snow, cutting in by the house where she had to swing wide. It was an awkward turn for the gate. If she missed it and crashed into the hedge she was done. She had to come close in to take the turn, and at her nearest he would be very near. He jumped for the running-board. The car jarred with his weight.

Sarah's heart jumped too, raced, and steadied again. She felt none of the things which an escaping heroine ought to feel when an arch-villain lands with a thud on the running-board of the car in which she is trying to escape. On the contrary the blood sang in her veins and her pulses drummed with triumph.

The gate loomed up—stone pillars, and a break in the hedge. The off-side bumper scraped and they were through.

Beyond lay the rough track over which they had jolted in the dark of their arrival. The snow softened its asperities now, but it was narrow—a mere cart track. She remembered bumping in and out of pot-holes—impossible to get up any speed.... And then at last the road turning right between its hedges—the road which led to the moor and safety.

John Wickham leaned in across the open window and said with a laugh in his voice,

"Well, that was a near thing—wasn't it?"

Chapter Thirty-Three

SARAH DID NOT even start. It seemed entirely natural that he should be there. He leaned in a little farther and said,

"I should push her along a bit now. I'll take over as soon as we get clear, but the road keeps skirting the farm and we can't afford to stop till we're really away."

"What do you mean?" said Sarah. "They couldn't catch us now."

He said in something like his old impassive voice,

"That depends. If anyone saw your lights and had the gumption to think of it, they could cut us off by taking the cart track from the stables—it comes in about a quarter of a mile farther on. Let's hope they didn't see your lights. You shouldn't have put them on."

"I couldn't drive without them."

He put a hand on her shoulder for a moment.

"Look here, I'll tell you when we're getting close to where the track comes in. If there's anyone there, you'll have to rush them. Go as fast as you can and don't stop whatever happens. They may shoot."

Sarah said, "Oh!" and heard him laugh.

"I shouldn't expect old Cattermole to hit a haystack, but I'm not so sure about the parson." His hand pressed down upon her. "Why did you run away?"

"Did you expect me to stay?"

"Yes, I did."

"After hearing with my own ears that you were in with them?"

One bit of Sarah was so happy and confident that she could enjoy letting the other half say these things. You don't mind reading a sad book when you are happy. It is only when you are sad that you can't, can't bear it.

He said, "Silly of me, but I really did think so."

"I heard them talking to you in the study. I heard them planning to frighten me, and you were to pretend to help me so as to get the papers."

"Don't you think it was a very good plan? It seems to be working out all right. I wanted you, and I wanted the papers, and it looks as if I was going to get away with them. And now step on it! That's where the track comes in—just at the corner. Rush it, and don't stop for anything!"

The road had been bearing all the time to the right. They would not come out upon the moor until they were past the boundary of Maltings. There was a high hedge dropping to a ditch on either side. Ice rattled as the low-hung branches brushed the roof of the car. A flurry of snow caught the wind-screen and blurred it. The hooded light struck two rough stone pillars where the track came in, right on the corner. A man shouted with a great bull voice, a torch flashed. And, quick and sharp on that, two shots.

Sarah had a moment of exhilaration, a moment of agonized fear. There was a loud bang which felt as if it were under her feet, and the wheel was jerked out of her hands. The car gave a lurch and went skidding and crashing past the farther pillar into the right-hand ditch and the hedge. She was flung violently sideways. Branches sharp with ice came thrusting through the window where Wickham had leaned. But he wasn't there any longer. The car tilted and settled. She fell against the branches.

That was all in a moment. She had shut her eyes when the crash came. Now she opened them and saw the beam of a torch come flashing in through the window on the other side. It travelled across her face and dazzled on her staring eyes. A voice said,

"She's alive all right. Here—take this!"

And with that the beam was gone and she was being pulled up out of the tangle of branches.

The voice was Mr. Brown's, and the hands which pulled her out— very strong hands—must be his too. They set her on her feet. The voice said in a booming whisper,

"Any bones broken?"

Sarah said, "No," and then wondered why she had said it, because she couldn't feel her body at all. For all she knew, it might be in pieces, or she might be dead. It came to her quite impersonally that it might be better for her if she was dead. Because if you are dead, you haven't still got to die, and something told her in plain, positive tones that these men meant her to die. They had murdered Emily Case, and they would murder Sarah Marlowe without any compunction at all.

Her mind was quite clear and she was not at all afraid. Fear belonged to her body, and for just this queer space between living and dying her body didn't belong to her. It stood there upon its feet, and it moved when she told it to move, but it wasn't her any more. She heard her own voice say,

"Where is he? What have you done with him?" And then, when no one answered her, it said again with a dreadful calm, "Is he dead?"

No one answered that either. The light from the torch went to and fro. She walked round the car, and did not know until afterwards that the Reverend Peter's hand was on her arm. The beam of the torch showed John Wickham sprawled head downwards in the ditch. His legs were under the car, his neck was turned awry, his face was down in the snow. He did not move. Someone went down into the ditch and jerked at his shoulder. The head fell over.

Mr. Brown called out in protest, "Don't touch him, you fool! It's got to be an accident, hasn't it?"

The voice which Sarah knew was her own said again, "Is he dead?" and close above her head in the darkness the Reverend Peter laughed.

"If he isn't now he soon will be. Neck broken, by the look of him."

The word echoed in some empty place—"broken". It echoed dreadfully. A broken neck. A broken body. A broken heart. There were so many things that you could break. And no way of mending any of them. John Wickham's body lay broken in a ditch, Sarah Marlowe's body stood here in the snow and felt nothing, and Sarah Marlowe's heart was broken.

It was then that she did feel something—the heavy compulsion of the Reverend Peter's hand on her shoulder. It brought her round so that she stood face to face with him. She could see him, huge and hairy against the snow. He said in a deep, threatening voice,

"What does it matter to you whether he's dead or not? He's the chauffeur, isn't he? What does it matter to you?"

Sarah said, "It doesn't matter."

She said that because it was true. Nothing mattered any more. Everything had come to an end.

He shook her a little, but without hurting her.

"Of course it doesn't matter to you, Miss Marlowe—how could it? But I'd like just to know what he was doing on the running-board of that car. If he's nothing to you, you can tell me that."

Sarah put up a hand and brushed it across her eyes, as if she could brush the darkness away. There was a darkness between them, and a darkness in her mind. But she could answer his question.

"I took the car out."

"Yes—why did you do that? It's Mr. Cattermole's car, isn't it?"

She said, "I wanted to get away—" Her voice died.

He made her feel the pressure of his hand again.

"Go on. You were going to explain how Wickham came to be on the running-board."

She stared up at him.

"He saw my lights—I had to put them on—I couldn't see. He came running—out of the yard. He jumped on the running-board."

"Is that true?"

She said, "Yes, it's true," in an exhausted voice.

After a minute he asked her sharply,

"What did he say to you when he saw us? Did he tell you to go on, or did he tell you to stop?"

Under the surface of Sarah's darkened mind a thought moved. It said, "He's dead. But if he wasn't dead, they would kill him if they knew he had said 'Go on'." She said,

"He tried to stop me. He said, 'Stop!' and he tried to stop the car. That's why we went into the ditch."

Mr. Brown gave his hearty laugh.

"Oh, no, it isn't—that's where you're wrong. You went into the ditch because I blew a hole in your front tyre. Well, Wickham didn't have much luck, did he?" He lifted his voice and called, "Hi, Grimsby—run the torch over that front wheel! I fired two shots, and both of them ought to be in the tyre. A bullet hole anywhere else would fairly give the show away. Go on—look lively!"

Grimsby had the torch. He turned it here and there upon the tilted front wheel. Presently he called out, "Both holes there, boss," and Mr. Brown called back,

"All right, change the wheel, and don't be all night! Can you manage?"

Grimsby said, "You'll have to give a hand." And with that Sarah was marched round to the other side of the car and pushed down on the edge of the running-board.

The Reverend Peter had disappeared, but someone else had taken his place, a shadow against the snow. The shadow had neither outline nor features, yet there was something horribly familiar about its aspect. If she had not been too much detached to feel, Sarah would have been shocked, because this shadow was Wilson Cattermole, and he had a pistol in his hand. It was Mr. Brown who had mentioned the pistol—"You'll sit still and you'll keep quiet, because he's got a pistol, and if you don't he'll shoot." It was like being warned that an ant was going to shoot you. She had always thought of Wilson Cattermole as an ant—dull, indefatigable, fussy. But an ant with a pistol was a monstrous thing and outside nature. She remembered Blake's dreadful drawing of the ghost of a flea. For a moment everything rocked on the edge of nightmare. Then she could speak again.

"Mr. Cattermole!"

Yes, that was it—he was Wilson Cattermole, her employer—not something out of a bad dream.

"Mr. Cattermole!"

There was no answer, but she thought that the shadow shifted. From the other side of the car Grimsby called out, "Shurrup!"

She waited a little and tried again, dropping her voice.

"Mr. Cattermole—*please*—"

There was no sign that he had heard her. Grimsby called again on a savage growl, "Shurrup, d'you hear!"

She kept quiet after that. There wasn't anything to do. It wasn't any good appealing to Wilson—even if he wanted to help her, they wouldn't let him. There was no help in him. She could feel him there, a hostile shadow, sharp, inimical, malicious. An ant could be all these things, but if she could have felt a shock, it would have shocked her. She had not thought of him like that. A little, dull man with a little, dull mind—earnest, fussy, painstaking. And now he held a pistol to her head in the dark, and a stinging hatred came from him like a poison.

She could hear them working to change the wheel. They went to and fro. The car lurched. She wondered how they would manage. The nose was jammed into the hedge. The wheel might be jammed too. But when the light had run over it, it didn't look as if it was jammed. It seemed to hang down over the ditch.

The car shuddered and lurched again. The shadow of Wilson Cattermole stood over her with the pistol in his hand.

Chapter Thirty-Four

It might have been a short time afterwards, or a longer time—Sarah didn't know. Mr. Brown came up with the torch in his hand. He had it switched on and hanging down so that it made bright shifting circles on the snow. But when he came up to her he turned it on her face and said,

"Where are those papers?"

When she did not answer, he put a hand under her elbow and jerked her to her feet.

"The game's up. Hand them over!"

He kept the light on her face, and saw her stare back at him without blinking. Something odd was there. Something odd about her all along—he had seen a man who had been shell-shocked look that way—as if she was walking in her sleep. He swore to himself. Easy enough to wake her up if it weren't that she mustn't be marked; and women were the devil that way—they bruised before you laid a finger on them.

He swung the light out of her eyes and back again, but she never blinked.

"Look here, Miss Marlowe, you're not doing yourself any good. You're in possession of stolen property—that's what you are. And what's it got to do with you anyway? Come—I'll make a bargain with you. We don't want to do you any harm—why should we? We only want our property, and we mean to have it. What's the good of fighting against the inevitable? It's exasperating for us, and it's going to be extremely unpleasant for you. Because, you see, we know you've got the papers, and we know you're bound to have them on you. Grimsby's just having a look in the car, but I'm prepared to bet he won't find anything there. You've got them on you, and if you don't hand them over, I'm going to hand you over to Grimsby to search, and I don't really think you'll like it. No, the game really is up, and the quicker you let us have those papers, the pleasanter it will be for all of us—except perhaps Grimsby."

Sarah stood with the light in her eyes and heard the words go by. They were just words. She heard him laugh, and then all at once he took her by the arm and brought her round to the other side of the car again. The beam of the torch went dancing over the edge of the ditch. It struck one of John Wickham's hands. It slid up the arm and dazzled against his hair. He was bare-headed. She couldn't see his face. Mr. Brown said in her ear,

"There he is—and he's dead. Did you give him the papers?"

"No—no—I didn't."

He brought the light sharply back on to her face.

"If you're lying you'll pay for it! You can't get away with it, you know. If you gave them to him, he'll have them on him, and we'll find them when we find him in the morning."

Grimsby had come up. He said in his coarse voice,

"Shall I go over him, boss? Paper's easy to spot—I needn't move him."

"No!" The word came like the crack of a whip. "No one's to touch him! Let him lie there and freeze! It's a sitter that way. He piled up the car, and we didn't know a thing about it till the morning—that's the tale. The way the door's hanging open he could have been shot out of the driver's seat. It'll look all right, even if anyone comes along and finds him before we do." He turned back to Sarah. "Now, Miss Marlowe, you see how it is. If you did give him the papers, we'll get them anyhow. If you didn't, you'll hand them over now, or we search you."

His voice reached only the surface of Sarah's mind. Words floated there: "John is dead. And I shall be dead too before anyone comes. They are talking in front of me as if I was dead already. They wouldn't do that if they meant to let me go." She felt no distress at the idea of her own death. It was all like a dream. The things which surrounded her, the people, even her own body, were remote and insubstantial. She looked with wide, blank eyes at the light.

"Wake up!" Mr. Brown's voice boomed in her ear. "You've got those papers, and we know you've got them. Hand them over"!

Under the surface her mind stirred. She remembered the sham pocket. She had rolled it up in the handkerchief from her neck and pushed it into the front of her jumper. It had slipped down under her breast. She could feel it there now as she took her breath.

For the first time since the car had crashed she began to think. The sensation of being detached from her surroundings persisted, but she herself, Sarah Marlowe, began to think again. The line which her thoughts took was an extremely simple one. John Wickham was dead. He hadn't wanted them to have the packet. She herself would soon be dead. It would be a good thing if she could save the papers before she died. Someone might find them afterwards. You never know. And John would be pleased.

Wilson Cattermole spoke for the first time. He said in his nervous, fussy way.

"Now don't you think we should go in? I really do feel—" (afterwards she thought that was the strangest thing of all, to hear him talking like that—a nervous irritable ant—a fussy, respectable valetudinarian ant)—"bitterly cold—most unsuitable—get in by the fire—"

She caught up the last word and considered it. If she could burn her packet, they would think it was the real one. But papers don't burn as easily as all that.

Mr. Brown said, "All right, all right," and swung her about. The beam left her face to light their way. They went in between the pillars and up the rough track towards the garage. There was a hedgerow on the left. The ice-coated twigs and branches creaked and rattled.

The hedge ran down to a deep ditch. She heard Grimsby caution Mr. Cattermole to keep away over to the right.

"There's a deep ditch on the left under the hedge."

A deep ditch—She kept that in mind. She put her hand down the front of her jumper and eased the packet out. Mr. Brown was on her left, she had her right arm free. She could see the hedge, all white and furred with snow. If she could throw the packet in amongst all that clutter of thorn and bramble, would it help? Not if they were to find it, because there was nothing there except the pages she had torn from the "Penguin", wrapped up in lining-paper. And they would guess at once that she had the real papers on her. There would be no other reason for making up a sham packet and letting them see her throw it away. And it would be no good doing it unless it took them in. If they believed it was the real packet and they couldn't find it—that was what was in her mind. If it fell where they couldn't find it until the morning....

Her thoughts ran hither and thither like creatures in a cage, searching desperately for a way out. This wasn't a good way—perhaps it wasn't a way at all. Perhaps the packet would catch amongst the thorns and be found and opened at once. Perhaps—

There wasn't any way out. But she would throw the packet into the hedge. It was too light—it wouldn't even reach it. She held it under her coat and thought, "I'll count twenty, and then I'll throw it."

It was the best that she could do. Between the brambles and the ditch, they might not find it till the morning. They might not even look too hard if they were sure that it was there. It was only a chance, but it was all that she could think of.

It wasn't a chance at all, but she would take it. She began to count in her mind, one—two—three—four—five—six—seven—eight—nine—ten—

Mr. Brown, still holding her by the left arm, stopped and called over his shoulder,

"Mind the old well as you come round into the yard, Cattermole."

The word dropped in on Sarah's counting and stopped it dead. A well—that would be much better than the hedge.

Wilson Cattermole said in his nervous, fussy voice,

"But you've got the torch. I really don't like this at all. It's dangerous—positively dangerous."

Mr. Brown laughed jovially.

"Oh, there's a parapet. You'd have to try quite hard to fall in. I was just being careful—I'm a careful man, you know."

"I don't call it careful to leave Wickham lying there in the ditch. You would not let us touch him. Suppose he is not really dead."

Sarah felt a momentary cold horror. He spoke in the trivial, fretful manner to which she was accustomed. A familiar thing bent to murderous uses—The horror passed. Mr. Brown said cheerfully, "I'd have a nervous breakdown if I worried like you. Take it easy, man. If he isn't dead, he's alive, and then one of two things happens—he's well enough to walk or he isn't. If he isn't, he'll freeze where he lies and be dead before morning. If he is, what happens?"

"That," said Wilson Cattermole, "is what I invite you to consider."

"All right, we're considering it, aren't we? Say he comes round and by a miracle he can get up and walk—the car's ditched, and it'll take more than him to get her out. What does he do? Comes back to the house of course. We haven't got anything against him, have we? He tried to stop the girl, by her own account. Why shouldn't he come back? And suppose he doesn't—is he going to walk seven miles to Hedgeley—or if he does, is he going to get there?"

"He might," said Wilson Cattermole.

"All right," said the Reverend Peter, "you go back. Sit up all night with the corpse if you want to—I'm not stopping you. The doctor can pick you up when we get him out in the morning." He turned to Sarah and said in a genial voice, "The doctor will be for you. You won't be able to say you didn't get every attention." He laughed. "As a matter of fact you won't be able to say anything very much by the time he gets here."

They had been standing at the corner where the track ran into the yard whilst this talk went on. Now Mr. Brown swung the torch up and sent the beam to the right. It shone on the low parapet of the well. There were two uprights, and a cross-piece from which the buckets hung. The open, empty mouth was black.

It was no more than a dozen feet away. Sarah pulled the packet out from under her coat and threw it with all her might along the line of the beam. It struck the coping. The light dazzled on the coral and green and brown of the handkerchief which wrapped it. It hung for a moment on the edge and was gone. The black mouth had swallowed it.

Mr. Brown said sharply, "What's that?"

Sarah said, "Your papers. You wanted to know where they were. They're in the well."

Chapter Thirty-Five

Mr. Brown burst out laughing.

"That's the spirit!" he said. "I like a girl with some go about her. I didn't think you had it in you. Pity we shan't have time to get better acquainted—it might have been amusing. But business before pleasure. And if by any chance you're thinking that you're one up over this, I'll just tell you that the bottom of a well is a very nice safe place for those papers to be. They might have got into the wrong hands, you know. That is why we were just a little bit anxious about them. You don't want your family secrets exposed to the vulgar gaze—something indelicate about it, don't you think? So they can stay at the bottom of the well until daylight, and if we can't get them up then, they can stay there until they rot, though I don't mind telling you I'd rather see them burned before my own eyes in our good kitchen fire. Family secrets had better go up in smoke, don't you think—especially when they are of a kind which your meddling Intelligence takes an interest in. You knew that, I suppose?"

They were crossing the stable yard diagonally. The lantern still burned on the coach-house shelf. Its pale golden light came a little way across the snow and lighted them.

They turned the corner of the haunted wing. Sarah said,

"No—I didn't know. She gave it to me. I didn't know what it was."

"Didn't she tell you?"

She shook her head.

"No. She put it in my bag. I didn't find it till afterwards."

"Then why did you hide it?"

Sarah spoke the exact truth.

"Because of the police. I was afraid of losing my job."

The beam of the torch ran ahead of them and showed the gate standing as she had left it, open to the courtyard. She could see it now, a solid wooden gate with a heavy bolt top and bottom. It seemed a strange thing that there should be bolts like that on the outside. Mr. Brown flicked the beam from one to the other.

"Wondering why they're outside?" he enquired. "Everyone does. The last owner had his wife here—mad for a dozen years before she died. He had the bolts put on. They used to let her out for a bit of air and exercise—quite safe, you know, because nobody could get away when those bolts were shot."

As he spoke he pushed her through the opening. There was just room for her to pass. To follow her he gave the gate a great shove with his shoulder. It creaked, moved a little wider against the snow which hampered it, and let him through. It creaked again as he banged it behind him. He had let go of Sarah now. Like the mad woman, she could not get away once the gate was shut. The two wings of the house and the block which connected them shut them in. The place was as secure as a prison yard.

Mr. Brown called out in his big voice,

"Hi, Grimsby, shoot those two bolts! You can come in by the front door—it isn't locked."

Sarah stood just clear of the gate. She wondered vaguely what would happen next. She thought they would kill her, and she wondered how. She wondered whether it would hurt. She thought it was a pity that she had not been killed when the car ran into the ditch.

There was a grating sound as the bolts went home. Mr. Brown turned round from the gate and took her briskly across the courtyard with his hand on her arm again.

The side door was unlocked. She remembered how she had come out, full of fear, and haste, and anger against John Wickham. All these things were gone. There was neither fear, nor haste, nor anger left. Everything had happened. She had only to die.

They went along the passage to the open kitchen door. Light and heat streamed to meet them. Mr. Brown said affably,

"You don't know how cold you are till you come in by a fire—do you?" And then he laughed, and Sarah felt again the touch of a horror which had no name or reason.

The kitchen was bright and very hot. There was a bracket-lamp with a tin reflector above the chimney-piece, and a standing lamp with a glass globe on the dresser. A big fire roared in the range. Mrs. Grimsby was pouring boiling water out of a kettle into a brown teapot with a bright blue band. She was vast and shapeless in a flowered overall and an old beige knitted coat. Her grizzled hair straggled untidily from an ugly bunched-up bun half way up her head. She had her back to them, and she went on making tea.

Another woman had been sitting at the kitchen table. She got up as they came in. As soon as Sarah saw her she knew who had played the part of Emily Case in the haunted room. There must have been a door in that corner by the fireplace, hidden by the panelling, and she had come through it to stand there and play the ghost. The battered hat and the black coat with the grey fur collar lay across one of the kitchen chairs. She wondered who the woman was. She was not really like Emily Case, but she had been chosen to play her part by someone who knew what Emily Case looked like. She was the right height, and the clothes were right—of course there must have been photographs in the papers. She had held a handkerchief up to her face.

Mr. Brown brought Sarah into the room with a genial air of triumph. He said, "Well, here she is!" as if he were announcing an expected guest.

The woman by the table looked at them. She had light eyes in a pale face. There was a sharp malice in them, and something else—was it expectancy?

"Delightfully warm in here, isn't it?" said Mr. Brown.

Mrs. Grimsby turned round with the teapot in her hand. She came over to the table and set it down. There was milk in a white jug with a broken lip, and an odd flowered bowl with sugar. There were two willow-pattern cups. In a detached way Sarah found herself feeling sorry for Mrs. Grimsby. She had the look of a woman who has forgotten how to smile. Her heavy face had no colour and no expression. All her movements were slow and burdened. She said without looking at anyone, "Two more cups, Annie," and began to pour tea into the two that were already there.

Mr. Brown laughed. Not loudly as he was used to do, but with a soft chuckling sound.

"Like a cup of tea, Miss Marlowe?" he said.

All at once Sarah felt a starved longing for the hot drink. She wanted it more than she had ever wanted food or drink in all her life before. She had begun to feel her body again, and it was shaking with cold. She longed to drink the hot tea and to get away into the dark where she could lie down, and be alone, and weep the numbness from her heart. She said,

"Oh, yes, please."

But Mr. Brown was laughing again, and the woman whom Mrs. Grimsby called Annie was joining in. They both laughed, and Mr. Brown said,

"I'm afraid—oh, yes, I'm very much afraid, that you won't get one. I'm afraid Mrs. Grimsby made a mistake. Just one cup, Annie. Miss Marlowe is not joining our tea-party—she has another engagement." He turned on Sarah suddenly with all his mock politeness gone. "You've been spying and playing tricks. I suppose you thought you could get away with it. Well, you can't. Do you know what I'm going to do with you? I'm going to have you stripped and put out in the yard—and that will be the end of Miss Sarah Marlowe. No one's going to lay a finger on you, except that I'm going to ask Annie and Mrs. Grimsby to take off that fur coat and the woollen suit you're wearing. If you make the very slightest resistance, I shall call Grimsby in to help them. I don't mind being quite frank—I don't want you to resist, because I don't want you to get marked. You see, there will probably be an inquest, and I don't want any awkward questions about things like that. It's got to be death from natural causes. I think a night in the yard in your underclothes ought to do the trick—don't you? And when you're too far gone for it to make any difference we'll put you to bed and have a doctor out to see you. He will find you surrounded by the kindest attentions. Miss Cattermole shall weep at your bedside. She has no head and a very kind heart. I am sure that she will weep most convincingly, and only a lunatic could imagine her being mixed up with anything shady."

Something went through Sarah like the stab of a knife. She said quickly,

"Does she know?"

Mr. Brown chuckled enjoyably.

"What a question! And you've lived with her for—what is it—the best part of five months! Does she ever know what's going on, even if it's right under her nose? Come, come—I gave you credit for more sense. If she knew anything she would certainly give it away—a born babbler. No, no, she will believe every word that dear Wilson says, and that I say. But she will weep over your death-bed and tell the doctor how fond she was of you, and how dreadful it is that you should be so ill but of course young people are terribly heedless."

A little warmth came up in Sarah. Even now, with everything gone and death only one step away, she could be glad that she had not to change her thought about Joanna.

Chapter Thirty-Six

SHE MADE NO RESISTANCE. The numbness closed down on her again. There was no one to whom she could cry for help. She could not struggle with Grimsby and Mr. Brown and have them put their hands on her. She stood without sound or movement whilst Mrs. Grimsby took her fur coat and Annie stripped her of her warm brown suit.

Annie fell back with the dress in her hand and laughed maliciously.

"You look nice like that—don't you? Fancy yourself, I shouldn't wonder—pink crêpe-de-chine, and a good eight-and-eleven a yard! Nice and warm it'll keep you out there too!" She leaned back against the table and shook. But there was no mirth in her eyes. They were hard and envious. "What about shoes and stockings?" she said, breaking off suddenly from her laughing.

Mr. Brown said, "Leave them—she mustn't cut her feet. Some of that ice has an edge on it like a razor blade. Now, Miss Marlowe, out you go!"

Annie laughed again.

"And she can keep her hat, just to trim her up a bit! Dinky, isn't it? All the very latest style, moddam, and suits moddam a treat! I don't suppose it ever came into your head when you bought it that you'd be wearing it with nothing but your step-ins to a January picnic in the snow."

"That'll do," said Mr. Brown. His hand fell on Sarah's bare shoulder. "This way, Miss Marlowe. And if you waste your time and get my temper up doing anything silly like trying to climb the wall and barking yourself, I'll send Grimsby out to keep you quiet—and you won't like that, you know—you won't like it at all."

He marched her down the passage, opened the door, and put her out on the step, all in a businesslike manner and without violence. But the violence was there. It would be used against her if she roused it. The hand lifted from her shoulder. The door was banged and locked. She heard the key grate, and the sound of Mr. Brown's footsteps going away. Going back to the kitchen.

At first she felt nothing but relief. To be alone and to be in the dark—this was what she had wanted. She moved to get farther from the house, and came within an ace of falling. The ground in front of the door was masked with ice. The overhang of the roof had kept the snow from covering it. She remembered that the rest of the yard was under snow and felt her way forward until her feet were firm upon it. Moving like that she came out into the wind. There was no force in it, only a light, deadly breath of utter cold. And she had no protection against it.

She found herself with the idea of taking shelter in the angle between the wall and the house. The wind came from that quarter. She turned and began to make her way along the side of the house. There were two windows letting out a very faint glow, and a streak or two of light where the curtains did not fit. They would be the windows of the kitchen. She had not noticed what the curtains were like at the time, but it came back to her now that they were of some red figured stuff. The light that came through them was red. It looked warm. She remembered piercingly how warm it had been in the kitchen. The light, deadly breath of the wind passed over her and left her shuddering.

Half consciously, she must have lingered near the lighted window. When she remembered to move on again there was a sense of time gone by. Time lost—the last time.... Time shall be no longer—that was in the Bible. She didn't know what it meant. No, she knew quite well. It meant that there was no more time for her. A time for sowing and a time for reaping, a time to laugh and a time to weep—that was in the Bible too. No more sowing or reaping for Sarah Marlowe. No more laughing or weeping. No more anything at all.

She stood there in the snow and felt her will to reach the end of the house weaken. What was the good of struggling? It wasn't any good. All the same she took a step forward, and another step, and another. The glowing windows were left behind. The snow was under her feet, dimly white. The house on her right was like a cliff, black and silent.

And then suddenly the silence broke. A small, familiar sound came through it—the sound of a window-sash being raised. It slid easily—a dark window opening in the dark wall. She stood still and turned towards the sound, but she could not see anything. Then there was the spirt of a match, bright against the blackness.

Sarah stood there, looking. She saw the little bright flame and part of a woman's hand—a heavy hand with thick, work-roughened fingers. The hand moved the match downwards until it met the wick of a candle. The wick flared up.

Mrs. Grimsby was standing there, close up to the window. The candle was on the sill in a flat blue china candlestick. It showed Mrs. Grimsby's heavy looming face and figure. She leaned on the sill and looked out. As soon as she saw Sarah she reached behind her and put down one of the blue willow-pattern cups beside the candlestick. Then she said in a flat, whispering voice,

"Here's your tea."

It was like a miracle, the black house opening to help her. The sill was quite low—four feet from the ground at the most. Sarah came and leaned on it, and drank the tea. It was so scalding hot that she hardly knew how to swallow it. She had to take it in small sips. Between the sips she could hear Mrs. Grimsby talking with a soft country accent.

"It's nobody's business if I bring my cup of tea through into my room. Many's the time I've done it just to get away from them—they won't think nothing of that. But I can't let you in. Cruel hard—and they'd do it some other way—you can't get from it."

The words flowed vaguely past. Sarah hardly noticed what they were. Mrs. Grimsby was kind. The tea was hot. She drank it sip by scalding sip. The two things thawed her a little—the kindness and the hot tea. Odd to put them together like that, but there it was. Even if your heart was broken and you were going to die, there was help in things like this.

She drank the last drop of the tea and set the cup back on the window-sill beside the guttering candle. She said,

"Thank you very much."

The candle-light shone on her face. "Looks like a child," said Mrs. Grimsby to herself. "Got that look in her eyes same as puppies and kittens and all that lot of young things. No sense in them—just looking at you—not even sense enough to be afraid. Oh my dear soul—what can I do?"

She picked up the cup and put it down somewhere inside the room. When she turned back Sarah had not moved. She stood there looking past the candleflame with those wide, dark eyes.

Mrs. Grimsby leaned out to her.

"See here, I'll give you something to put round you against the cold. You keep close by the wall out of the wind, and so soon as they're all asleep I'll come round outside and pull back the bolts for you. There's no more I can do than that, and they'd kill me if they knew."

The blank eyes changed. Something came into them. They focussed on Mrs. Grimsby's face.

"Will you really?"

Mrs. Grimsby nodded.

"I'll pull back the bolts. Can you get to Hedgeley, do you think? It's all of seven miles."

"I can try."

Mrs. Grimsby nodded again.

"I'll get you something," she said, and went back from the window. Sarah watched her.

She pulled out a drawer, groped in it, and came back with an immense hand-knitted vest. It was old, and had been washed so often that the wool had matted. When Sarah put it on it came right down to her knees.

Mrs. Grimsby opened another drawer. This time she came back with a pair of thick grey flannel bloomers and a large safety-pin.

"You'll need to take them up round the waist," she said—"I'm stout. It's a pity about your own clothes, but they took them up to your room and I dursn't go for them. That Annie have got eyes all round her head. Grimsby's niece, she is, and no more feeling than a ferret. I'll give you a scarf and my coat. That's the best I can do."

The scarf was thick, the coat a cheap cloth one but so voluminous that it wrapped twice over in front and kept out the wind. It came down to her ankles. She said in what was almost her natural voice,

"I can't thank you properly. You're saving my life—you know that."

Mrs. Grimsby nodded.

"Get you along into the corner and set down. Here—as well be hanged for a sheep as a lamb. I'll give you a blanket, but you must give it back when I let you out."

Sarah took the blanket and watched the sash come down. Through the glass she saw Mrs. Grimsby pick up the candle, take it over to the chest of drawers, and come back to pull the curtains. The rattle of the rings came to her. The room was shut in, and she was shut out.

She went along the side of the house as far as the corner and huddled down there with the blanket pulled round her.

Chapter Thirty-Seven

MISS CATTERMOLE STIRRED and opened her eyes. She felt confused and giddy, and for a moment she did not know where she was. There was a feeling of strangeness. Not her own room or her own bed. Colder than Thompson ever allowed her room to be. And she wasn't undressed. She was lying on the outside of a strange bed with a strange eiderdown drawn up under her chin. And her head was much too low. She liked plenty of pillows, and here she was with only one, and a shocking crick in her neck.

She pushed back the eiderdown and pulled herself up on the bed. The room was full of yellow lamplight, but she did not see the lamp until she looked to the right. There was a bedside table, and on the other side of the door a big dark chest of drawers with a lamp standing on it.

By the time she got as far as that she knew where she was. They were staying with the Reverend Peter Brown, and this was his best spare room. It was her room. Sarah was next door. There had been a séance in the haunted wing, and she had fainted. But she couldn't think why. There must have been some malefic influence, because she had never done such a thing before. They must have carried her here and put her down on the bed just as she was. No, not quite—because she had been wearing her fur coat. She raised herself a little more and saw it lying across the foot of the bed.

She pushed the eiderdown right back and got up. It was very bad for a good coat to lie all in a heap like that, and as her conscience would certainly never permit her to buy fur again, she must take all the care of it she could.

She hung the coat up and went over to the dressing-table to see what time it was. A few minutes short of midnight. She wondered whether the séance was over. It came to her that she would just look into Sarah's room and see if she was there. Deep in her own thought it was strange to her that she should have waked from her swoon alone. It was not what she would have expected of Sarah Marlowe. Sarah had always been most attentive.

She opened her door and looked out. The wall-lamp burned across the landing.

When she came to Sarah's door she found it ajar. The room beyond was in darkness. She went a little way in and stood there, peering at the bed and listening to hear if anyone breathed. There was no sound at all, and when she came right up to the bed it was empty.

She went back to her own room and fetched a candle.

What the candle-light showed her was very puzzling indeed. Sarah's fur coat hung over the back of a chair and Sarah's brown woollen suit lay folded on the seat. Her pyjamas and her dressing-gown were laid out on the bed. But where was Sarah? Her underclothes were not there, and nor was she. It was inconceivable that she should be walking round the house in her underclothes, yet it did not seem possible to escape from the idea. She had brought only the one suit, and it was here. Since Sarah was not here, it was impossible not to believe that she was somewhere else in her underclothes.

The thought of the bathroom presented itself hopefully to Joanna. Not really very nice to go along to the bathroom without your dressing-gown in a strange house, but it was so very close that perhaps this was what Sarah had done.

Candle in hand, Joanna proceeded to the bathroom, and found it empty.

As she came back, the confusion in her mind was shot with fear. Where could Sarah have gone, and where could she possibly be, without so much as a dressing-gown to cover her? When she came to her own bedroom door her hand was shaking so much that she felt unable to go on holding the candle. She set it down on the chest of drawers beside the lamp and went out on to the landing again.

Mr. Brown's door stood open, and Wilson's ajar. A light still burned in the lower hall. After hesitating for a little on the top step Joanna began to descend the stair, her long black velvet draperies trailing behind her. She held the banister and leaned upon it as she went. The trembling of her hands had spread to her whole body. All the evil that she had felt in this house seemed to be waiting for her at the bottom of the stair, yet it did not occur to her to turn back, because she had to find Sarah.

When she had reached the hall she stood there looking about her. The dining-room and drawing-room doors stood open facing one another. She turned to the right and went towards the den, and before she had taken half a dozen steps the sound of voices came to her, as they had come to Sarah a few hours earlier. She hurried forward, and then stopped dead. The door was not quite shut. She could see a thin streak of light along its edge, and she could hear what was being said on the other side of it.

It was the words she heard that stopped her. They were spoken by the Reverend Peter Brown. They were horrible, unbelievable words. She heard them quite distinctly, but she didn't believe them. He said,

"You took a risk over that Morgan business. Better drop it. Tell your sister he's dead and have done with it."

She didn't believe it, but just to hear those two words together, "Morgan" and "dead", made her feel quite sick with pain. And why should Wilson tell her that Morgan was dead? She had seen him only yesterday morning. She heard Wilson say,

"I thought it very ingenious. And you know, Paul, there is a certain pleasure in acting a part when you can act it on your own stage, make your own entrances and exits, write your play."

"Too ingenious." Mr. Brown's voice was brutally direct. "Too ingenious by half. Never be more elaborate than you need. The whole of this Morgan business is just a wanton elaboration. I never liked it, and you've got to cut it out."

She heard Wilson snigger.

"Kill Morgan—my own twin brother? Oh, Paul!"

The Reverend Peter drew at his pipe.

"Did you ever really have a twin?"

Leaning against the jamb of the door, Joanna was shaken with a spasm of anger. Morgan—her darling Morgan! How dared he?

Wilson sniggered again. She hadn't heard him laugh like that for years, and she had always hated it. He said,

"Of course I had. You just ask Joanna! She never really cottoned to me very much, but she adored Morgan—in fact she does still. That is why he comes in so usefully. Do you suppose she would have pretended to be frightened and got Sarah down out of her room to keep her company—for me? Not a bit of it! She would have wanted to know why, and what did it all mean. But Morgan had only to ask."

"When did he die?" said Mr. Brown abruptly.

Joanna's heart gave a sickening lurch against her side. Wilson's voice seemed to come from a long way off, but she heard it quite distinctly.

"A couple of years ago, in Australia. I didn't tell her then, because I knew she would make a fuss, and later on I saw that he might really be very useful. The risk was negligible. If I could play the part well enough to convince Joanna, there really was no risk at all, and as it proved, I did play it well enough. Joanna was delighted, and there was Morgan—a most convenient scapegoat if anything went wrong. Take the other night. If Sarah had returned to her bedroom before I had completed my search for the packet and had found me there in my own proper person, there would have been a most damaging scandal, and she would have left the house before breakfast. But if she had found Morgan, it would have been Morgan who had to leave. She would have complained to me on my return. I would have deplored my brother's behaviour and assured her that she would never be exposed to anything of the sort again. She would not have had the slightest suspicion that I was involved. Green put through a call to her, you know, whilst Morgan was there, and played her over a nice recording of my voice, all about posting a letter to you. She would have sworn in any court that I had been telephoning to her whilst Morgan was in the drawing-room with Joanna."

Joanna Cattermole listened to all this with something more than her usual vagueness. She was to remember it afterwards. At this time there was nothing in her mind but pain—the kind of confused pain which follows upon a stunning blow. Morgan dead—two years ago in Australia—Wilson said so. And he had played at being Morgan to deceive her. If she did not take in the words, she took in the fact. With horror, but without surprise. Because long ago when they were all quite young he had pretended to be Morgan and taken her in. It had hurt and frightened her very much. Now he had done it again. And Morgan, her darling Morgan, was dead. She couldn't believe it.

She forced herself to listen again. Perhaps it wasn't really true. Perhaps Wilson would say so.

But they had stopped talking about Morgan. She caught Sarah's name, and remembered that she had come down to look for her.

It was Mr. Brown who was talking. He said,

"We shan't have any more trouble with her. A night in that yard in her underclothes ought to finish her all right—I should think it will touch zero before morning. And then before she's quite gone Grimsby can take the motor-bike in to Hedgeley and call old Dr. Smith. He's been past his work these two years, but he can still sign a certificate, and that's all there'll be for him to do by the time he gets here. We can show him the car piled up, and Wickham in the ditch at the same time." He laughed and drew at his pipe. "There won't be any trouble. All he'll want is to get back to a good hot fire. I suppose there'll have to be an inquest, but weather like this is enough to account for anything." He laughed again. "We're in luck!"

She heard his chair grate on the floor as he pushed it back. She shrank and trembled against the jamb. The room was full of evil. If he came across to the door now and opened it, the evil would come with him and drown her.

But he did not come to the door. She heard him go over to the fire and kick it with his foot. With an oath which shocked Miss Cattermole very much he said,

"I wonder if she's unconscious yet."

Chapter Thirty-Eight

JOANNA STRAIGHTENED UP. Her mind was terribly confused, the impression of evil very strong. She had to get away—now, quickly, before the door could open. She caught up her long velvet skirt and went, hurrying but careful to make no sound. Up the stair and back to her room—that was her first thought. And then when she had reached it and the door was shut she sat down on the edge of the bed and tried to think. The lamplight was yellow and soothing. There was something steady about it. She tried to steady her thought. Morgan was dead—a long time ago—two years. Two years was a long time. He was dead, and Wickham was dead—poor Wickham. And Sarah was not dead yet, but they wanted her to die. That was the wickedness that she had felt in this house. They wanted Sarah to die, so they had taken away her clothes and put her out in the yard to freeze.

She found herself on her feet, and she heard her own voice saying in a shocked, frightened tone, "Oh, no, they mustn't—I won't let them!"

For once in her life she knew what she must do. She must find Sarah, and she must take her her clothes and help her to get away. She was not confused any more. She saw these three things quite clearly. They were like three steps in a stair which she had to climb. Get Sarah's clothes. Find Sarah. Help her to get away.

One step at a time, and the first step first. It was the easiest one. She took the candle into Sarah's room again and fetched the warm brown suit and the fur coat. When she was out on the landing with them, the second step had to be taken—she had to find Sarah. Mr. Brown had said she was in the yard. There was a yard between the two wings of the house. She knew that, because Mr. Brown had talked about it that very evening when Sarah was out of the room. There was this part of the house, and the haunted wing which was older, and they made up three sides of a square, with a wall to close the fourth side in. Mr. Brown had told them tales about this courtyard. One man had kept bloodhounds there, and when his daughter ran away from him with her lover he had loosed the hounds and hunted them to their death. Another had a poor mad wife. She had been used to walk in the courtyard, with the walls and a barred gate to shut her in. It was an evil house, full of old sorrow and sin.

She thought, "They have put Sarah in the courtyard and shut her in to freeze and die."

She held the brown suit and the fur coat over her left arm, and the candle in the other hand. The coat was heavy, but she hardly noticed the weight. Her mind was quite taken up with how to get into the courtyard and let Sarah out.

She came down the stair again and into the hall, but this time she turned to the left. She pushed her way through the baize door and left it to swing to behind her. She found herself at one end of a narrow flagged passage. In front of her on the left there was a stair that went up between walls. She could only see the bottom step, the rest was shadow. A little farther on on the right was the open kitchen door, and, facing her at the end of the passage, what she had counted on finding there—the door into the yard. She had not thought about it consciously, but she had been quite sure that it would be there. There always was a door leading into a yard from kitchen premises. In a small house you would have to go through the kitchen and scullery to get to it, but not in a house like this.

She went past the stair and past the kitchen door. The kitchen was dark and warm. There was a little glow from the sunk fire. When she came to the door into the yard she set her candle down on the floor and unlocked it. It was only locked, not bolted, and the key turned easily. When she had opened the door she picked up the candle again and stood on the threshold looking out.

Sarah did not know how long she had been in the yard. Just for a little while the hot tea had warmed her, and Mrs. Grimsby's kindness. Then the glow faded and an icy, bitter cold pressed in upon her. It was not just the cold of frost and wind. It was the cold of separation and betrayal. She seemed to have come to an end. Presently Mrs. Grimsby would come and draw back the bolts and let her out into a desolate wilderness. What was she going to do there? Walk until weakness betrayed her and she fell in the snow to freeze. That she could reach Hedgeley seven miles away did not seem possible. She could find in herself no strength, no determination of the will, no passionate desire to live. Any one of these things might have taken her there, but she had none of them. Her strength was sapped, her will quiescent, and her desire to live had drained away. She was very cold. The blanket kept slipping. If she hung it over her shoulders, the frost struck upwards from the ground and numbed her. If she folded it under her, the cold struck at her very heart. In the end she stood and clutched it round her. Every now and then she walked a little, moving along in the shelter of the wall with her feet on the snow.

She had been as far as the gate, and was coming back, when she saw Joanna's candle and stood to stare at it. Of all living things Joanna Cattermole was the last she could have looked to see, standing there in the open mouth of the passage with the candle in her hand. The flame of the candle moved in the wind. The wild, light halo of Joanna's hair moved like blown thistledown. Joanna's eyes peered vaguely into the snowy dusk.

All at once Sarah began to run. She stumbled on the blanket and caught it up. She came slipping and stumbling and running into the circle of candle-light and held by the jamb of the door to keep herself up.

Miss Cattermole let Sarah's clothes slip down upon the passage floor. She put a finger to her lips and said,

"Hush—hush—we mustn't make any noise. I've brought your clothes." Then, with a sudden note of curiosity in her voice, "My dear, what have you got on?"

Sarah came past her and shut the door. It shut out some of the cold. She looked fearfully at the kitchen door and saw that it was open, and the room dark behind it.

Miss Cattermole held up the candle and looked at her with astonishment. She did not know quite what she had expected to see, but the sight of Mrs. Grimsby's second-best coat, black, voluminous, and almost trailing on the ground, surprised her very much. Above its ragged fur collar Sarah's face quite white, her little pill-box hat slipped into something more than the fashionable tilt, and the veil dragged down over a falling strand of hair.

Sarah let the blanket drop and began to unbutton the coat.

"I've brought your clothes." Joanna spoke in a breathless whisper. "Oh, my dear, you must get away quickly. We ought never to have come here. I told you there was evil in this house. You must get away quickly. They are very wicked men."

Sarah nodded. She let the coat fall on the top of the blanket and began to pull on her own skirt and jumper over Mrs. Grimsby's grey knickers and thick woollen vest. Then she picked up her coat and slipped into the soft, warm fur. A long shudder went over her. All this time she had not spoken, and still she did not speak.

Joanna Cattermole put up a thin, shaky hand and tried to straighten the little crooked hat.

"I don't know what to do," she said in a whispering voice. "They were in Mr. Brown's room talking—downstairs, in his den—but he called him Paul—he did it twice. It seems strange when his name is Peter, but Wilson called him Paul. If we go through the hall, perhaps they will hear us. They were talking, you know, and they said you were in the yard. You know the door doesn't shut, and I listened, and they said you would freeze, and they said—oh, my dear, they said that Morgan was dead!"

Sarah spoke for the first time. She said,

"But he was here. I heard his voice this afternoon."

Joanna fell back a step and shook her head.

"They said he had been dead for two years. It couldn't be true—could it? But they said it. They said Wilson had dressed up and pretended to be Morgan. It was for some bad purpose, my dear—to get some papers out of your room. He told me to say I had had a dream, and to keep you with me as long as I could, but I thought it was one of Morgan's practical jokes—he was always so fond of joking. I wouldn't have done it if I had thought there was any harm in it. I wouldn't have done it for Wilson—but I thought it was Morgan."

Sarah said, "Stop!" She put a hand to her head, felt the loose strand of hair, and pinned it up. Then she said slowly,

"Mr. Cattermole spoke to me on the telephone whilst you were in the drawing-room with Mr. Morgan."

Joanna shook her head.

"It was a gramophone record—they talked about it. They didn't know I was listening. They said Morgan was dead. Oh, what are we going to do?"

Sarah was being forced back to life and thought. Joanna's effort had spent itself. She stood confused and helpless with the tears running down her face. Sarah took her by the arm.

"Will you do just what I say? You will—won't you?"

Joanna nodded.

"I want you to go back to your room. You needn't go into the hall at all—this stair comes out in the passage. Take Mrs. Grimsby's coat and blanket with you. They'll kill her if they know she helped me. You must find a way of giving them back to her tomorrow, and tell her if there's anything I can ever do for her, I'll do it. Now go quickly! And thank you a million times!"

"What will you do?" said Joanna with a sob.

Sarah kissed her.

"Get out of the dining-room window," she said.

Chapter Thirty-Nine

SARAH DROPPED FROM the window ledge and, steadying herself, looked back. The dining-room was dark behind her. She had closed the door into the hall. She tried now to close the window, and succeeded in pulling it down to within an inch or two of the sill, but there it stuck and there she had to leave it. It did not matter—nobody was likely to come into the room until the morning. She wondered how far the night had worn. Then she turned resolutely and made her way towards the stable yard.

She came soon upon the track which they had trampled down when they came back from the car. She set her feet on it with relief. It was much easier to walk on than the untrampled snow. But there were seven miles of snow between her and Hedgeley.

She stopped thinking about Hedgeley. It did not matter. She thought about the car, and John Wickham lying there in the ditch. And with that she turned the corner of the haunted wing.

A yard away on the frozen track someone moved, tall and black against the white dimness of the snow. John Wickham stood above her and said her name, and when she put out her hands with a soft, desperate cry the hands which took them were living hands. They held her up with a hard, insistent clasp. His voice said,

"I was coming for you. Good girl! Now we've got to hurry."

Between one breath and the next everything was changed. The effort of despair was gone. She felt a rushing joy, an invincible sense of life and hope. They went quickly and without words until they were clear of the stable buildings and well away on the cart track. He kept his arm through hers and held it close. Then he said,

"I had to get the car out of the ditch. It's been a job."

Sarah said in a dreaming voice, "I thought you were dead."

"Well, I wanted them to think so. Anyhow there was no harm in trying it on. I wasn't quite sure whether they'd think I was trying to stop you going off with the car, or aiding and abetting, and if they thought that, it was all up with us both. So I thought I'd be a corpse. I really was a bit knocked out to start with, but fortunately I came round before they got a torch on to me, because I was able to do a very useful imitation of a broken neck. I reckoned they would want the smash to look as natural as possible, in which case they would do just what they did do and leave me be without touching me. I let them get well away and then started in getting the car off the bank. The front wheels were hitched up, and I was afraid they'd drop when I began to back her away, so I had to fill in the ditch with snow and ram it down to make a track. I couldn't go at it too hard—I was afraid of starting that damned scratch again."

"Are you all right?" She turned to peer at him, seeing only height and blackness against the snow.

He laughed.

"Don't be a fool! You know, I'm tired of telling you that. I told you it was only a scratch."

An almost unbearable happiness warmed her.

"I don't believe everything I'm told."

And then they were coming out between the pillars on to the road and the car loomed up.

To remember in what desolation she had stood there no more than an hour ago was strange.... It must be less than an hour.... The earth had broken under her feet and the sky had fallen in. Now she was back in a safe world. It was the nightmare which had broken and let them through.

As the car moved and the hedges began to slide away on either side, she thought, "It's true—we're going to get away." There was nothing to say about it. She leaned back and saw the beam of the hooded light make a shining path for them.

When they came out on the moor she drew a long sighing breath. Now they were safe. Now surely nobody could catch them. This time she spoke her thoughts.

"They can't catch us now."

"I don't know about can't—they won't."

"Where are we going?"

"To Hedgeley, I think. Look here, is there anything you can charge them with if we go to the police? I want them pulled in, and at once, but I don't want to play my stuff in a local police station. But if they used any force to you—"

Sarah looked straight in front of her.

"They took away my clothes and shut me out in the yard to freeze."

His left hand came down hard upon her knee.

"Sarah!"

"They reckoned I'd be unconscious by the morning. When I was almost dead they were going to put me to bed and send Grimsby for a doctor. They weren't sure how much I knew about those papers. And then of course there was Emily Case. I suppose one of them killed her."

He nodded.

"Yes—Grimsby. Sarah, have you got those papers? They're awfully important."

"Yes, I've got them. I threw a sham packet down the well when they were taking me back, and they think they know where they are, so they're not bothering. I tore some pages out of a book in your room and wrapped them up in the lining-paper out of a drawer and my neck-handkerchief. I threw them down the well, and Mr. Brown laughed and said it was a nice safe place. So then they didn't bother me any more—they just wanted to be rid of me, and to make sure I'd freeze in the yard."

He said, *"Sarah!"* again, and then, "How did you get out?"

She told him.

"Mrs. Grimsby saved me really. You won't let her go to prison, will you? She thought they'd kill her, but she helped me all the same. John—what is it all about? What are those papers? They tried to kill you for them, and they did kill Emily Case, and they were going to kill me. What is it all about?"

There was a moment's silence. Then he said,

"Can't you guess?"

She said soberly, "I've been guessing ever since Emily put the packet into my bag. Now I want to know."

"Did you look at the papers?"

"Of course I did—a lot of names and addresses all over the place, and a photograph of a bald man called Paul Black or Blechmann."

"A photograph of the Reverend Peter Brown."

Sarah cried out.

"Oh! Joanna said that Wilson called him Paul! But he isn't bald—he's simply smothered in hair."

"You can get away with a hairy wig much better than one with a civilized hair-cut. Paul's as clever as they're made. Lots of hair, lots of beard, untidy clothes—beard, tobacco, folk-lore—don't you see how it all hangs together? Professors and parsons are his long suits. But didn't you notice that he hadn't any eyelashes? That's why he wears glasses. He doesn't need them, you know—his eyes are as good as mine."

"Who is he?"

"Head of Hitler's Fifth Column over here. And the names and addresses are those of his agents—key men. I had a fake attack of influenza and went over to get them. Thanks to another man's extraordinarily clever work I succeeded. But I hadn't much start. I passed the packet to Emily Case after I was stabbed, because I wasn't sure of keeping my senses and I knew they'd be on the look-out for me in Paris. They'd have had me too if a friend of mine hadn't turned up in the nick of time. As it was, I couldn't get on until next day, and the first thing I saw when I landed was a headline about Emily Case."

Sarah took a moment. Then she said,

"Who are you—really?"

"Well, my name is John Hamilton, and I expect you can make a guess at my job."

"Then you didn't rob a bank?"

"No. The real John Wickham did though."

"Oh, there was a real John Wickham?"

"Oh, yes—dossier as given you by Wilson Cattermole. He died in prison, and I was discharged in his place. The same general description would fit us both. You see, my employers thought it might be a good thing to keep an eye on Wilson Cattermole. Wilson was all set to give some poor criminal a second chance, so it was arranged that I should be that criminal."

"Why did he want a criminal? He isn't a philanthropist."

"Quite right. He wanted a criminal because he was engaged in shady business. Once a man's been in prison he's apt to shun the police. Wilson wanted a chauffeur who could be trusted to shun the police. A man like that would be in his power—if he accused him of stealing, he'd be done for. I was given a pretty strong hint of that sort the first time I took him to Maltings."

Sarah thought about that.

"He pretended not to know Mr. Brown—they were carrying on a correspondence as strangers—"

"And meeting once a month down here. They've got a wireless installation in that haunted wing, you know. Very clever people, but I think we've got them now. Well, here's Hedgeley. We'll knock up the police and pull a string or two. Let me do all the talking, and don't say your piece till I give you a lead."

Chapter Forty

HEDGELEY POLICE STATION had quite a busy time for the next hour. The wires hummed. A Chief Constable was got out of bed. There were conversations with London. And presently, after a longish wait, a car drove up from which Mr. Wilson Cattermole, Grimsby and his niece, and the Reverend Peter Brown were decanted.

Sarah found it all rather vague in her recollection next day. There was a very hot fire in the charge room.... If you sat close to it, you scorched, but if you moved away, the fierce cold that beat against the windows set an icy touch upon your spine.... There was a large red-faced policeman—he looked too big for his uniform—and there was a long, thin one with a beaky nose.... The Chief Constable had a bright striped muffler and a pair of keen blue eyes.... All their faces seemed to float in a thick white mist—they kept coming and going.... She made a statement, and when it had been read over to her she signed it—but she couldn't see the paper, or the pen, or her own name....

And then John was asking her about the papers and she was looking at him blankly, because the words were just words. When she tried to think about them they slipped away from her. There had been papers in an oiled-silk packet—John had been stabbed for them—Emily Case had been murdered—Sarah Marlowe had just escaped with her life....

But the papers—that was what John kept on asking.... She had told Mr. Brown that they were at the bottom of the well, but that wasn't true. "Sarah, where are the papers? You said you'd got them. Where are they?"

She had held them back from everyone for so long that it seemed as if she had no strength to let them go. Not now—not like this. The fire was so hot—her head went round.... She heard John say, "It's no use—she's all in. I'd like to take her over to the hotel and get them to put her to bed...."

There was an interval, and then she was in a strange bed in a strange room. Someone had undressed her. There was a fire, and something hot to drink. Then sleep. She went down into it and lost everything.

When she woke up there was a cold daylight in the room. An engraving of Queen Victoria's marriage hung upon the opposite wall in a narrow gilt frame. Underneath this picture upon the mantelshelf there were two large sky-blue vases with a raised pattern of gilt knobs. Between the vases was a clock in a wooden frame carved with edelweiss. The hands of the clock stood at half past ten. Sarah gazed at them. If it was half past ten on Monday morning, she had been asleep for about eight hours. The events of the last few days presented themselves to her with a curious effect of having happened to someone else, a long time ago.

She got out of bed, dressed herself, and went downstairs. As she turned towards the door of the stuffy sitting-room where she and Joanna had waited on the Saturday which seemed to have slipped so far into the past, John Hamilton came out. They stood for a moment and looked at each other. Then he took her back into the room and shut the door.

"I was coming up to see if you were awake."

Sarah said, "I'm starving."

She felt shaken—uncertain of herself and of him. The strange current which had always run between them was there, stronger and warmer than ever before. Sarah had met it with resentment, with resistance, with shame, and joy, and terror. Now all these feelings dissolved and were transmuted. The current flowed strong. And then all at once they were back where they had been yesterday. His hands fell on her shoulders and he was saying in an urgent voice,

"The papers—where are they? There simply isn't any time to be lost. You were all in last night. You have got them, haven't you? You said you had."

"Oh, yes, I've got them."

"Hand them over then!"

She stepped back from him and pulled off the little pill-box hat. The crumpled veil gave it a disreputable air. He stared at it, frowning.

"What's this?"

"My hat. The papers are sewn into it—they're the sides of the pill-box. It was the safest place I could think of, and nobody guessed."

Mr. John Hamilton emitted a loud triumphant war-whoop and embraced her.

"Sarah, I've kept on calling you a fool. I take it all back. You've been clever enough to diddle Paul Black and get away with it, and there aren't many people who can say that. When we're married—"

Sarah disengaged herself. Her cheeks were burning and her eyes shone.

"Who said we were going to be married?"

"I did. You heard me. I'll come back and talk about it later. They want these papers and they want them quick."

He put an arm round her, tilted up her chin, gave her a long, hard kiss, and ran out of the room, banging the door behind him.

Sarah looked at it. He had taken her hat. He had kissed her without a with your leave or by your leave. Her knees wobbled disgracefully.

She sat down on the nearest chair and said, *"Well!"*

THE END

Made in the USA
Monee, IL
27 February 2022

91992458R00118